Book One of the Garth Trilogy

Of Angels and Eagles

L F McDermott

First published in 2016 by Lynette McDermott in conjunction with Lynbara Investments Pty Limited

Sydney Australia

Design: Lynette McDermott and DocMaster Publications
Cover Photo: Frank Allen, Marine Artist
Back cover Photos: Frank Allen, Marine Artist
Printed by DocMaster Publications

National Library of Australia
Cataloguing-in-Publication data:

Author: McDermott, L.F.
Title: Book One of the Garth Trilogy (Of Angels and Eagles)
ISBN: 978-0-9946057-0-2 (paperback)

Website: www.lfmcdermottauthor.com

Dedication

It is said in studies of human genetics that every living person today descended in an unbroken line on their mother's side from "Mitochondrial Eve" who lived over 100,000 years ago ... so perhaps you and I are related...?

This book is dedicated to us, to you, to family ... to Susannah and Edward, to Jacob and Ann...

...to all of you!

Prologue

In the 1700s in Great Britain four souls were born, four souls no more and no less important than any other. In the years that followed circumstance conspired to bring them all together, to an improbable location, as distant from their imaginations as the likelihood of inhabiting the moon or the stars.

Chapter 1

1783-1788

She emerged from the *Dunkirk* hulk, a cool breeze whipping about her. Shivering and squinting at the relative brightness of the daylight, she shielded her eyes and tried to cover her shoulders with what was left of her frayed dress and as she did she thought, *I am 24 years old, I have no family, I will forget my past, I will embrace my future. With this chill wind I am baptised, for today is my new beginning*, and she dared herself to think there might be a real chance at a fresh life.

The iron chain, thick and heavy around her ankles, scraped and rubbed against her uncovered skin as she and the other wretched women shuffled from the hulk to the cart. In Plymouth, the cool March wind of 1787 carried with it the faintest whiff of dianthus flowers and as Susannah breathed deeply she looked up seeing the flower box on the window sill above, heavy with purple blooms. Sometimes in her dreams she had smelled the sweet scent of a rose, but now the fragrance was real, the chill wind not only brought hope, it had brought back to her the power of her senses and with them the dianthus fragrance of spring.

I am in the open air, she thought, *anywhere has to be better than the last three years in the foul smelling Dunkirk*. And although her ankles ached and she shivered from the cold, she silently celebrated having traded the bowels of the hulk for the fresh air and chains.

Her dreams of late had been filled with visions of endless rolling waves and high flying birds and she had wondered if they were premonitions of her liberation, prompting her to spend most of her waking hours imagining the future. There were not many recollections from her past life in St Giles that brought any comfort. She had once experienced the tender touch of a kind gentleman and from time to time she had sat quietly in the Fields Church but her thoughts were mainly filled with daydreams of what her life would be like when she became free.

The guard kept shoving her roughly forward from the *Dunkirk* to the waiting dray, 'you're off to the bottom of the world,' he sniggered.

Under her tangled hair she smirked back at him, for as far as she was concerned his sarcastic slur held no threat. She had already been to places uglier and blacker than hell and his threat aroused no fear in her.

Like animals they huddled together against the cold, the open cart exposed to the gusts of wind that blew about the remnants of their clothes. Some of the women had virtually no clothing at all, just shredded cloth tied about them and as they struggled to cover their bodies their ineffectual attempts were met with jeers from their gaolers. As the horses pulled the cargo of dishevelled prisoners through the streets they attracted derisive taunts and looks of disgust.

It was hard to see the woman beneath the grime and filth of those lost years but if one were to look past the matted hair and rags they would see Susannah, although somewhat gaunt, was still as beautiful as ever.

As the cart approached Portsmouth, Susannah wondered what the bottom of the world would be like.

****

A striking mariner in a blue and white uniform with brass buttons and a three-cornered hat stood on the dock watching as the women grappled with their bits of clothing and dragged their chains as they got down from the cart. Other marines in red uniforms fussed around him.

'Look at him,' Susannah said to the woman ahead of her. 'He's the one in charge. They're all bowing and scraping to him.'

'I hear they are taking us to a dangerous land, where black Indians roam,' the woman replied.

Susannah almost smiled, 'I'm not afraid,' she said. 'We have been living between hell and purgatory, nothing can be worse than where we've been.'

She had heard talk that hundreds of convicts were being sent to this place, at the bottom of the world but Susannah did not dread the new land. Still there was to be a long journey at sea and she knew from her time in the confines of Newgate prison and the *Dunkirk* hulk, small spaces and many people could mean death and disease. What Susannah didn't know was that the man in blue, Captain Arthur Phillip was ready to take every care with his cargo to ensure they reached their destination alive. He was not just the captain of one ship, but the leader of a fleet, a fleet in the great part comprising what some called the scum and refuse of society, who were the passengers of this first fleet to traverse the Southern Ocean to settle the Great South Land.

He looked for all to Susannah like a determined man. Although small in stature the man in blue commanded an air of authority and if she had known his thoughts she would have also known he was a man who wanted to succeed, who was shocked at the state of the prisoners who were being herded on the docks before him, that he wanted to do his best to make things easier for them and to prevail in his mission to colonise for Great Britain the land they called New Holland.

As Susannah made her way onto the *Friendship* anchored at Portsmouth, she and the other convicts had their shackles removed. She rubbed at her reddened skin and looked quizzically at the guard, 'We don't have to wear the irons?'

'The captain says you will not be chained,' the guard replied. 'So long as you behave yourselves.'

Susannah smiled a small smile, grateful for the instant lightness of her step. She looked about the harbour, it was an unusually warm day, then turned back to the guard.

He had a kindly look upon his face. 'What day is it?' she asked him.

'Tis May 13.'

She figured the year must be 1787. 'And are all those ships leaving with us?'

'Aye, all eleven of them.'

When she was sluiced down with water and handed a clean garment, she felt the relatively fresh water on her skin and although brief, it was like a heavenly bath and as she discarded her rags she thought… *a promising start*.

Susannah's dreams of rolling waves and high flying birds seemed about to become real and she wondered whether those parts of her dreams that saw her walking through trees, the likes of which she had never seen before, thick and green, tall and straight surrounded by water the colour of topaz, would also evolve into reality.

Whilst the ship remained anchored in the harbour in the days leading up to the fleet's departure, Susannah noted one marine in particular who strutted about, his nose in the air, left hand resting against the small of his back in a superior stance *he looks full of his own importance*, she thought.

'You,' he commanded, pointing past Susannah to Elizabeth Dudgeons, who had been Susannah's former partner in crime. 'You, stack those rations!'

Elizabeth looked sideways at the marine.

'You talking t' me?' she spat back at him.

Susannah looked at the kindly guard and whispered, 'who is that one?'

'Tis Lieutenant Ralph Clark. He's an important officer, you'd best heed what he says. He don't like you convict women.'

'Sailor take that whore and put her in irons! And any one of you other whores who dares to speak with impertinence to me will end up the same as she.'

'Sees I told ya. He don't hold back when it comes to punishment. You mind ya'self around that one,' the guard whispered back to Susannah.

'Put the others into groups of six,' Lieutenant Clark ordered. 'Put one in charge of making sure they keep their groups area below deck clean. That same person will also weigh the rations to make sure everyone gets equal.'

Susannah made a point of not looking the lieutenant in the eye. *I want no trouble,* she thought. But part of her was glad of the order the lieutenant was trying to put in place. The last thing she wanted was to be a part of more chaos.

The lieutenant pointed to one of the women who was crying. 'Stop that one snivelling,' he demanded of one of the other women.

'That one', 'whore' … the way he speaks about us, Susannah thought *it's as if we are less than human. And what is it about him, that look he has? Tis as if he is bitter against the world.*

If Susannah could have read and had been privy to his journal she would have known the extent of his resentment. The lieutenant had seen service in the American Revolutionary War and although he had volunteered for duty on this journey, he had done so only in the hope that it would afford him a promotion. He was there out of sufferance and saw the task of overseeing convicts as beneath him. In his pursuit of status, he had been forced to leave his wife and son and so he was indeed bitter and disappointed.

At the end of each day he wrote in his diary. The oil lamp affixed above his desk flickered as he turned his bitterness into words.

'The Captain has ordered we should treat the convicts humanely; he is far too lenient. Those scoundrels are spoilt! These Convicts! I believe few marines or soldiers going out on a foreign service under Government were ever better treated, if so well provided for as these Convicts are.'

Each day Clark skulked about on deck, seemingly waiting for a chance to ridicule someone. Susannah dared not look his way. His glances stung of contempt, his eyes narrowed with vexation and whenever the prisoners were mentioned by him there was vehemence in his voice. Susannah resolved not to draw his attention, although the way he looked the women up and down, as if they were lesser beings, did stir her ire and if she had been on the streets of Piccadilly or in the tavern, she'd not have hesitated to give him a tongue lashing. But she restrained herself and she remained silent. Still there were others on board who could not control themselves, amongst them some of the surviving mutineers from the Mercury and Elizabeth Dudgeons.

Susannah thought about how in Newgate prison Elizabeth had been in constant trouble with the guards and so Susannah decided she would try to steer clear of her. Elizabeth attracted unwanted attention and Susannah did not want to be drawn into her group or feel the wrath of Clark.

Elizabeth was always trying to inveigle Susannah into some scheme or another, to make deals with the sailors for favours but Susannah resisted, sometimes finding a dark corner in the hull to secrete herself away from Elizabeth's mischief.

Her feelings about Elizabeth proved to be well founded as less than three weeks out from port, Elizabeth was too friendly with some of the seamen who had let her out of the bulkhead. Lieutenant Clark appeared on deck just as a fight broke out between Elizabeth and one of the other women, the screeching and scuffling attracting his attention.

'What's that ruckus?' He turned to see it was the same woman whom he had reprimanded when first they came aboard.

'Put that whore in chains,' he ordered.

Susannah watched as Elizabeth kicked and yelled at the guards as they shackled her. Still Elizabeth did not learn her lesson and when the same occurred not less than three weeks later Susannah heard Lieutenant Clark's harsh words and cringed at the thought of being the target of his scorn.

'I'll not have you disobeying me,' he said as he took a deep breath and paced in front of Elizabeth. 'I am in charge and you will yield. One way or another you will come to heel and take note the rest of you, this is what will happen to you if you follow this one's example.'

When the irons were fixed onto Elizabeth's ankles she cursed and spat in Clark's direction. *Foolish!* Susannah thought, *there are many months left to journey and she has now well and truly made herself a target.*

'Take her to the flogging post.'

Elizabeth was dragged to the spot, all the time cursing at the lieutenant. Susannah gasped and she and some of the other women went to turn their heads away from the sight.

'You will all watch' he ordered, and Susannah was forced to look on as the flagellator administered the flogging with a rope.

Susannah flinched at Elizabeth's groans and the sound of the rope against flesh. With each blow feelings of pity and sorrow rose within her. After the punishment Elizabeth was tied to a pump on deck and left, red welts ridging across her back, the stain of filthy tears down her face.

Susannah heard Clark say to one of the marines, 'she has long been fishing for it, which she has at last got to her heart's content!'

What kind of a man is this that feels pleasure at such things? Susannah thought.

Susannah waited until the marines had moved away and despite not wanting to draw attention to herself, she poured some fresh water into a cup and took it to Elizabeth. Kneeling beside her briefly and holding the cup to her lips she whispered, 'for the sake of God, stay out of strife Lizzie. The lieutenant has it in for you.'

Still within a month Elizabeth tried to persuade Susannah to join in a mission to ingratiate themselves with the sailors by offering their bodies in exchange for rum.

'I'll not be in it Lizzie. If we keep out of trouble, we'll have a better chance when we get to where we are going.'

'Do you not want to forget our woes Susannah, a little rum to lighten your head and help us forget?'

But Susannah refused. 'Whatever good mark I can make I will. I'll not be drawn into your mischief and Lizzie if you know what's good for you, you'll be putting away this silly plan.'

Elizabeth argued with her then turned her attention to the other women. When a fight broke out again Elizabeth was dragged kicking and screaming into the hull and was soon back in irons. Susannah shook her head, *stupid girl*, she thought, *all for the sake of liquor and lust.*

After her last troublesome behaviour Elizabeth was kept down below, mostly in irons and every time she saw Susannah she called out to her which drew the guard's attention. When Elizabeth was in chains she was less a bother but when she was released from them Susannah made it her business to avoid Elizabeth as best she could.

As they sailed the open sea the vessel pitched and swayed but unlike others who suffered for weeks with seasickness, Susannah found her sea legs early. She was careful with her rations and kept herself as clean as she could. She made sure she went up on deck as often as permitted and when she did she breathed the fresh air deeply, tilting her face to the sun. In this simple act she found pleasure. It was hot and oppressive when they sailed in the precincts of the equator, not at all what the convicts were used to and, to make things worse, they desperately needed fresh fruit and vegetables by the time they reached Rio. When Susannah saw them being brought on board she took heart at this, for it was an affirmation that the captain indeed had every intention of trying to make sure that disease was staved off and the passengers revitalized.

Susannah's dreams persisted, thick green forests, songs echoing through a valley, her own voice mixing with another's, one she did not recognize. Like the unknown place and the unknown voice, the dreams were pervaded by an unknown smell, fresh and salty all at once and the fragrance lingered in her nostrils momentarily even after she woke and again she wondered, would this come to pass.

Susannah's resolve to be well behaved had its own reward for whilst the *Friendship* was in Rio, after three months at sea, she was transferred to the less problematic *Charlotte* and away from Elizabeth and, much to Susannah's delight, away from Lieutenant Clark.

As she moved from one ship to another Susannah looked up in awe at the mountains that rose out of the harbour. At the mouth of the bay stood a peak, higher than any landform Susannah had ever seen before. She thought it splendid and imagined herself standing at the top, looking out, *oh what you could see from there* she thought, *up there the breeze would lift you like a bird.* And she thought perhaps when next she slept she could conjure a dream of flying from that mountain top.

She was amazed at the place and indeed, as the journey continued, she was amazed at every place she saw, the things she heard, the sounds of the different places, the calls of different birds, the languages and she was astonished at the world that existed outside of London.

She listened to the conversations of the sailors and took in the names of the places they stopped at. She marvelled at the landscapes, at sights so unlike those she had known, at the different dress and customs of those who came aboard. She had never before heard of Teneriffe or Rio de

Janeiro or of the piece of land known as the Cape of Good Hope. She had never travelled outside of London, but here she was, now traversing the oceans and was part of what she began to see as an adventure, a world away from Britain.

Susannah wished she could read and write for if she had been able to she would have written many things down. Instead she committed all she could to her memory, for some day she would tell her children about this voyage.

But in between where she had come from and where she was going, the ocean seemed endless and if it were not for the fact she knew land existed on the other side, she would have been tempted to think there was no limit to it.

Down in the bulkhead the quarters were crowded. It was hot and the stink of body odour, urine and excrement filled whatever space there was. The smell at times was so rank that Susannah sometimes found herself with her nose up to a gap in the deck trying to breathe in a little air from the outside. Most covered their noses and breathed through their mouths to try and avoid the smell of the rancid air but it seemed some had just become used to it.

Whenever fresh water was provided to wash in, there was almost always a fight about who would use it first. Susannah tried to push her way through or bargain in some way to use the water when it was cleaner, instead of having to use the dregs but unless there was an officer supervising, invariably there were loud arguments. There seemed to always be a racket of noises, fighting, swearing, grunting and moaning and to Susannah, it seemed that every time there was a crack in the cacophony it was filled with the whimpering of a child.

The atmosphere was heavy and difficult to bear, so much so that even in inclement weather she spent as much time on deck as she could. And although the vastness of the ocean seemed daunting she never tired of looking out at it and feeling the breeze, breathing in the fresh sea air, and having the sun on her face. If it rained, she took off her bonnet and let the fresh water wash through her hair and over her face, rolling up her sleeves and hitching up her petticoat to let the raindrops fall on her skin and cleanse her.

She had promised herself she would do whatever she could to stay as healthy as possible. She looked about her and saw she was one of those who possessed great natural stamina and whilst some perished on the journey or became ill, she remained well, those years as a guttersnipe, as a prisoner in Newgate and on the *Dunkirk* had made her resilient.

She continued to believe her future would be brighter than her past. Not even the great storm the ships battled through on New Year's Day 1788 dampened her positive outlook. Even though the winds were against the ship with the waves rising up like mountains, flooding the decks and water seeping into the bulkheads, Susannah thought, *this will pass, I will survive.*

It had been two hundred and fifty days since leaving Portsmouth. A long, arduous journey, with weeks when nothing but seabirds and occasionally another ship from the fleet could be seen. Indeed, some around Susannah wondered if they would ever make it to this Great South Land. The supplies were nearly exhausted and fear began to creep in, people were hungry and worn down. So, when the cliffs and beaches of the new land came into view a sense of relief swept through the fleet.

Anticipation spread and Susannah stood amongst those who were allowed on deck as the ships made their way into a wide blue bay. She let her gaze drift across the shimmering water from shoreline to shoreline, *what a fine sight, not a building to be seen, no foul water...no filthy hulks*! And with deep breaths of optimism she turned to the woman beside her, 'here we are, the bottom of the earth,' she said, 'and it looks grand!'

It was not the landscape of her dreams, not the green thickly wooded place with tall straight trees and hills and valleys that her mind's eye had conjured but still to Susannah it was beautifully refreshing.

For an Englishman the line of ships made a splendid spectacle but when Susannah looked more closely, casting her eyes toward the land she saw black figures on the shoreline and she couldn't help but wonder what they were thinking.

The *Charlotte* anchored alongside the other ships in the vast basin they called Botany Bay. Broad and open, by the afternoon high winds howled across it, setting the surface alive with dancing whitecaps.

She saw some of the officers rowing to the sandy shore, among them she recognized the blue uniform of the captain. Later she saw the frustrated faces of the lieutenants and even when the word was passed that Arthur Phillip was not satisfied with the location, that it was too exposed and lacked fresh water and they would have to move on, even then Susannah's mood was not spoiled.

After six days anchored in the bay the ships set sail again. As the *Charlotte* left Botany Bay she sailed dangerously close to the rocks. Susannah noticed the rushed pulling of ropes and changing of the sails and the closeness of the rocky headland. 'Have we come all this way only to be wrecked!' she heard someone exclaim. But her faith was unflinching, from somewhere deep inside her she knew they would not come to grief and the urgent grappling of ropes and sails was relieved in an instant when *Charlotte's* sails caught the breeze full on at the vital moment, hauling her away from the rock face and out to the open sea.

****

'... the finest harbour in the world, in which a thousand sail of the line may ride in the most perfect security ...' 3 July 1788 Captain Arthur Phillip; letter to the Marquis of Lansdowne

One by one the eleven ships navigated their way into a harbour north of the bay, a harbour which lay beyond two towering sandstone headlands that Susannah thought stood like giant watchman on either side of a watery gate. The water sparkled silver, beckoning, and she thought, *I have been through the gates of hell and found my way out, perhaps now I have been delivered to the gates of somewhere close to heaven...* for inside the heads was a colossal shimmering waterway and unlike the Thames of London or the harbour of Portsmouth, there was not a single sign of grime.

The fleet anchored in a protected cove with deep water close to shore, where a fresh water stream ran down the gently sloping hillside to the bay, a place Captain Phillip called Sydney Cove, in a harbour that the mariner James Cook had named Port Jackson.

Susannah watched keenly as some from the ship called the *Scarborough* rowed to shore, amongst them a young man who captured her attention. She watched as he and others cut down trees to make a clearing and was impressed with his robust looking physique, his broad shoulders, *he has a lean and healthy look about him*, she thought, a smile on her face.

From the *Charlotte* the trees looked like nothing she had ever seen, they were not the straight tall green trees of her dreams, they were all shapes and sizes, more brown than green, gnarled, with curling branches and many looked like they had been there forever. There was no sign of any flowering plants but the bush held its own attraction, it looked tough and enduring.

This coupled with the clean blueness of the harbour had Susannah immediately admiring the place.

For several days she watched from the ship as an area of ground was cleared and some makeshift dwellings erected together with the assembly of tents. Later when all the remaining male convicts and women convicts went ashore, Susannah was seated on the ground with the others in a large circle. Amongst the crowd she spied the good looking man with the broad shoulders who had felled the trees in the days before.

As the soldiers marched in unison they formed a circle around the convicts and began to play the fifes and drums. In watching the circular march Susannah caught the gaze of the young man, he smiled at her. It was not the kind of smile that one of her customers may have shown her, it was not a smile of ardor and anticipation, it was simply the smile of a young man seeing her as a young woman, unknowing of her past, of her morals and with no overt look of lust, just a naïve grin from a handsome lad to pretty girl.

At first Susannah thought the pomp and ceremony was just puffery but when Arthur Phillip spoke it filled her heart with promise. He raised his voice and spoke with genuine conviction, commanding the attention of the crowd.

'Good people, I am a man of vision, and I do not doubt that this country will prove to be the most valuable acquisition Great Britain ever made. We

have come here today, to take possession of this fifth great continental
division of the earth, on behalf of the British people, and have founded here
a state which we hope will become a shining light among all the nations of
the southern hemisphere. How grand is the prospect which lies before this
youthful nation. I give you, success to the colony...'

For the first time in her life Susannah felt real purpose. She was part of something. With this rag tag group, she would make her future.

Chapter 2

1788-1789

'We arrived in this country in the end of January, 1788; the weather was then very fine, though warm; the sea and land breezes pretty regular, and Farenheit's thermometer was from 72° to 80°. In February, the weather was sultry, with lightning, thunder, and heavy rain; this sort of weather continued for a fortnight, with few and very short intervals of fair weather; a flash of lightning fell one night near the camp, and struck a tree near to the post of a centinel, who was much hurt by it; the tree was greatly rent, and there being at the foot of it a pen in which were pigs and sheep, they were all killed. Towards the latter end of the month the weather was more settled, little thunder, lightning, or rain, and the thermometer from 65° to 77°': From the Historical Journal of transactions at Port Jackson and Norfolk Island.

Arthur Phillip charged his Lieutenant Phillip Gidley King with the task of putting together a small party to settle on Norfolk Island. King took recommendations and began compiling a list of convicts to take with him.

The lieutenant was well aware of the fear among British authorities that the French could occupy Norfolk. Even His Majesty King George wanted to prevent this. He also knew Norfolk was studded with tall straight pines and an abundance of what appeared to be flax plant, and harvesting these to make masts and sails for the new colony formed part of his orders.

Phillip Gidley King was a man of humble birth, some considered he was not a 'gentleman' in the traditional sense because his father had been a draper, but he joined the navy as a captain's servant when he was just twelve years old. By the time Arthur Phillip chose him as his Second Lieutenant for the First Fleet, he had already spent seventeen years earning his stripes. Phillip held a high opinion of King and entrusted him to establish the subordinate settlement on Norfolk Island. King's struggle for recognition and promotion within the ranks left him with an understanding of what it meant to try and better oneself and, to give the settlement the best chances of success, he had to choose the best candidates.

Examining the records of prisoners, King knew what he wanted, *no trouble makers*, he thought. *I need strong and co-operative convicts I can hopefully come to rely upon.*

Nine male and six female names were on his final list and he set about having them kept apart. Susannah found herself amongst them wondering where this place Norfolk Island might be.

'I don't want to leave the others,' one of the women said.

'We've been singled out for good purpose. It's meant to be. Don't worry yourself,' Susannah said confidently to her.

When King gathered them together he encouraged them and although he spoke with the power of his position, he was re-assuring, saying they would not be harshly treated and that after their term of transportation had expired if they wanted they could return to England. Susannah had never before been spoken to by someone in authority in tones such as these and she thought to herself, *I am not the least bit worried about ever returning to England* and much to her delight, amongst those chosen to sail to Norfolk was the broad shouldered young man.

Susannah thought King almost fatherly and smiled to herself when he said if reciprocal affection grew between the male and female convicts they could marry under the authorisation of the surgeon, *if affection is to grow between me and anyone,* she thought, *I hope it will be with that fine looking young man.*

It was a Thursday, the summer heat rising from the harbour in a fog, the morning of Saint Valentine's Day, just over two weeks since they had arrived at Port Jackson. *A day for lovers*, Susannah thought and she wondered whether she possessed the key to unlock the young man's heart, *after all*, she thought, *if I am to live in some remote place I want to spend it with someone I have an attraction to.* Along with the excitement of this possibility other emotions percolated within her. She felt special, she had been selected, she Susannah Gough, wearing a fresh dress and bonnet, had been selected as part of this human endeavour.

She was not filled with trepidation as were some of the other twenty-three men and women who boarded the *Supply*. To be away from the rest of the colony, to be alone on a distant island seemed to some at the very least precarious but to Susannah being part of this small contingent filled her with greater purpose, *of all those women I am one of the few chosen. The lieutenant sees worth in me, I'll not be taking it for granted.*

She stood on deck, feeling like a lady in her fresh dress, shackle free and waving to those on shore. The *Supply's* sails were hoisted, flapped and then ballooned into life, filling with the wind of this new world, billowing and sending them on their way.

Susannah savoured the journey, the atmosphere was relaxed and at times almost recreational. As soon as she had the chance and being aware that the handsome man could probably form affection with any one of the other women on board, she wasted no time and sat right down beside him to make sure she was the one to whom his attention would be drawn. As they ate their rations she struck up conversation.

'So what is your name, and how is it that you came to be here?' she asked dipping her head to one side.

Edward thought her bold but there was indeed something about this one that relaxed him.

'I am Ed Garth… and it was a case of mistaken identity.'

'Of course it was,' she grinned cheekily.

'No, tis not a lie.'

'Well then Ed Garth you'd best tell me about it.'

The moon was low on the horizon, bright and full. Susannah looked at the way it was rising, an orange ball, like the eye of a giant peering over a shelf towards them. A breeze blew warm and delicious. As the moonlight rested on Edward's face she found herself feeling the pleasure of it all and looking at him intently, waiting for him to speak.

'It was a job I'd had done before, taking cows to market for a fee and this job seemed no different from any other, except this was the first time I had been in the employ of a Mr Hamilton of Highgate. In fact, I had only met the man the day before. The morning had started well, I was in good spirits and I remember as I steered the cows down the Hampstead Road I was whistling as the sun rose and nodded good day to the watchman at the smallpox hospital near the turnpike at Cold-Bath-Fields. If I knew then what would happen I would have stopped right there or turned back around, but it seemed a day like any other. I left the cows with the man I was asked to deliver them to at Smithfield market and went to the King's-head tavern for a pint of beer. Do you know the place?'

Susannah nodded.

25

'Not more than an hour later as I was chatting and drinking with some friends a stranger came into the tavern angrily calling out my name. He accused me of stealing his cows. He had a peace officer with him who seized me. I couldn't believe what was happening to me. I have to say I was truly frightened.'

'Ed Garth, there is nothing to be ashamed of in being frightened,' Susannah said. 'When I thought I might be hanged I feared hearing the crack of my own neck.'

'I had never stolen anything in my life. I'd never had to. My family had a farm in Malmesbury and I'd grown up with plenty to eat and a roof over my head. It was only after the farm servants began leaving and going into the cities to work that the farm suffered and I needed to move away to earn myself a living. After I was arrested I had help from a family friend I had been lodging with in Hampstead and I had a fancy lawyer act for me, a Mr Peatts. He was very good, catching my accuser, Mr Rhodes out with his questioning.'

'A fancy lawyer eh... I was my own lawyer!' Susannah winked and Edward smiled at her, recognising her cheekiness.

'It was just before Christmas and I sent word for my family not to travel to London for the trial. I was sure I'd be proved innocent. But the judge, Lord Loughborough was sitting up there in his long white wig and red gown and I could tell he was barely listening. I could tell he had heard the same pleas of innocence over and over and wasn't in the mood to hear another tale of mistaken identity. Mr Rhodes went on with some long winded story about being a cow-keeper and his father being a cow-keeper and seeing his cows being herded away from the sale yards at Smithfield and being told by the seller that it was me who had brought them to market. He said to the court he had never been mistaken in identifying a cow and how he could pick his cows if they were a thousand miles off, in the midst of a thousand beasts. Can you believe it? Mr Peatts looked at the judge when he said it and even the Lord raised his eyebrows at that. I even had four witnesses who vouched for my good character and honesty but later I heard some of those in the jury knew Mr Rhodes well and didn't wish to count themselves amongst his enemies. When the jury found me guilty I was in shock, I couldn't move and then when the judge declared I should be hanged, I swear I nearly collapsed.'

The moon moved slowly across the sky and as he continued, Susannah felt Edward's mood become more sombre.

'I had believed the hangman would be the last man I would see, that I would die never having felt the embrace of a woman or having heard the laughter of my own children. If it had not been for Mr Herring and Mr Peatts putting forward my plea for mercy I would have felt the roughness of the hangman's rope about my neck and dangled from the gallows. When I got the news that my sentence was no longer to hang but to be transported for seven years to Africa I was surely relieved but I knew this meant I may

27

never see my family again. Later they decided I should be sent to New Holland, even further from Britain. I didn't want to bring shame upon them so I made sure their names had not been written on my charge sheet. I suppose the folk of Malmesbury think I have simply disappeared.'

Edward's face showed sadness. His eyes momentarily stared past Susannah into the night. It was as if he were contemplating his own supposition and his genuine sincerity drew emotions of compassion and longing from within her but whilst she rested her hand upon his arm in empathy and whilst she was sorely tempted, she knew it was not the time to offer him her lips.

Although his eyes were the bluest she had ever seen and his countenance most appealing, she knew enough that his mood was melancholic. She also knew that whilst he may have found her attractive, he was a deep thinker and if she made it known to him that she would not mind if he kissed her, he may in that moment have interpreted the gesture as superficial lust and it would not necessarily be something that would capture his ongoing fancy. So with the moon now high in the sky they found a place to sleep and she left the want to kiss him for another day.

So she took her time, revealing slowly and surely, day by day her qualities to him. She listened to him, spoke optimistically of the future and encouraged him. She laughed heartily and smiled often, showing him those parts of her that for so many years had been secondary, she was opening herself up to him as a person, not just as an object of desire and in doing so she reassured herself, *I am worth more than just what my body has to offer.*

Part of Susannah wished the journey never to end for she thought she was making steady progress with her intended but when the island came into view and she saw the beauty of the place they had been sent to, she was overcome with gratitude at being brought to their destination. As they approached she stood again on deck observing the coastline, the ocean rushing relentlessly to the base of the high ragged cliffs, bursting into foam. And there, right in front of her were the images that had come to her in her sleep, the tall straight green pines, thick and woody, covering the island.

'This is the place,' she whispered.

'What do you mean, what place is that?'

'Ed Garth, this is the place in my dreams.'

He looked at her, amused. There was something about her that made him lighter, she charmed him, she was enchanting and he couldn't help but be infected by her manner.

When they sailed to the north shore they were met with the face of ancient, volcanic crags, greeted with tall rocky outcrops, mini islands in effect which littered the coast, crowned green and white with lichen and grasses. These rocks were the nesting place of thousands of birds that swarmed from their high spires, watching and waiting for the opportunities of the sea, diving and screeching with what Susannah regarded must be the sheer joy of their existence.

Susannah watched as Lieutenant King and another seaman climbed into a longboat and were lowered to the sea. They tried to row ashore but the swell was too large and the risk of being tossed upon the rocks too great. As they turned back to the ship Edward stood by Susannah's side, he placed a hand lightly upon hers.

'How on earth will they be able to access this land?'

With that small gesture Susannah knew there was a mutual affection between them and she inwardly congratulated herself at having been measured in the way she had endeared herself to him, not throwing herself at him but letting him come to her and like her for who she was beneath her skin.

'If anyone can get us safely to land, the lieutenant can. I have faith in him,' she said and she looked at Edward placing her other hand on top of his.

She did sometimes wonder why he had not attempted to seduce her or even succumb to her subtle advances. He admitted to her that at Port Jackson he had spied her dark hair falling from her bonnet and she had immediately caught his eye but on the *Supply*, whilst others around them paired up in earnest, sharing each other's bodies completely, he had held back. *He is shy, still sad and perhaps he hasn't had a woman before... yes that may be it,* she thought. *He was just sixteen when he was gaoled...perhaps that is it*. She certainly hoped so, even though he had not acted upon it, she wanted him to desire her. She had never met a man that hadn't desired her.

If the prospect of living in this apparent Eden was somewhat daunting for Edward, it was not so for Susannah. Unabashed, she was inspired and enthusiastic. Even when the mood of many on board became tempered as the days passed without being able to find a suitable place to lay anchor and go ashore; even when it seemed the only bay that looked as if it might be entered endured an almost relentless, breaking surf against a reef, even then, her spirit was not dulled.

For many days they circumnavigated the island. The coastline was dotted with small white beaches, where turquoise water broke heavily on the sand, hissing its warning that this was not the place to land. Susannah saw the worry on King's face, his furrowed brow, but she also saw resolve as he waited patiently for the seas to become calmer.

A tall peak was prominent in what looked to be the centre of the island, forming the upper part of an otherwise unseen underwater ridge that stretched submerged between New Caledonia and New Zealand, part of a continent that eighty million years before had sunk thousands of feet to create a new ocean floor. King called the peak Mount Pitt, the peak from which many freshwater streams came to life, making their way to the ocean shores. During those days of waiting, rain came and water streamed down the northern shore forming two splendid waterfalls that cascaded from the steep cliffs into the sea, rainbows forming in their mist. As she marveled at the colours, Susannah thought, *surely this must be a good sign.*

The island lacked a natural harbour. However, close to the southern reaches of the island there was another small isle which, together with the main island, formed an entryway to a large bay that opened up onto the shore. Here the land sloped downward more gradually to a sandy beach partially protected from the strong northerly wind and it was in that bay they found the refuge they sought. But a large rocky reef lay at varying depths across the face of the cove. Susannah knew virtually nothing about harbours and coves, other than some were more beautiful than others but she could see in places the rocks below the surface and realised that if they were to land safely the ship would have to be carefully negotiated through the reef and anchored in exactly the right spot. Even though she could feel the tension on board, she did not lose heart, she had trust in Lieutenant King.

On a day when the weather had calmed Lieutenant King called his men into action and they began jibing and tacking at quick intervals to bear through the maze of submerged rocks. There were anxious moments but finally King gave the command to put down the anchor and the ship stopped her heaving and lulling, sitting relatively securely and quietly in the bay. King and his party went ashore in longboats, making their way

32

through a gap in the underwater ridge which led through to the beach. Smiles spread across the faces on board the *Supply*, Susannah was sure her smile was amongst the broadest.

The weather was warm and the water looked clean and clear. To Susannah the scene was invigorating. She stood leaning against the deck-rail of the *Supply* and, as she had done when she first started her journey, she lifted her face toward the sun, the sea spray of the Pacific Ocean annointing her. The sight was breathtaking, the breeze was lively and rustled through her hair and in that moment she was moved to tears, a moment she thought she would never forget, an euphoric moment when all the misery of her past slipped away and all the promise of the future consumed her.

Susannah had joked to Edward she would make history, that she would be the first of the women to stand on the sands of this 'paradise island' and with her enthusiasm he saw a wild freshness which struck a chord in his heart.

Edward and some other male convicts went ashore ahead and, as he had done in Sydney Cove, he set about clearing trees. Later as Susannah climbed aboard the longboat she was bursting from the depths of her soul, nervous flutters jiggled in her insides and she let out a squeal of delight. She leaned out over the edge of the longboat, feeling the water with her hand and looked at the shore with anticipation. In her eagerness as the boat reached the shallows she jumped into the knee-deep water wading to the shore placing her feet firmly on the beach.

'I am the first!' she called out. 'The first Englishwoman to set foot on this land!'

Edward looked up from his toiling and watched as Susannah leapt into the water wading with her heavy, sodden dress through the shallows until she stood proudly on the sand with a smile so wide even Lieutenant King noticed. Her joy was irresistible and Edward found himself laughing aloud.

She removed her petticoat, draping it across a low lying bush, took off her shoes and sat upon a large rock, drying herself in the heat of what seemed like a new sun, brighter and warmer than the sun that had shone over London.

She thought of her dreams, of the rolling waves and seabirds, of the tall green trees and she wondered whether the dreams had been the consequence of things she had somehow heard and not at the time taken note of, or whether they had come from some unearthly place, whether everything that had ever happened to her had merely been a stepping stone to leading her to this destination. She looked at Edward and found herself wondering what her future dreams may reveal, if Ed Garth would feature in them and for a moment she conjured up a daydream about lying in his arms.

It was March, ten months since she had left Portsmouth and as the Union Jack was hoisted on the shores of the beach later that day, Susannah looked at what surrounded her, *this place is as close to paradise as I could ever have imagined,* she thought, *here really is my new beginning.*

King surveyed the scene and decided that the ridge overlooking the sandy bay would be a suitable place for the government buildings to be constructed. These buildings would oversee the settlement, a settlement that would be called 'Sydney Town' after Lord Viscount Sydney, a man who believed convicts should be given a chance to make a new life.

That night King wrote in his journal, '*At day-light on the 6th, I left the Supply with two boats, having in them all the persons belonging to the settlement, together with the tents, a part of the provisions, and some of the most useful tools; all which we landed, and began clearing a small piece of ground to erect the tents on: the colours were hoisted, and before sun-set, every person and article belonging to the settlement were on shore, and the tents pitched. Before the colours were hauled down, I assembled my small colony under them, (Lieutenant Ball and some of his officers being present,) and drank the health of his Majesty, the Queen, the Prince of Wales, and success to the settlement: and, as we had no other way of testifying our loyalty, we gave three cheers on the occasion*': 6th March 1788.

Although the *Supply* was relatively small she brought with her the huge energy of a group of outcasts with promise in their hearts. To Susannah the promise was truer than anything in her life had ever been. Whatever imaginings she may have had they had not been of grand houses, jewels or fine clothes, they had been of fresh air and freedom, of food and shelter, of love and rebirth and this place held that potential for her. She could not remember ever having joined in with three cheers for anything before and although the cheers were meant to be an affirmation of allegiance to the King, to her it was a heralding in of expectation charged by the enthusiasm she had for her future.

Tents were erected, King and his men in their tents almost side by side with the convicts. There were no walls or prison cells, King was relying as much upon the convicts as he did upon his own men to build this outpost and he treated them in a way that he hoped would bring out the best in them.

Susannah shared a tent with a few of the other women who had not yet paired up. Most other women were already with a man and in fact some of the mariners had themselves formed relationships with some of the convict women.

Susannah was keeping company with Edward but he seemed preoccupied. Although he paid her attention he had not been driven, as most of the other men were, to satisfy his sexual desires and from time to time she questioned whether her initial instincts and attraction to him had been misguided. But then he would do something or say something which brought her focus back, a gesture of taking her hand when she least expected it, or calling her 'my dear' and in those first months she settled for growing their intimacy on a level that, whilst initially had been unfamiliar to her, now felt comfortable and rewarding. They grew a friendship and as they did she waited patiently for him to realise there was no need to hold back on his physical desires.

By the beginning of June, a large area of ground had been cleared and permanent dwellings were beginning to take shape. The men had built a catamaran to fish from and some crops had been planted and whilst there was progress, the first months had not gone by without hardship and tragedy. There had been many days of gale force winds and rain and so taking out boats for fishing was often problematic. Bringing the boats back into the cove was always fraught with the danger of capsize and when one of the marines was drowned after falling off the catamaran in rising swell, his body disappeared only to be washed up some days later on the shore, leaving everyone to deal with the sadness of losing one of their few. Despite these physical hardships and tragedies, Lieutenant King saw promise in the settlement and refused to be discouraged. Susannah too would not allow herself to be disheartened. With fresh water and fresh air, she believed anything was possible.

It was the birthday of His Majesty the King and whilst Susannah felt no allegiance to royalty she was happy to celebrate his birthday for she had heard that the lieutenant planned for all in the settlement to be included in the celebrations.

She saw torches being lit and watched as piles of debris were set alight, making for bonfires that lit up the darkness, sparkling and crackling as the small community gathered. A fiddle was found and some of the men and women, including Susannah, were of fine voice and before long they were all singing and dancing.

In the fire glow and dancing a jig with Edward, Susannah delighted in the reality of her freedom.

'We both were in Newgate, then you were on the *Ceres* and I, the *Dunkirk* in Plymouth,' she said. 'And now here we are, singing and dancing, forgetting our pasts, who would have dared to think that?'

'Aye, two years in Newgate and then the hulk. I made a friend there, his name was Jacob. We helped each other, protected each other from those who would try to prevail upon us to take our food and the few belongings we were allowed to keep. He also could read and write and he used to write often to his sweetheart. Jacob came with me on the *Scarborough* but now sadly he is left back at Port Jackson. He was a good friend. Tis a pity he is not with us.'

'People come and go in our lives. When you struggle from day to day, when you are just trying to keep food in your stomach and find shelter, people use you and true friendships are hard to come by so you were lucky to have had him while you did. And you Ed Garth, you at least had a family. I had none. And tell me, did you write your family, or perhaps you had a sweetheart yourself?' She said, caressing him lightly on the shoulder and dipping her head to the side, a questioning eyebrow raised coyly.

'I had no sweetheart and at first I did write to my parents but then I worried that it would bring them too much pain. I have always hoped one day I could go back to them, make out to those in Malmesbury that I'd been away working at sea. I had vowed to myself that once my sentence was over I would take back my life and go home.'

In these few words Susannah saw the reason for Edward's seeming reluctance to commit to her. He was homesick for England and the family he left behind and had not let go of his want to return one day.

'You seem full of life to me Ed Garth. You have kept well. How did you manage that in the confines of the cells?'

He puffed up his chest and with a cheeky grin upon his face and a hint of humour in his voice he held his arms up, flexing his muscles and clenching his fists.

'I was lucky. I'm strong, good with my hands,' he winked. 'They set me to work in the warehouses and government stores on the banks of the river and wealthy men paid the gaolers for me and some of the other fit men to labour for them. I liked it. I knew it was good for me. They also fed me more and it meant I could get away from the foul air.'

Susannah looked at him, his shoulders were broad, but he was otherwise lean and sinewy. His leanness belied his physical strength. She had seen him work, and she knew he was tough and strong.

'And your journey Ed, how did you fare in those months? I did not suffer from the seasickness. I was queasy a little then it passed.'

Edward sat back down next to her, the stars of the new sky adorned the heavens and fires made from deadwood dotted the cove.

'It took me some days to find my sea legs. On board we were released from our chains and I was able to get some fresh air. For the most the meals were good. Fresh fruit kept the scurvy at bay and some who were sick when the journey started even seemed healthier at the end. I felt like I was in another world, eleven ships sailing on seas far from England. I heard them say we travelled over 15,000 miles. I had never imagined how far that was, that there could be a place so distant.'

'It was the same for us,' said Susannah. 'It seems the captain wanted to try and get us all here alive and healthy and even when the storms were fierce he guided us well.'

'Aye, I think he was a good leader,' said Edward. 'But by the time we rounded the place called Van Diemen's Land, there was virtually no fresh food left on our vessel and when we sailed into the great harbour at Port Jackson I the saw natives in canoes, waving sticks of fire above their heads. A sense of dread overcame me as I'd heard tales of cannibals in the Pacific and of savages in Africa but the next morning when I was ordered to row ashore with some officers and other convicts, the natives were friendly. They smiled at us and by the afternoon the blacks were dancing with some of the marines and one of the officers had set up an easel and was painting the scene; so odd and peculiar.'

Susannah looked closely at him as he told his tale, his long brown hair and beard, his blue eyes, the shape of his arms, his shoulders and back beneath his shirt and she imagined the thrill of being in his embrace. She found herself staring at him, desiring him and before long her cheeks flushed at the thought of it.

He spoke his words like nothing she had heard before and she imagined if she had ever read a book it would have a voice such as his.

'Well Ed Garth I can say that right now I feel like a free woman, King treats us more like settlers than prisoners. And I know he has encouraged the men to build dwellings with promises that if you stay after your sentence expires he will grant you land on the island. Imagine that, your own land, from the cells of Newgate to the hills of Norfolk. I would never

41

have thought such a thing possible, although in my dreams I saw myself here, walking through valleys and amidst these tall green trees.'

What manner of creature is this, he thought, *whose dreams come true, who sees wonder in almost anything...*

As they sat beneath a myriad of foreign stars, the Via Lactea, that milky patch of sky that rings the Earth, Susannah thought to tell him everything of her past, but she hesitated, *one day I will tell him my story.* But for now she simply impressed upon him.

'I know you miss your family and you have thought you would return to them, but perhaps Ed, we are the lucky ones after all.'

****

That night Lieutenant King wrote in this diary.

'The 4th June 1788, being the anniversary of his Majesty's birth-day, I caused it to be observed as a holiday. The colours were hoisted at sun-rise; every person had a good dinner, of the produce of the island, and I gave the convicts some liquor to drink their sovereign's health: the evening concluded with bonfires, which, exclusive of the joy we felt at the return of his Majesty's birth day, and the celebrating it in this distant part of the globe, we with pleasure saw some large piles of wood burnt that had been a long time collecting, and which were a great incumbrance to us.'

42

Chapter 3

1788-1789

'It's taking shape, our little town, is it not Ed Garth?'

Susannah was sorting seed and plants as Edward dug the garden bed around Lieutenant King's dwelling. She liked to watch him work, the way his flexed muscles made lines upon his skin, the veins in his arms rippling across his biceps. She felt the warm glow of blushing on her face and she turned her head away from him, embarrassed at her own thoughts. Although she had been with many men, there were few she had desired, but Ed Garth sent the blood coursing through her and set her stomach dancing with nerves.

'Aye, tis' said Edward, 'and the land we've cleared will soon bear its first harvest. We're all busy making the settlement a place to grow crops and livestock and not just for ourselves but for the colony at Port Jackson. The governor says we're to make ourselves valuable!'

All around them Susannah could see cottages and structures replacing tents. A number of clear paths and tracks were taking shape and on the flat land the livestock were now penned. The settlement extended up the hillsides, which was no easy undertaking on an island consisting of many hills, valleys and steep ridges all thick with pines.

'And what are these seeds and plants the governor has given to us Ed, do you know?' she asked.

He continued to fold the earth, 'there are carnations and roses, lavender and dianthus in that seed mix, and the small plants are all kind of flowering growth. It seems Lieutenant King is homesick for his cottage garden.'

Ah dianthus, Susannah thought and when the new ground was ready she followed Edward's instructions as to how large to make the hole, how deep to push the seed into the earth and how far apart to plant the seedlings. It seemed to her that he knew how to do most things for she had watched him write and draw, build and plant and fish and heard him talking to some of the officers about where he thought crops should be planted to avoid the wind that regularly swept the island.

One by one she placed the seeds into the warmth of the rich black dirt, smoothing the soil back over the top and watering each planting. Never before had she been given a task to make things grow and she was surprised how much pleasure it was giving her. She knew there would be satisfaction in seeing the shoots emerge, watching as they grew, nurturing the plants into flowers. It did not matter that her fingernails were black with dirt, nor that her hands were rougher than a lady's, she felt content and at peace with this small world they were making.

Edward turned to Susannah, 'I think the lieutenant is impressed with you, you're never one to say no to a job and he sees that you do your work with no complaint or hint of irritation.'

'No, Ed Garth it is you he is impressed with. You put down the foundations for his cottage. You built it fast, giving good instruction to others and now we are planting his garden, just as he will like it. I heard him say to one of the marines that you had an eye for building and showed 'ingenuity', which I gather is a good thing,' she said grinning. 'And he speaks to you with respect.'

Edward pondered upon her words. There was a time when he believed he would have been successful, never thinking even for a moment he would be convicted of a crime he did not commit, and in that success he knew he would have commanded the respect of others. Lieutenant King respected him, it was true but he was still a convict.

When Edward had finished the digging and Susannah had planted her seeds, she went again to collect water. There was no want for fresh water on the island, as many as five streams flowed from Mount Pitt, crystal clean water the likes of which Susannah had never seen before and each time she drew water she took the opportunity to wash her hands, drink from the stream and splash her face. Fresh water was a luxury she would never take for granted, a gift she would forever be grateful for.

As she made her way back from the stream, she noticed Edward leaving the governor's cottage and making his way up the hillside. She had seen him do this almost daily, disappearing through the same little track he'd worn through the bushes.

What is he doing wearing that same path down day after day, she thought. She had not asked him, hoping he would offer her some reason but he hadn't and this time he had left without waiting to say good evening. When she finished the watering she followed him, through the gap in the thick briar and bush to the east of the island, to higher ground. The day was warm and she hitched her skirt up, tying it into a knot at the front, freeing her legs to walk more easily and to cool her. It took her some effort and little streaks of perspiration escaped from her temples and trickled to the side of her mouth.

She saw him ahead in a clearing and, partly hidden behind a shrub, she watched him cutting and carrying wood. Just below the ridge she could see a cottage beginning to take shape. In a spot that not only afforded some protection from the wind but also in parts provided a spectacular view across the valley to the ocean and toward the two smaller islands off the southern coast.

He raised a hand and wiped it across his forehead and Susannah stood mesmerised at the sight of him, until the sound of the 'ya ho' call of the island's curious native owl broke through the surrounding bush and Edward looked up seeing her.

Trying not to show her embarrassment at being caught spying on him, she walked toward him, deliberate, confident and thinking *what have I to lose* '…A fine spot to build your place. And Ed Garth who would you share this dwelling with?'

He just looked at her and smiled.

She was impatient. Yes, she had in the past weeks offered her lips to him and he had not only responded but he too had initiated many a kiss but whilst she had felt an eagerness in him, he still held back. She wanted for him to welcome her to his bed, to ask her to be his wife. But she saw he was still often preoccupied and deep in thought.

Now she felt inwardly quite annoyed he had not simply said *you Susannah, of course you.* And then she thought, *perhaps this measured holding back is a little struggle for power?* But before she could take him to task she saw from the corner of her eye the *Supply* leaving the cove and she turned to watch.

'Look there Ed, they are sailing her back to Port Jackson.' Susannah pointed to the vessel as her white sails hauled the *Supply* through the gap in the reef.

'I hope she makes it back safely,' Edward said. 'She's our contact with the outside world.'

'What are you worried about?' Susannah said, lifting her hands to her hips. 'We can always build our own boats, can't we?'

'I'm not so sure,' Edward said. 'The pine wood is too soft to be the mast of a large vessel. I know, I can feel it when I work with the timber and that which King thinks is flax good enough to make sailcloth from…well I cannot see how that will work. I think it's too light.'

Edward picked at some flax, showing it to Susannah and feeling its texture.

'Maybe my friend Jacob would have known how it could be done, this treating of the flax for the making of sails. He was a silk weaver back home. But still I think the plant is too weak for the task.'

'Well then Ed Garth, we will just have to stay here forever!'

She hoped for a smile, but Edward's gaze was drawn back to the *Supply* and a crease appeared between his eyes.

'Without the *Supply* we are without any means of escape, we are being left alone, and Susannah, I am worried about the crops, I have seen grubs on them.'

'Ed Garth, you worry too much. We have all we need here.'

Edward let it pass but in his days on the farm in Malmesbury he had seen the damage caterpillars could do and he was indeed worried.

They spoke a short while longer but there was only a little sunlight left and when Edward did not offer for her to stay, she reluctantly returned to her shelter. He did not entice her to remain with him that night, nor in the nights that immediately followed. He sometimes became distant in his mood and although he sometimes embraced her and even when at times she lay in his arms on his bed, feeling his arousal, he restrained himself. She could not quite believe he was not like other men. To Susannah he seemed to worry too much.

Within the passage of a few short months, what Edward had said came true. The pines on Norfolk proved unsuitable for large masts and the flax not suitable for sails and, although the many crops sewn in the rich soil were initially luxuriant and successful, this success turned to disappointment with the infestation of destructive flies and with grubs devouring the plants.

As if the pestilence was not enough, from time to time fierce sea winds blew strong across the island and in August of that first year, just as some of the produce was about to yield, a storm like a hurricane thrashed the island, causing grain to be ripped from the crops and for the harvest to suffer badly. The wind blew the vegetation flat to the ground and the rain fell in torrential sideways sheets, turning the streams into torrents, flooding the lower ground and causing waterfalls to form and gush walls of water down the cliffs of Cascade Bay.

When the rain stopped Edward thought it looked for all like devastation but Susannah refused to let herself slip into the same kind of melancholy she sometimes saw on his face and the faces of others.

'The crops will grow again. The sun will shine and the wind will ease. We should not lose heart.'

She often accompanied Edward to his spot on the hillside where his dwelling was nestled and yet still he did not ask her to stay with him. Of late she saw in him constant concern for the future, a concern that did not come naturally to her and his conversation was full of woe.

Still she somehow knew that this side of Edward was not the only side of him, not the one she had seen before and which she still saw from time to time and she re-assured herself that he remained the man she should be with.

Edward held Susannah's hand.

'There is no disease here and no natives to contend with but if the crops continue to fail more hardship is going to fall upon us. The stores of grain and livestock are running low and there has not been one ship come to replenish us.'

'Well we will have to work harder. The sea is full of fish. There are the mutton birds and the turtles, there are plenty of them. And the soil grows plants well, the grubs will move on or die. We will get over this. We can survive without supplies from Port Jackson.'

Edward just shook his head.

'Yes, there have been turtles but they have proved to be few and far between and now the mutton birds are disappearing. To make matters worse a nest of rats was found in one of the bags of flour. I fear Susannah if a ship does not come soon with more supplies we will all be in serious trouble.'

Edward was showing signs of despairing and he was not the only one. King too was deeply worried sending men to catch as many fish as they could to smoke, but sometimes the seas were too large to venture out and the men resorted to catching whatever remaining birds they could find.

It was five months from the day when the flag had been raised on the sandy shore and Edward seemed more consumed in his thoughts than ever, the frown on his brow deeper than before. He thought if he just had enough grain he could cultivate in secret a small field of wheat near his dwelling, just large enough to manage one small harvest and he believed with his vigilance he could protect the crop from the pestilence. It was nearly spring and he was given the job of carrying a large bag of wheat from the main area of the settlement to Arthur's Vale, a newly cleared piece of land near where he had built his dwelling.

As he passed by his cottage Edward hesitated. *Surely a few handfuls will not make a difference to the field at Arthur's Vale* he thought and looking around him, making sure no one saw, he scooped out some wheat and left it wrapped in his bedding.

Although he had tied up the bag again as best he could the officious public servant taking receipt of it noticed.

'Why is this not full?' he asked.

Edward had thought it would not be obvious, that a few small scoops would not be missed, but having been caught out he felt compelled to tell the truth.

'I have saved some to plant in case a crisis befalls us,' he said hoping the officer would let it pass.

'You'll have to explain your actions to the lieutenant.'

Susannah was tending King's garden when she saw Edward and one of the storekeepers speaking with King in an animated manner. Leaving the garden, she made her way to where they stood and in horror listened.

'You did this understanding we have no knowledge of when a ship will arrive with more supplies!'

'I did this knowing if a ship did not arrive and the grain stores were depleted I could cultivate a small crop and that it may help,' replied Edward.

'I cannot have men taking matters into their own hands. You have left me no choice. If I let you get away with this, others will not be deterred.' King turned to one of his marines, 'Choose a convict to administer a flogging. Edward Garth for your transgression, tomorrow you will receive 100 lashes...'

Even when she had been under the threat of her own hanging Susannah had not felt weak but now, with King's words ringing in her ears she felt her legs quivering and heard herself saying, 'No, please governor! Ed is one of your best!'

But King did not relent and Edward was ordered to present himself the next morning.

Susannah had witnessed the administering of such punishment upon others, indeed some who had endured floggings had nearly died. That night she could not sleep and lighting an oil lamp she walked from her quarters into the stillness of the night to Edward's cottage. As she approached, she saw him standing at his doorway. Her heart ached for him and she held out her hand to his, squeezing it lightly.

'Oh Ed of all the things...' and whilst he said little, it was not necessary to speak, for more was being said by the silence.

She stayed the night in his cottage, not with the expectation that he would make love to her as she had for so long yearned, but to comfort him and hold him as they fitfully dozed, the pall of what would happen the next morning, hanging over them.

The next morning, she followed Edward as he was escorted to the centre of the main settlement. She could see him steeling himself for his ordeal with both resignation and apprehension on his face. This was the second error of judgment he had made, the first to take cows to market for a man he did not know. For the first he had paid with his freedom, the second would be paid for with his flesh.

There was silence amongst the community. All were made to assemble for the purpose of watching. King had ordered this to demonstrate that everyone was required to submit to his authority. If he punished one of his favorites, the rest of the colony could be sure they too would be punished if they committed any such indiscretions.

The short whip hung from the flagellator's hand, nine strands of leather, knotted in intervals along its length, designed to bite into the skin. Edward was stripped to the waist and suspended by the wrists beneath a tripod of wooden beams.

Susannah held her hand to her mouth, stifling the sound of her tears. She thought the first lash would be the hardest to bear, the one that would make a man flinch the most, carrying with it the sound of that initial crack of the

54

leather on virgin skin. She hoped that a numbness would set in soon after for she knew the skin usually split after the first several lashes and she prayed his backbone would not be exposed.

As each one of Edward's lashes were counted aloud the impact grew worse and the flesh began to welt, then bleed and pieces of his skin flung loose from his back as the cat o' nine tales was whipped back and forth. Susannah could barely look but felt compelled to share his ordeal, praying the whole time for some intervention to ease his pain.

With every lash he grimaced and winced in agony but he made no sound. Susannah knew he would not, the silent code of convicts had always been not to utter any words or to cry out, no matter how hard the punishment was to bear. As the doctor stood by waiting to see if Edward displayed any signs of expiring, Susannah wept openly staring from King to Edward in disbelief and sadness.

Edward remained conscious throughout his ordeal but his knees buckled, sweat and blood dripped from his body and the skin on his back peeled open. King himself inwardly winced at the sight.

The lashes were called out, one to one hundred and for Susannah it seemed the end would never arrive. With each lash she flinched and with every crack of the whip on flesh, she felt the nausea rising. Blood ran down Edward's back, inside the legs of his pants and she could see it seeping out the bottom of his trousers, dripping into his shoes. She had seen floggings before, some men had not survived and she found herself praying silently that Edward would not be one of their number.

When he was finally helped down and led away to the surgeon's tent, Susannah ran to him, King directing her as she did, that she was to tend his wounds.

Gently he was laid upon his stomach and carefully, tentatively Susannah applied brine to the lesions. At first he winced at her touch and as he did her salty tears spilled over her cheeks and onto her hands. Susannah mopped his brow and tended his lacerations with such tenderness that Edward's pain was soothed and he eventually slipped into sleep. As he slept Susannah pondered, blaming herself.

If I had been with him, if I had just prevailed upon him to take me into his home, this would never have happened. I should have insisted, I should have shaken him into action, to forget his past and any longing to go home, if I had just made him release himself into my heart and arms this would not have happened. Here we are now months since arriving and I should have told him of my past and I should have convinced him of our future together. I should have been with him. I would never have let this happen.

In the week Edward spent in the surgeon's tent Susannah barely left his side. She looked after him and distracted him, finally telling him the stories of her life, promising herself that when this trial had passed, she would make him realise his future was with her.

At first she was not sure he was listening but he nodded for her to continue and each day when she cleaned and tended his wounds she told him a little more.

'I imagine Ed with this awful time you have thought of your mother. She would have stroked your forehead and wiped away your tears. There'd have been comfort in her touch. I don't remember my mother. If it were not that I knew where babies came from I would have thought I had just somehow happened on to this earth, dropped from somewhere and gradually just understood I was alive.

I used to watch other children with their mothers outside those upper class grand terraces. I used to imagine myself as one of those girls whose mother fixed their bonnet, smoothed their dress and plaited their hair.

As a wee girl I had no-one to love me. I didn't know what it was to love someone else. I thought I felt it once, love that is. There was a boy who shared a mouldy blanket with me on the floor of a room in a falling down house. We took shelter there together for, I think it was months and then, one day I woke up and he was gone. I never saw him again.

Did your mother help teach you things? Did she read you stories? I don't even know how my name is spelt. I can't read or write proper words. I know some letters but I don't know how to put them together to make sense.

I've always been called Susannah Gough. I don't know why or who gave me the name. I don't care much for Gough but I like the way Susannah sounds, it rolls off the tongue, don't you think?'

Edward listened, allowing the sound of her voice and the touch of her fingers to soothe him. She moved long strands of his hair away from his face and traced her fingers along his arms. She didn't expect any answers to her questions, she spoke to comfort him there was no need for answers.

'Someone, I can't remember who, told me I was born in the year 1763. I lived my whole life in St Giles in cahoots with other guttersnipes and as we grew we did what we had to put some food in our stomachs and clothes on our backs.

In the end it was my body that saved me. I was shapely and I'm sure I don't have to tell you Ed that even without a pretty face a woman can sell her body. Some say it was wrong but it was my saving.'

Edward looked at her, her words mingling with his dreams. He thought her beautiful. She had long, shiny dark hair, which she twisted into a knot on the top of her head, a few strands escaping around her face and her eyes were pale and blue like the sky of a midwinter's day. Her skin was clear and her body more than appealing. She spoke with her common London accent but he knew her mind was sharp.

In and out of sleep he saw her, in visions of the present and tomorrow.

'Did your mother sing you lullabies Ed? I may not be able to read or write but you know I can sing' and she began to hum and then sing, in a tone that healed and tempered his pain and for those few moments, others outside the tent stopped what they were doing and listened.

She thought she saw a small tear escape from the corner of his eye and drew closer to him and kissed him on the forehead, a soft motherly kiss.

'On the day I was arrested I saw a little girl. She was crying. It was a wailing mournful sound. She was being dragged by an old woman and the girl was crying out to her mother who was walking away from her and disappearing down a foggy lane. The child was calling out 'Mumma Mumma, no…' I could see the child was all a panic and it tugged at my heart. As I passed by her I wondered had I been forsaken that way. Had my own mother just left me like that? And you know Ed, somewhere inside me a feeling rose up. It was a feeling I knew, from when I was a wee girl myself. I'd kept it, I felt it in here,' she said placing her palm against her heart, it was a sad feeling from some other time, tucked away.

'When I saw the woman take the child into a tavern I remember thinking that at least she would have a roof over her head, maybe they would treat her well. But when you are on the street Ed no-one treats you well. You get cunning and you steal because if you don't you die. And you learn that gin shops and taverns offer warmth.

As I grew up the taverns were full of sailors and men wanting to spend their money on grog and women. I knew some looked down their noses at the likes of me but any woman who grew up as an orphan on those streets would have had no trouble making a choice between going hungry or selling her body.

I decided I would not act like the street walkers. I didn't swear or lift my petticoat in alleyways. I copied the ladies who came into London from the country in grand carriages. I copied the way they held themselves and the way they spoke and I tried to be choosey about who I gave my custom to. I earned enough money to buy cloth to make one special dress and I thought I looked better than the tramps in the streets.

It was that same night I saw the child when I went to the Cart and Horses at Piccadilly that I was arrested. I used to work with another girl there. Her name is Elizabeth Dudgeons. There was a room in the tavern where we took our customers and that night there was a very drunk wealthy looking gentleman who was pawing at me. Elizabeth and I took him to bed. He was barely undressed before he took his pleasure and then fell asleep without paying us. So Elizabeth and I took it upon ourselves to go through his pockets. I can't say I am ashamed Ed, for I am not. You may not agree but all I did was done in need.

When he woke up he came roaring down into the bar. Elizabeth hid under a bed but he had found her and dragged her up to me. He stood at my toes and demanded I let him search me, which I did. He slid his hands all over me, under my clothes and through my hair but he found nothing. I thought I had gotten away with it but he came back later with a peace officer and I was forced to the cells. It would have been no use me taking flight, everyone around about knew me. I thought I would just lie; what choice did I have?'

Each day Susannah recounted more of her story and as each day passed Edward became less constrained by his pain, opening his eyes longer and looking forward to the sound of her voice.

'Elizabeth was trouble from the start, she cursed all the way to the cells drawing attention to us and when I had to respond to nature's call there was no privy. But it was not that which caused the hoots and yelling of the other prisoners, it was when I had to search through my own business to find the coins I had swallowed that the ruckus began and it got the attention of the guard who pounced on me. I didn't know what to say I blurted out something about the money being my cousin's home from the sea and me keeping it safe for him. But the gaoler just laughed and took the money, eight guineas they said it was that I'd swallowed!'

Susannah knew there was a chance that Edward would be repulsed by what she was saying but she had come this far with her tale and thought there was little point holding back the whole truth.

'I knew that others had faced the noose for crimes less than this. I'd always heard talk of God and the hereafter. I don't think I am scared of death. I didn't think so at the time. I thought if I am to die and meet my God and if He is merciful He would not judge me harshly. If He was all knowing as they preached, then He we would know I only took what was fair. No, it was not death, it is not death I fear Ed, it is having this life taken from me.'

As the days went on Edward found himself re-assessing his outlook on life. He listened to Susannah and saw more clearly how she viewed her own existence. To her it was a gift to be made the most of and he found himself embracing what he started to call in his head 'Susannah's truth'.

'When I went before the Judge I told him I had nobody to vouch for my character but God and him and that I had not a friend in the world. Perhaps he listened and maybe I found a merciful place in him, for it was not a sentence of death but seven years' transportation to Africa that he brought down. I did not blink an eye when he made his sentence, but I was inwardly grateful at having my life spared.

I'd hoped that my transportation would be swift, I had no desire to spend endless days in the putrid cells. But like the gates of hell itself, the gates to Newgate were waiting for me. The prison was riddled with disease. People were starving in there and the violence was worse than what I'd seen. The gaol seemed to go on and on further into the earth and the floors were wet and rats scurried everywhere. But I know Ed you have been there too and were witness to the suffering just like me.

I kept to myself. I know you had Jacob, but I befriended no-one and I even kept my distance from Elizabeth for she was always in trouble with the gaolers, giving cheek and trading favours. No, I stayed away and I tried to stay alive.

Once when I held my hand out through the bars into the street in the hope of some tiny morsel of food, I was handed a small tin cup by someone with fresh water in it and I guarded that cup so fierce. I used it to catch the rain to drink. When people were coughing and sick around me I covered my mouth and nose with a rag and literally held my breath as much as I could so I didn't get sick. But when winter came the freezing stone and wet forced me to huddle with others. I don't know how long I was there but it was nearly half a year before they took me out.

What a fuss some of those women made, crying about not wanting to leave and saying they'd rather be hanged than shipped away to Africa, a place where they said there were wild animals and cannibals. But I was glad. There was nothing that I loved that I would be leaving behind.

We were taken onto the *Mercury* at Gravesend. I was happy for the fresh air the ship's deck offered but down below it was no better than Newgate. Down in the hull there was no room to move and when the hatch was closed there was barely a sliver of light or breath of air.

A little while after we'd set sail, I could hear a huge commotion on deck. People were yelling out and muskets were firing. Some of the convicts had rose up against the crew and when they opened the hatch I found myself rushing to join them.

I knew I had wanted to leave London but I'd never been to the countryside and it looked a picture. We weren't far from land and I began to imagine stealing some clothes, living in the forests or somehow earning a living from sewing or as a maid, or if needs be a whore, far away from the sour air of London. I even thought about trying to swim ashore myself but I didn't know how and besides I had no want to end up dead in the English Channel.

They'd lowered some of the longboats and in the ruckus I managed to struggle down the side of the ship into one.

There was confusion and a frenzy of movement. The rowboat shook and swayed with people leaping into it and bodies falling about it. I held on tight. I'd seen death many times before, horrible deaths but this seemed somehow worse, here were healthy people falling into the freezing water. They couldn't swim and they'd gasp for air before slipping under. Twas a terrible sight.

Before we knew it guards in boats were bearing down on us and before we could reach land we were stopped.

They told me later if I had made it to shore I'd have been hung because I would have been said to have escaped but as I had not left the longboat I did not suffer that punishment. If I'd known I could lose my life by hanging I wouldn't have taken the chance, for as miserable a life as I had lived, my life was still a life worth living.

I was sent to Exeter prison and then the *Dunkirk* hulk. It was there I spent about three more long, miserable years.'

Edward knew of the hell of the prisons and the hulks and he had seen the way women were treated. Susannah's sorry tale resonated within him and as the heat and pain of his wounds gradually subsided, he found himself coming to know her well, like he had known no other person and each day his feelings for her grew stronger. He thought he had become somewhat immune and hard to the world but this was a woman he found himself caring for deeply.

'Ed, I know I was a prostitute but it was out of necessity. On the hulk the guards took us when they felt the urge. It was violent and depraved. Some of the marines forced themselves on us, raping us in vile ways. I tried to cover my face and avoided looking at the gaolers but one day I was forced into a corner against the rocky cell wall. He had my face pinned hard against the stone, a sharp edge of rock tore at my cheek and soon I could taste blood in the corner of my mouth.

He had reefed up my dress and was pressing himself upon me. In that instant I recalled having been told by a kindly guard that a new code of conduct had come into force and I turned my face to him so he could see my eyes. He was breathing his foul breath upon me and before he could do what he was about to, I told him I would protest to the superintendent but if he stopped I would remain silent; if he didn't stop he would have to kill me to silence me. He let me go. I couldn't really believe it. After that whenever he saw me he sneered and cursed at me. He was the last person to speak to me before I was led away from the *Dunkirk.* He said to me that I was going to the bottom of the world. The laugh is on him eh Ed?'

Seven days after the flogging, as Edward walked away from the surgeon's tent, they saw in the distance the *Supply* approaching. Had the ship arrived a week sooner with the much-needed fresh provisions, the temptation for Edward to take matters into his own hands may not have arisen. As they passed by King's dwelling, King looked out to the approaching vessel and back toward Edward and even as King felt relief at the sight of the ship, it was with some heaviness in his heart that he watched Edward go by.

It was still some weeks before Edward could return to normal duties. The night before he was due to resume his tasks Susannah looked upon his wounds. They were healing well, they had scarred over and were no longer painful to touch but hard ridges of skin formed in streaks across his back and the sight was enough to make her cry knowing the pain he had suffered.

She took Edward by the hand and out of his cottage into the open air.

'Look up there Ed Garth, those are the stars of our new world, they shine for us, as does the fullness of the moon above your little house. It's time to live our life. I'll not ask you to marry me and I'll not wait for you to ask me. It is our time, married or not.'

And under the canopy of unfamiliar stars and the shine of the radiant moon set firmly in the granite sky, she undressed, the complete reveal of her shapely body silhouetted in the moonlight.

He no longer held back, he knew death could come at any time, the whipping had brought that reality. Any reluctance he had felt about forming a relationship with Susannah and any concern he had that he would have to leave her when he returned to England vanished, he would not leave her, he would not go back. No longer would he allow consternation to occupy him or restrain him and he ardently took her into his arms and into his bed.

That night was a night like no other. There were no restraints or inhibitions, it was unbridled fervor, a mixture of passion and love that released itself through their bodies and hearts. To them they were the only two people on the face of the earth. Susannah was skillful and mature, yet she submitted to his lead, the blend of their attributes leaving them breathless, time and again until finally, entwined they succumbed to sleep.

Chapter 4

1788-1790

A shard of light pierced the timber shutters, the morning call of birds broke the air. Her dark hair lay loose across his chest as her head rested there. With the new day Susannah felt new hope, *this is the first morning* she thought, *the first morning of our life together*.

From that day Susannah saw a change in him. His serious side remained but more and more, the likeable and self-assured traits which Edward possessed emerged with the confidence he felt in his place by her side.

They were in love, as fully and deeply as any two could be. There was a combined ambition in their coupling and, there was happiness. She thought for them both when she thought that soon the flogging would become a distant memory and she knew that Edward's once longed for wish to return to England had finally for all time been abandoned.

Edward had brought with him one possession from his family, a bible. As she sat with him at the kitchen table he had carved out from the pines, Susannah noticed it, picked it up and opened it. There was writing etched upon the front cover.

'What does it say Ed?'

He began to read it aloud. When he had finished she was determined to commit the story to her memory, practising it over and over in her head.

69

The way the words went together. For she was not sure if she would ever learn to read and she wanted to remember it. She was by now convinced they would always be together and imagined if she and Edward ever had children of their own she would be able to tell them this tale. She memorised what he said, recalled it to herself and believed the story that she would tell their children one day would go something like:

Your father hailed from royalty. His ancestors had lived in Garth castle. A castle that stands on a rocky point above the Glen of Keltney Burn in Scotland. It was built hundreds of years ago by one of the royal Stewarts, a son of King Robert II of Scotland. King Robert II had married the daughter of the hero Robert the Bruce and the Garths are descended from these Stewarts of Garth, whether from Walter Stewart the Earl of Athol, Alexander Stewart or one of the many sons of Robert the 2nd, no-one is sure.

It was said that Walter Stewart was not impressed with his nephew James 1st. James, who had become King of Scotland. He had fought with the British against the Scots and Walter hated him for this. On James' return to Scotland the Earl plotted a coup against him. Although James was murdered, the coup itself failed and many of those related to the Stewarts fled Scotland, one such ancestor taking the name Garth from the 'Stewarts of Garth' of Perthshire, where Garth castle was built. It is this unnamed ancestor, that settled in Wales in the town that became known as Garth, from whom you are descended.

70

Three hundred and fifty years after the Stewarts fled Scotland Susannah listened and impressed the story forever in her mind. She was sure that the brave blood of Robert the Bruce ran through Edward's veins.

****

With the arrival of the *Supply* came replenished stores and co-incidentally some months of renewed success in the crops. The settlement was no longer on the brink of disaster and promise rose again.

Edward bore the scars of his flogging and although the memory of the punishment still played upon his mind in nightmares that sometimes wrenched him from his sleep, with Susannah by his side he now carried a new sense of purpose. He was her husband; their future together was what he would look forward to.

In the days when his flesh had burned with pain, she had cared for him with such genuine devotion he had been moved by her and from this his love had grown. Now, each night when she gently massaged lotion into his back and sang with a voice so sweet he felt sure it came from God himself, he was full of adoration for her. He recognised the bond they now shared, a bond forged from the love and tenderness of a woman who would not be beaten down by circumstance.

Sometimes he simply watched her as she went about her chores, the way she tried to make things nice for them both. She took care in the way she did things for him, always smiling, never complaining and he noticed and was warm with gladness.

They were living in Edward's timber and stone cottage. Sometimes Susannah found herself running her hands along the twisted timber frames of the windows or the backs of the chairs, the little details whittled into the work, admiring what Edward had created from nothing and she breathed deep gulps of joy and sighed, closing her eyes and thinking of where she now was and of how she now belonged.

'Twas some unearthly force that brought us here Ed. Although I find it hard to forgive the governor for your flogging, he has given us hope for the future. He has let us make the most of our land and with the promise of land grants, it gives us good reason to do our best. Who would have thought Ed Garth that you a farm boy from royalty (she winked) and me an orphan, would end up together in this unlikely place; I'd call that fate.'

And Edward thought this another of Susannah's truths, that indeed it was some supernatural plan that had delivered them there.

She began to dream of children at her skirt, of walking about the island with them, treading well-worn paths. In the past she had listened to older prostitutes tell of how they chose their times for sex to minimise the chance of falling pregnant and Susannah had followed those instructions closely, for at the time she had no want to bring a child she could not care for into the world. Now she felt secure, both in her love and circumstance and she abandoned herself in unbridled lovemaking at will.

In timely fashion Susannah's belly swelled with new life. She was astonished by her own feelings. She cherished the life growing inside her, this fruit of love. Edward made a crib for the child, shaping and bending the timber upon which the cradle rested into arcs for rocking, smoothing the roughness of the wood back so it was soft to touch, whittling a delicate feather design into the small headboard, lovingly molding a bed for his first born child.

And when her labour began in the spring of 1789, Susannah rode the waves of her contractions, breathing through the pain and discomfort. As the pain grew stronger she fleetingly thought about mothers who had died in childbirth, *but I will survive this and so will you my baby.*

Healthy groans escaped Susannah's lips as the child was born, followed by silent tears of delight as she held her baby. *Unlike those motherless babies who were taken into a world where they would never know their mother, your Papa and I will raise you and we will care for you and love you.*

She thought she had never felt anything as soft, the babe was like silk against her breast. She looked at Edward.

'Thank God for our good fortune.'

The room filled with the sucking sounds of the tiny bald creature who, with her eyes wide open, was looking at her mother as if she'd always known her.

'I'd like to call her Mary,' Edward said beaming at Susannah and their daughter. 'After my mother.'

'Of course Ed Garth. If I knew my mother's name, I would join it with Mary.'

Susannah looked at their child and she was grateful she had endured the trials of Newgate, the hell of the *Dunkirk* and the journey to the other side of the earth for it had delivered her to the man who had fathered this delightful creature and who would father the rest of her children, someone she loved beyond measure and in awe she realized love came effortlessly.

In that moment she wondered, *did my own mother ever love me, did she ever hold me with this same emotion?* And she allowed herself to believe she had.

****

The summer came and went, after the initial hardship there was success in the harvest but with the arrival of more people and after a season of high winds and rain the crops suffered and with more mouths to feed the stores were again running low. The governor had announced all would be on stricter rations from the stores, warning against anyone being tempted to steal. Susannah knew there was no chance Edward would think of trying to take things into his own hands again, the flogging was still raw in their minds and whenever she ran her fingers across the scars on his back she remembered his pain.

Unlike the others, Susannah did not fret. She believed something would happen to make things better, just as it always did. It had been two years since they arrived, *an anniversary* she thought, *even though things are not perfect, they are worth celebrating*, but to her disappointment no-one seemed in the mood for celebration, worry was etched upon their faces.

Susannah was walking the ridge near Edward's dwelling, collecting palm fronds to make a rug for the floor. Mary was swaddled against her back, bundled into a cloth she had wrapped and tied over her shoulders and around her waist. Mary gurgled in Susannah's ear, blowing bubbles of contentment, wetting the side of her mother's face. The delight that Mary's baby-speak gave Susannah brought a song to her lips, the sweet sound contradicting the mutterings of worry that had been taking place for days now in the valley below.

It seemed a sense of doom had begun to seep into the community but Susannah held fast to her confidence that all would be well and as she raised her head to look towards the sea her voice stopped mid song. All within coo-ee heard Susannah's cry.

'A ship, a ship is coming!'

And baby Mary let out a squeal of fright at her mother's sudden loud voice.

'And there is another!' she called as the wings of white appeared on the horizon.

As the word spread people in procession made their way to the shore. Smiles of relief and chatterings of anticipation percolating throughout.

The *Supply* came into the bay safely but the swell was rising and the *Sirius* waited.

'I don't like their chances of coming in now, the swell is too high.'

'Surely their captain will not attempt it Ed, the word would have been given to him that the reef is dangerous. Surely he wouldn't try now.'

'The *Supply* has raised the flag to signal not to enter so I would think not, but sometimes it isn't until you are in the thick of it that you realise it is too late.'

Although there was obvious relief at the ships arriving, the sea was too rough to remove the stores and anxiety about bringing the *Sirius* into the bay could be seen in a line across Governor King's forehead. As they realised the *Sirius* would not enter that day, the crowd dispersed and Edward and Susannah heard the governor speaking to one of the marines who had rowed ashore earlier from the *Supply*.

'I hope whoever is in command of her has been well informed about the reef.'

'Sir, it is Captain John Hunter and Major Ross in command. They indeed know what they are doing. Also Ralph Clark is on board, he was appointed Major Ross' lieutenant, so between them they know how to manage a ship.'

'I hope you are right, but even with all their collective skill they may not be able to negotiate a reef such as this.'

Susannah gasped, 'Ralph Clark!' and immediately she felt a shiver up her spine.

The *Sirius* waited off shore and each morning the people waited to see if this was the day the ship would enter the bay.

Captain Hunter sailed the vessel to the north-east side of the island, where, at Cascade Bay there was one spot where a rock some distance into the sea was surrounded by deep water. He spoke to his officers.

'If we can land marines and convicts alike on that rock they can then be transported by longboat to shore.'

Captain Hunter and Major Ross watched from the bow of the *Sirius*, anxious and holding their breath as the swell broke over the longboats again and again causing the women and children to shriek with terror.

Somehow, through those long moments of anxiety and through the rocking and near overturning of the boat, those offloaded made it to shore.

Around 200 people were landed at Cascade Bay but none of the stores could be unloaded. Cascade Bay was miles from the main town at Sydney Bay on the southern side of the island. The tired and somewhat nervous passengers began to make their way along a track which they hoped would take them to the town, but it was not long before the sun began to set and they found themselves trying to find a place to sleep in the woods as night fell.

The next day Susannah was amongst those who saw the bedraggled travellers emerging from the bushes.

'Oh my Lord Ed, there's so many!'

'And every possession they have is on the *Sirius*. Who knows when they'll be able to offload everything from the ship?'

For three days Captain Hunter kept the boat in the open sea. On the day he decided to bring the ship into Sydney Bay, he observed it seemed a fine and pleasant day with a light breeze. As he drew nearer he saw the *Supply* lying at anchor in the bay and observed the signal upon the shore that boats might land.

Inhabitants old and new assembled on the shore when they noticed the ship was about to make its way in.

Edward knew the waters well.

'The swell is stronger than the wind and it belies the true conditions. The water seems calm but if you look closely you can see the rips,' he said pointing out to Susannah the direction of the currents.

Without the experience of ever having entered the bay Captain Hunter found himself on a course he could not turn back from. The *Sirius* lowered her mainsail and moved towards the cove. When the ship began navigating its way in, it was accompanied by frequent tacking.

All the inhabitants knew the danger of the reef and of the maze of sunken rocks through which the ship needed to pass to find the best place to put down anchor and they also knew the ship had supplies to alleviate the stores, so the cargo was precious to all.

Edward thought the maneuvering of the vessel was somewhat clumsy, but he breathed a sigh of relief when at last the anchor could be seen to be lowered, only to have that relief stifled as the *Sirius* struck the reef before the cable was secured.

Susannah's hand went to her mouth, in horror the crowd watched as water flowed fast into the hold and as the sailors frantically cut away the masts. There was hurried activity on board as all were employed in getting as much of the provisions as possible out of the hold and on deck.

Instead of dropping the seas were becoming heavier and with each surge of swell the boat listed and rocked.

'If she stays there she'll capsize for sure,' Edward said to Susannah as he looked towards the governor and his men. 'They don't have time to launch any longboats, the waves are rising too quickly.'

Governor King began giving orders from the shore, pointing at some of his marines and calling men by name to swim out to the ship to fix a cable to it.

'Be careful Ed!' Susannah called out as she watched him and others wading at first, then swimming, towing a heavy rope towards a large empty cask that had been dropped from the ship and was floating, being tossed about by the waves. Already attached to the cask was a thick hawser secured to the ship.

In the rough surf they grappled with the rope but finally managed to tie it to the cask, hauling it and the cask on to the land, then fastening the rope to a sturdy tree. As soon as the rope was sound, three and four people at a time began making their way down the side of the ship into the surf and across the reef towards land, clinging to the hawser and being assisted by those who waded onto the reef from the shore.

Edward helped in bringing people ashore, battling through the waves and dragging them onto the beach then grappling his way out again through the surf. It was there, in the swirling water, in the melee of whitewash and struggling passengers that he saw the familiar face of his old friend and swam hard towards him. Jacob was being flung about on the ragged rocks, holding on for dear life to the rope, the waves crashing over his head. He was tired and straining against the pull of the rip but when he saw it was Edward who had come to rescue him he tried to find some renewed strength.

'Edward!' he gasped and reached for his friend.

Exhausted he held on to the line with one hand and Edward with the other. The tide was rising, the water becoming deeper and both of them were hurled about as the waves sucked in and out over the reef. Jacob's arms ached with the effort, his legs lacerated on the coral and his lungs hungered for more air.

'Nearly there my friend,' Edward shouted over the roar of the surf. 'Hold on!'

Susannah watched from the shoreline, Mary on her hip, her free hand held to the side of her head, occasionally lifting it up to the heavens in a prayer. Not since the flogging had she been so afraid.

Edward and Jacob battled their way through the swell, sometimes waves washing over them, Susannah holding her breath until she saw their heads bob above the waves. It seemed an eternity before they reached the beach and when they finally fell upon the sand, bone-tired and breathing hard, Susannah rushed to Edward draping Mary's blanket about his shoulders.

'Thank God you are safe,' she said holding him against them both.

Mary began to cry, but it was a ragged laugh that escaped Edward's lips and when they had enough energy Edward and Jacob embraced as the friends they were, smiling broadly at each other.

'Remind me to teach you how to swim my friend,' Edward said, his arm draped about Jacob's shoulder.

They removed their shirts and trousers to dry. It was then Jacob noticed the scars on Edward's back and Susannah saw the way Jacob looked at Edward, the disconcerted crease across his forehead. Jacob had seen these scars on others and knew they were the permanent legacy of a flogging. He would leave the asking for another day, for now he was grateful to be alive and in the company of his old friend.

Jacob was one of the last to reach the shore that evening. The remainder of those who had not made it to land stayed on board the ship overnight, it was too dangerous to continue to haul people in the darkness and the rising tide.

Few provisions had been brought ashore. The great majority of the stores sat on the deck of the *Sirius* as she rocked and creaked upon the reef.

'You must stay with us Jacob,' Susannah said. 'Our home is a little climb though, up the hill through the bushes.'

'You have a home of your own? I had heard of King's kindly leadership and before we were shipped from Port Jackson we were told of his promise to provide land grants if we stayed after our sentences had expired, but it seemed too good to be true.'

'Indeed it is true my friend,' said Edward. 'I've built our home in the hope that the land upon which it sits will one day be mine.

And tell me of those who command the *Sirius*?'

'Tis Admiral Hunter, Major Ross and his Lieutenant Clark,' said Jacob.

'Ralph Clark.' Susannah interrupted. 'Dear heaven, he was the marine who hated us on board the *Friendship*, he called all the women whores and had one of the women flogged regularly. He was a dreadful man. I remember the gossip on the ship how he missed his wife so much that he kissed her picture every day and that it was wearing away due to the ardor of his lips!'

'He may miss his wife but he has taken one of the convict women as his mistress and brought her here with him,' replied Jacob.

'We can only hope she may have mellowed his mood toward us women,' said Susannah. 'Enough for tonight though, you and Ed must eat and then sleep as they'll no doubt want all men to help with getting those supplies off the *Sirius* tomorrow.'

That night Susannah made a bed for Jacob on the floor but early the next morning Edward was up building a bunk for his friend to sleep in.

Over the following days, when the tide was right and the surf less treacherous, more people were brought ashore. Eventually the weather eased, the surf smoothed and although there was a continual break of waves against the ship, those who could swim were engaged with the task of making their way out to her and floating casks, which contained the much needed provisions, across the reef to the sand.

To prevent opportunists pilfering, Edward and Jacob were ordered to stand guard over the provisions once they were brought on land.

'Tis a miracle that not a soul was lost but still tis a sorry sight Jacob,' Edward lamented as they both watched the ship listing to one side. 'As they lighten her load she is being lifted and dropped more heavily onto that reef. I fear she will be broken up and there I'm afraid she will stay.'

As the ship leaned more to the side provisions washed off the deck, some floated under their own steam to shore while others were dashed upon the rocks and lost, claimed by the perilous reef.

In no time the ship was torn apart, the remains of her hull forever wedged amongst the coral and underwater ledges of Sydney Bay.

If they had read Lieutenant Clark's diary during those days before the *Sirius* was finally claimed by the sea, they would have known what he thought of the whole sorry event:

Cut a way all her mast gracious god what will become of us all, the whole of our Provision in the Ship now a Wreck before us I hope in god that we will be able to Save Some if not all but why doe I flatter myself with Such hopes there is at present no prospect of it except that of Starving. What will become of the people that are on board for no boat can goe along Side for the Sea and here am I who has nothing more than what I stand in and not the small hope of my getting anything out of the Ship for every body expects that She will go to pieces when the tide comes in soon.

Saturday 20 have been up all night as has every body in the place Soon after the Ship went on Shore trunks, Boxs beds &c what was nearest at hand was thrown over board in hopes it would float on Shore a great dele has come on Shore but as Yet nothing of mine Captain Hunter and between 30 and 40 of the people came on Shore on a graiting made fast to hauzher and the Remainder are coming on Shore as fast as the[y] can as Yet there is nobody drownd or lost I was very near been drownd Yesterday when I was going of on the Raft to assist the people that were coming on Shore almost drownd on of the Convict who could not Swim, fell of the Raft and pushd me along with him, in which case we Should both have been drownd if I could not have Swimd for the Raft went over us both and I was obligd to

85

Swim back to the Shor with him holding fast to me by the waisband of my Trousers.

****

It was not long before news spread that King was to sail the *Supply* back to England and Major Ross was to be the new Commander on the island with Lieutenant Ralph Clark his second in charge.

There was trepidation amongst the community. Some were fearful of what the new command would mean for them. King had been mostly an empathetic and kind man who led them with real care and concern about their future, whereas Major Ross was an unknown to them and as Susannah knew, Ralph Clark had sometimes been a ruthless officer.

Lieutenant Clark had been a prisoner of the French and was tough. He argued with Arthur Phillip and other officers back at Port Jackson as had Major Ross and it was rumoured they had been sent to Norfolk to prevent further conflict between them and Arthur Phillip, but Phillip's relief at not having Ross about was Norfolk's dread, for with his arrival, the wrecking of the *Sirius* and the departure of Governor King, Ross proclaimed martial law.

The settlers were not used to being treated as convicts and a real dejection began to develop amongst them. One evening after the last retrievable stores from the *Sirius* had been brought ashore, Edward, Susannah and Jacob ate their evening meal together.

'With King gone things will be different. Ross is unyielding and he thinks we are treated too well. What's more that lieutenant of his, Ralph Clark, he is a severe officer also.'

'I told you what he was like,' said Susannah, a grimace upon her lips. 'He had no regard for the women and treated us poorly. It was nothing for him to publicly call the women whores, even those who were not.'

When she had seen Ralph Clark come ashore her memories of her time on the *Friendship* crept back.

'I wonder whether now he has taken a convict woman as a mistress will he have changed his view. Perhaps once he sees how women like us have been made respectable and provided good homes for their families he will soften.'

Jacob looked across the table at Edward.

'And what of King's promise of land grants, do you think Major Ross will follow through with that pledge?'

'Surely the governor will still require the Major to adhere to this promise. I think Ross wants us to be able to fend for ourselves so we are not dependent on the government stores. He wants us to keep growing our own food. All we have to do is what we have been doing. It is the lazy ones that should be worried. Lately, I've seen how Ross treats those who work hard.

He seems to have no quarrel with them, with us and so the martial law should not affect us.'

Susannah looked to Edward. 'I think the governor will be missed by us all,' she said. 'But it is Ann Innet I feel sorriest for. She has been King's wife since we have been here and she had his children. What will become of her? She loves him and he her.'

'They say he has found another husband for her. She would never have been accepted as his wife back home and besides, I hear rumour he may have another family waiting for him in England. Tis a sorry state but they both would have known this would happen,' said Edward remembering the ambition he once had to return home.

'And Lieutenant Clark's mistress, Mary Branham, no doubt he also he will leave her and any children they may have one day and return to his wife and child in England. After all he nearly wore out the picture of her kissing it every day.' Susannah chuckled at the image of the lieutenant in her mind and wondered if he still did that with his mistress by his side.

'And Jacob, what of you? Ed says you had a sweetheart you had to leave behind?'

Susannah was not shy in speaking her mind and was curious, it came naturally to her but she could see Jacob's sadness at the question and thought perhaps she should not have been so direct.

'Aye, I had a sweetheart, Aileen. She lived no more than two blocks from my family at Webb Square. Every day I would detour past her house on my way to work. I worked in Duke Street at John Gearing's weaving business, you might know the place. I'd lived in Shoreditch my whole life, baptised at St Leonard's Church.

I knew lots of girls. I have to admit I always had an eye for a pretty girl but there was only one for me.'

Susannah was sure this stocky young man, with his shock of blonde hair, strong jawline and granite-blue eyes could have had his pick of pretty girls.

'We had known each other for as long as I can remember, we grew up together. Our families thought we would marry and that is what we had planned to do. I saw us living in a fine terrace one day amongst the homes of the master weavers.

We'd go for long walks down Threadneedle Street and Petticoat Lane and on Sundays up along the City Road, past the Old Eagle Public House and hear the bells of St Mary's. We lived among the places in the nursery rhymes that we sang and had grown up with.'

Susannah found herself thinking, here was a lucky childhood, unlike her own, another man who could read and write and make things, another man similar to her Ed and she hoped he could find a good wife among those on the island. But, just as Edward had once been homesick so Jacob still was and she could tell it would take some special woman to make him see differently.

'I'd seen my father make a good life for us. My brothers and sisters and I had gone to school, had jobs and I used to dream of a day when I would open up my own warehouse and import and export cloth. We had connections in France and I was hopeful I could one day make a go of it. Years before my father's grandfather had fled France with the protestant Huguenots who had escaped to England amidst religious persecution and they settled in Spitalfields, but we still have family in Paris.

I knew my trade well. I'd struck my own path and instead of taking the easier road working with my father in the upholstering business, I obtained work at Gearings. I'd been there for three years leading up to that terrible day. It was five years ago now, in 1784.

I learned the skills of spinning fine yarn and of choosing the best silk. My bosses Mr Gearing, Mr Vaux and Mr Taylor saw talent in me and valued my work but unknown to me, my colleague William Cole also saw this and was jealous. William Cole was a greedy and devious man and it was he who brought about my downfall.'

Susannah thought about the way Jacob spoke, like her Ed he spoke as an educated man and thought lightheartedly *Ed Garth you're lucky this one didn't come along first.*

'I had noticed from time to time that yarn had been cut and some missing and commented to Cole about it. In my naivety once Cole knew this he set about planning to kill two birds with one stone, to get rid of me and at the same time to deflect any suspicion from himself about missing cloth.

On Christmas Day he strode brazenly to Aileen's home and straight out accused me of stealing silk. I was furious and told him I'd give him a hiding if he didn't leave. He was clever in that he picked an important day, feigning shock at his false discovery and making everyone think he must be telling the truth if he were to make his accusations so confidently on that day of all days.

But later when Aileen and I were visiting our neighbours, Cole went to my home saying I'd stolen cloth and demanded to search the house. My brother-in-law humoured him and allowed him into my room. It was there he pretended to find the cloth. The truth is he must have secreted it in. My mother was angry and ordered him out and he came straight to where Aileen and I were taking afternoon tea, shoving his way through the front door as soon as it was opened, accusing me of hiding in the pantry when I was just retrieving plates and threatening to have me hanged if I did not go with him to the Crown.

I was sure I would be able to expose Cole for the liar and thief he was but John Gray the peace officer took no heed of my story and it was then I was taken to Newgate.'

Susannah looked at Jacob, 'We all know what a hellhole that place is.'

'It wasn't until the new year of 1785 that my matter was heard. I stated my case but Cole and Mr Gray both lied. They must have been in it together. They said I had confessed and intended to sell the yarn to a Mr Jones who was a patron of the public house on the corner of Petticoat Lane and Cox's Square.

I had a lawyer who called five witnesses, all attesting to my good character but it was to no avail.'

'You two and your fancy lawyers,' Susannah winked at Edward.

'I will never forget the cries of my mother and Aileen and the tears even in my father's eyes. Like Ed I was taken to Newgate and then the *Ceres*. Aileen and my family visited me in the cells but it left them dismayed. They brought fresh fruit, clothes, soap, books to read, all to try and bring me some small comfort, but I dare not tell them that what was given to me was mostly stolen by overbearing violent prisoners… that is until Ed teamed up with me. Together we could fight off any would be thieves. We shared our food and meagre possessions and gave each other the encouragement we needed to survive.'

'Yes Jacob, it is true, we saw each other as brothers and victims also of an unjust system, so we made a pact to stick together and it was with sadness that we were separated. Still when I said good bye to you at Port Jackson I hoped one day we would meet again and here you are!' said Edward.

'Once you were around Ed, even though it was gaol, it was a comfort to have a friend beside me. Still, I spent long nights in the damp and grime of those cells imagining myself warm and happy in Webb Square, vowing that as soon as my sentence expired I would go back home. Do you remember Ed the folk songs we sang? And how sometimes other voices throughout the hulk would join in, the voices of other sad and melancholy creatures.'

As if transported back in time, he began to sing, a song which Susannah also knew and their three voices rang out through the night.

'The trees they grow so high and the leaves they do grow green

And many a cold winter's night, my love and I have seen.

Of a cold winter's night, my love, you and I alone have been…'

'Tis a fine voice you have Jacob but those songs bring tears and tis better we sing happy songs,' Susannah said with a wry smile. 'Still go on with your tale, it sounds like as sorry a tale as any can be.'

This one needs shaking from his downheartedness, she thought

'When we were finally moved for transportation my family and Aileen came to the docks. They were all weeping and I know Aileen was holding fast to my vow that I would one day return.'

'And then we ended up on the *Scarborough* eh, Jacob. She was a large vessel that one. Do you remember how we stood shoulder to shoulder on

93

the deck eight months later when we saw the fierce looking naked indians amongst the trees at Botany Bay and watched them holding up fire sticks in the air above their canoes?'

'Aye, I was uneasy but there was no violence then, not that day but sometime later, after you left Ed, the natives were no longer friendly. There's been killing on both sides.

And the lightning storms, like the one we had at Sydney Cove not long after the women convicts were brought ashore, they were frequent right through the next couple of months, striking trees and even livestock.

Do you remember Ed that night of drunkenness when the men and women were wild?'

Susannah looked at Edward, wondering had he joined in that night while she had been kept apart waiting with the other women to travel to Norfolk.

'I had been separated by then and didn't take part in any of that,' said Susannah quickly trying to distance herself from the debauchery which had unfolded that night.

Jacob looked at Susannah, 'You were fortunate. I found myself tangled up in the arms of a large bosomed woman who made a bee line for me amidst the bolts of lightning, the crashing of thunder and the singing and swearing, grabbing me and dragging me to her tent.'

Susannah and Edward began to laugh.

'Thankfully the next day order was swiftly returned and I was able to unleash myself.'

Susannah could understand completely how a woman could be wanton towards the handsome Jacob, but still she had to admit to herself *as handsome as he is, my Ed is more so and what's more he no longer has a distant sad look in his eyes.*

'Two weeks after we went ashore, when Ed was chosen to go to Norfolk Island, I implored Lieutenant King to let me join him, but I was denied.'

'Implored?' Susannah raised her eyebrow, *a fussy word* she thought.

'As I watched the *Supply* disappear from view that day I remember my heart was heavy and thinking, Aileen, my family and now my only real friend are gone…and asking, what curse is it that I have upon me to be removed from everyone I love?'

'But here you are now Jacob, with us and we will find you a woman,' Susannah said confidently.

Jacob sat back in his chair and Edward began to chuckle at Susannah's boldness.

'And what of Port Jackson Jacob? I hear it is in dire straits, worse than here,' asked Edward.

'After you left, I wasted no time in proving I was a valuable worker. I wanted to follow you to Norfolk. I ploughed fields and felled trees, volunteered to explore the great river that feeds into Port Jackson and planted crops at a place up river that Captain Phillip calls Rose Hill.

During that year the *Supply* came and went between Norfolk Island and Port Jackson. The stores from each settlement were shared but by the end of that year it was rumoured both settlements were heading towards famine.

The colony at Port Jackson was suffering, the initial promise of thriving crops and farming at Farm Cove was spoiled time and again through the harsh weather, fire and pests, too much rain or not enough.

As I said, some of the natives had become hostile and it became dangerous to venture anywhere too far from the settlement on your own. Their good nature seemed to wear off as they realised we had come not just to visit but to stay.

Still I witnessed the humanity in them. I saw black women cry at the lashing of the convicts and a native they called Manly, he was gentle and played with the children at the settlement. I also saw their fishing and hunting skills and was glad of the native who accompanied us up river to the place his people called Burramatta, 'the place where the eels lie', for it was there richer soil was found and a new settlement created where they were able to plant crops in better ground. I used to travel to and fro along the river from Burramatta to Port Jackson bringing crops grown up river back to the main settlement.

Although the harvest up river was beginning to be productive and although the *Sirius* had not long returned from the Cape of Good Hope with new supplies, soon enough the provisions again diminished and convicts began stealing. The governor sought to reduce the number of mouths to feed and decided the colony should be divided. That's when I was chosen with some other convicts and marines to come to Norfolk, to relieve the burden at Sydney Cove and at the same time deliver some supplies that had been saved for your settlement.

And as you say, now I am here.'

Susannah thought Jacob spoke like one of the marines, his sometimes *frilly words* and she chuckled to herself. *Yes*, she thought, *he will make a fine husband for someone, once we can make the sadness in his eyes disappear*.

Jacob stayed with Edward and Susannah for a short while until Edward helped him construct his own small dwelling in the valley, down the hill below. There was a spot next to a babbling stream that trickled its way through rocky banks towards the sea and Jacob saw this patch of ground as a pleasing location.

He and Edward collected stones for Jacob to make his fireplace, chimney and walls, Jacob thinking if he was to stay then this dwelling would last more than a lifetime.

'Thank you for welcoming me Ed, for helping me. You indeed seem happy my friend, radiating joy in fact.'

Jacob saw Edward no longer showed signs of the grief he had in those early days in Newgate and on the *Ceres* when they had talked of their families. He was living as Susannah's husband and Jacob could see, despite the hardship that still surrounded them, Edward was counting his blessings.

It was apparent to Jacob that Susannah's enthusiasm for life had seeped into Edward's being. She was herself an affirmation that hope can become reality.

'Jacob Bellett' she said to him, 'it has been your fate to come to this place, just as it was ours. There is a woman waiting for you, you just have to find her, after all who could resist a voice like yours.'

She smiled, thinking not only was it his voice that a woman would find appealing.

'You will make a home here, just as we have.'

'Tis another of Susannah's truths Jacob,' Edward said, encouraging this friend.

Still, Jacob found it hard to reconcile and whilst he quietly conceded to himself that perhaps one day he too could be happy if he stayed, he was also tormented by his vow to return to Aileen and what's more he could not ever imagine loving anyone as much as he loved her.

Chapter 5

1790

Just days after Jacob had arrived, he and Edward watched as Governor King took command of the *Supply* sailing her out of view, falling over the edge of the horizon. It was then Jacob asked about the scars and listened astonished as Edward spoke fondly of King, the man who had ordered such severe a punishment as to mark Edward for the rest of his days.

'I hold no grudge against him. He did what he had to do.'

'You're a better man than I. I don't know that I would be so forgiving.'

'It was the flogging that made me realise I must live for now and hope for tomorrow. It made me see my Susannah as someone I could not leave. She loves this place and I saw that she loves me. When I came out of the haze of pain, it was Susannah who brought me solace, not the thought of returning to England, not the thought of returning to be with my family. I suddenly understood, I belonged with her, no matter where that was and she, she has no want to return to England, you could not drag her back there, so, it is here we will stay.'

Jacob did not really want to face a life that meant he would never return to his home and to his sweetheart. He had convinced himself that Aileen would wait for him and had written to her reaffirming his love and promise to return but had never received a letter in return, whether that meant she had written back to him or not, he did not know. Jacob carried the burden of the vow he had made, at the same time holding on to the love he had for her. He felt uncomfortable talking about it, it just unsettled him further.

'Now Ed, what of our plight with Major Ross in command. With the sinking of the *Sirius* and King having left on the *Supply*, what lifeline do we have to the outside world?'

'I ask myself the same thing but I find if I let myself listen to Susannah, she always has a positive answer, she is my perfect foil,' Edward smiled. 'And she sees past the problem. Even though she was not schooled she is wise and has taught me to trust in hard work and determination, to have faith we will be able to not only endure but live our lives well. I see it as another of her truths. So even though there are more mouths to feed, there are also more hands to clear land and plant more crops…we will fish, catch birds, plough the ground. As Susannah says we will more than just keep body and soul together, we will live life.'

'But there are three hundred more people since the arrival of the *Sirius* and with the great majority of provisions on the *Sirius* being lost, surely the burden on the colony will grow and although the soil is good and the crops growing, we are still troubled with the regular fierce weather and the persistent grubs.'

Jacob paused then lowered his voice,

'I have noticed tensions are beginning to rise. While some of us have the satisfaction of being able to live in dwellings we have built on land we have chosen and eat food which we grow ourselves others and some of the newcomers, who have few skills, are discontent and prone to causing trouble.

Whilst Governor King started out the settlement with his band of trusties like you and Susannah, some other convicts who arrived on later transports don't appreciate the good things the island has to offer. You know there has recently been the rumblings of a rebellion. Governor King quelled those uneasy stirrings in his own way, the new governor is quite ruthless and means not to let any possibility of an uprising. Some resent Major Ross's bringing in martial law and are railing against it, egged on by the newcomer convicts who Ross treats like prisoners.'

Edward felt the line between his brows deepen.

'I can see why the major needs to be stricter but I think if we carry on the way we have, he will have no quarrel with us. Hopefully once he sees that we are productive and once we have some more success in the crops there will be no need for him to keep the martial law going. But he does need to give the new ones more incentive, give them what they need to try for themselves, like Governor King did.'

'I hope you are right Ed and I do think he does have everyone's best interests in mind but the sobering truth is at the moment, there are just too many people to feed and not enough supplies for everyone to have a reasonable helping.'

A few evenings later, Edward and Jacob were sent to hunt Mount Pitt birds, but returned to Edward's dwelling empty handed, disappointment on their faces. Susannah looked at Edward raising her eyebrow in question.

'So where are the birds?'

Edward had often caught the birds for meat for the settlement but where once the birds had nested in abundance and as many as eight birds could be caught at a time, they had now become scarce.

'We saw not a single bird,' replied Jacob. 'And, nobody knows whether word has managed to get back to Sydney Cove about the wreck of the *Sirius*. We don't even know if those at Port Jackson are aware our settlement still survives. And with things so dire back there, they may have even deserted us.

What's more, plagues of caterpillars are infesting the crops again. It's as if they come out of thin air, appearing almost overnight, first a few and now thousands upon thousands. The major has given orders that all our urine must be collected and spread over the fields!' Jacob said with eyebrows raised and a grimace on his face.

'That I think is a foolish idea,' said Edward. 'It won't deter the grubs!'

Susannah could see Edward's dismay.

'Well, what about the fishing boats. Ed some of the small boats you have built they can still withstand a fair swell.'

'Yes the major has given orders that all boats be employed to catch fish but the tides are still unfavourable and it is just too dangerous right now.'

Susannah looked at the men.

'Yesterday I spied a ship Ed. I was wishing it toward the shore but it just passsed us by. But one will come soon, I'm sure of it and just the other day another cask washed up from the *Sirius* with seeds and grain in it so that will boost the crops. Meantime we have the fish and what remains in the smokehouse. It is temporary. We should not lose hope. As surely as the sun rises we will pull through. It may take time but it will happen.'

Edward ran his hand through his hair and stroked at his beard, deliberately and slowly.

'It's a matter of how much time we have.'

In the days that followed, copious amounts of urine were collected and applied to the crops but just as Edward had predicted, this experiment served no good purpose and the majority of crops failed.

The main diet became salted pork and rice and there was little fresh produce. There was fear scurvy would break out and that the sick would not get the nourishment they needed to stave off death.

For some weeks the tides and swell combined to prevent the task of fishing and as June came and went many thought the settlement doomed.

'I fear we have been forgotten,' Jacob said one night as they sat around the fire at Edward and Susannah's cottage. It was August and baby Mary was gurgling and trying to pull herself up on Susannah's skirt. The fire was not to warm them, for it was rarely that cold, it was lit so the pork could be held over it and the dripping fat caught and applied to bread. The pork itself was so old now that to be able to eat it Susannah had resorted to boiling it up, *but still* she thought, *it is food and it will do the job for now.*

'They say things are dire…without a ship soon it could mean ruination for us.'

'For heaven's sake Jacob,' Susannah said. 'This is not dire straits. If we have to pick the oysters from the reef itself and eat the pepper plant by the handful, we can and we will. We will not go hungry, dire is not this! Dire is the way you live and the swill you have to eat in the likes of Newgate or the *Dunkirk*, or the scraps you pick up from under the tables of the wealthy in the streets of London. The opinion of the powers that be of dire is governed by their once overfull bellies!

My sentence has expired. I am now a free woman. One less hindrance and I for one am not giving up on us. I don't believe they have forgotten us. They have not brought us all this way to desert us. Even if they do not care for us, they would not leave Major Ross and his men high and dry. They will come. I know they will. There are still plenty of fish in the sea and fresh water to drink. We will survive and another ship will arrive.'

'Ever the optimist Susannah. What a find was she eh Jacob?' Edward said, trying to embrace Susannah's passion. Jacob felt reassured by her confidence and began to think how much easier it would be for him if he had a woman like Susannah by his side, if he had Aileen by his side.

That night, with dreams of white winged ships and tall fields of maize and wheat Susannah's sleep comforted her.

The next morning, five long months after the *Supply* had left, Edward and Jacob were working in a potato field harvesting a meager crop. The sea was like velvet, looking soft and pink in the hue created by the rising sun, when out of the mist a ship emerged like a ghost, she did not steer away but sailed toward the island. The call went out and the crowd began to gather on the shore, tears of joy in the eyes of the women and sighs of relief in the voices of those who watched as the ship approached.

The aptly named *Surprize* had arrived. Later from the haze a second ship emerged, the *Justinian,* and an atmosphere of anticipation permeated throughout the colony.

'What did I say?' Susannah chided Jacob as they watched with the others as the vessels tacked up and down outside the bay.

'Dare I say you were right… but we do not know what these ships bring with them,' said Jacob. Although relieved, he could still not let go of his doubts. 'Look, the same difficulty is being visited upon them as was upon the *Sirius*. It is no easy task to steer those boats safely into the bay and lay anchor.'

Edward held Susannah's hand and spoke, his familiar frown upon his face.

'Governor King knew the bay well, the lie of the reefs but for every new commander it is an unknown.'

Major Ross with some of his marines stood ready to order assistance. He knew first hand that negotiating the reef, the anchoring and coming ashore was a demanding task and the memory of the sinking of the *Sirius* was raw in his mind.

All could see the swell was rising and again the onlookers were anxious, no-one wanted to see another ship and her supplies dashed upon the spiral rocks that lay beneath the bay.

Eventually both the ships entered safely, dropping anchor. But instead of waiting for the seas to ease the longboats were lowered and people began to climb into them, trying to row their way across the reef through the choppy waves. It was precarious, the swell intensifying and becoming more treacherous.

Edward looked on with the others, as the longboats were tossed around.

'I cannot understand how it is not conveyed back to those who come here that the conditions must be just right before coming into this bay and trying to come ashore. It is as if no-one bothers to tell the next lot. Look there, that boat has just been swamped and look another!'

When people began falling into the sea an urgent call came from Major Ross ordering all able bodied men to assist in bringing people to shore.

Men and women floundered about in the surf. Out of the foam a mother appeared holding her child, struggling to stand in chest high water on the rocky floor but the rip was too strong, dragging her off her feet, her child cruelly snatched from her arms by the waves. The mother's screams could scarcely be heard above the crashing surf and in an instant, the child was gone.

Susannah pointed to the woman and Edward let go of Susannah's hand. He was a strong swimmer and made his way to her, again Susannah prayed for his safe return, looking up to the heavens. Edward reached the woman but could see no sign of the child, she had disappeared. Jacob also waded out and helped those struggling, bringing them one at a time to where they could more readily stand and clamber across the reef. Finally, when there was no-one else left to save, Jacob and Edward collapsed spent upon the shore. Around them passengers from the vessels either sat or lay trying to recover from their ordeal.

Susannah looked to where the child had been swept away, but there was no trace of the little one, *she has been swallowed up by the sea…*

'Dear Lord… the poor thing and the mother, she was trying so hard to hold on to her baby.' Susannah held Mary a little tighter as she looked at the mother who was pale and sobbing. The woman's distress set up an ache in Susannah's heart and tears sprang to her eyes.

She made her way to the mother, sat beside her, her arm across her shoulder. The woman was desolate, weeping uncontrollably and sitting beside her, holding her hand was another young woman, who cried with her, a new arrival trying to comfort the devastated lady. Susannah beckoned them to come with her to the hospital which they did and later, when the mother had been administered rum to calm her, Susannah spoke to new girl.

The sun shone strongly, with the sky as blue as cobalt and with the ironic splendour of Norfolk surrounding her, they left the sorrowful mother with the surgeon and walked up the hillside.

'I would say welcome but the delight I first felt when we saw your ships coming out of the fog this morning has been sorely worn by this cruel day. I am Susannah. I can't offer you much but I can offer you a place to stay until you have your lodgings sorted and, I can offer you some tea. Until we get the supplies off the ship there is little to go around in the way of food but it will improve. I'm sure of that,' Susannah reassured.

'I am Ann,' she said as she looked back towards the *Surprize,* thinking of the heartbroken mother. 'Her child is gone, lost somewhere out there. I hope the poor little soul did not suffer.'

Susannah could find few reassuring words.

'It would have been quick, unlike the grief which will last, perhaps forever.'

'Despite the cruelty of the day, it is a beautiful place. This morning when we saw the island I drew deep breaths of hope. I saw the crowd gathering along the bay and everything seemed as if it would be well, but sadly …' she paused, 'not for those who were lost in the waves.'

'It has been a tragedy indeed. Others before this day have drowned out there, the seas can be dangerous across the bay. Still we find the strength to keep going, we must. Come with me and Mary and I will show you where things are. Won't we Mary?' Susannah said to her daughter who smiled at the stranger. Ann let the child wrap her little hand around her finger.

Susannah pointed to the men along the beach,

'See that one, that is my husband Ed and that's our friend Jacob. They will stay behind and see if any stores can be brought ashore. We are farmers, fishers and builders here. Major Ross lets us do whatever we need to keep ourselves fed and to grow crops, not just ourselves but to help provide Sydney Town when we can. But he is strict, since there've been more people on the island he has made martial law and he won't tolerate any theft. We have been low on stores and all food is precious but things will get better and, we have plenty of fresh water.

We have been saved from starvation at least once by the arrival of a sea bird that comes in numbers and nests in holes in the ground. We have eaten their meat as well as their eggs. We call it the bird of providence, but Ed, he says they are just mutton birds. Still they are not bad eating. So they may fly here again and that would make for a little more food.

You'll be given tasks to do but if you behave you will not be monitored like a criminal. There are no cells here.

So tell me where you are from, how is it that you happen to be here?'

As always Susannah was direct, but she had a sense about this girl, she liked her and wanted to know her better. Patience was not one of Susannah's greater virtues, endurance yes, patience not so and she was a curious as ever.

'I was lucky I think. The ship I travelled on to Port Jackson was a ship where there was a lot of freedom. We were all women, told we had been chosen to come here to find a husband… so that is what I understand my job to be,' Ann said, a slight smile forming on her lips.

Susannah took Ann into their cottage. 'Tonight you can stay with us, I'll make up a cot for you.'

Later when they retired for the night Susannah could not remove the image of the childless mother from her mind.

'The day has been tragic Ed. Everything seems so different when you are witness to such things.'

She stared into the darkness,

'But I like Ann, and Mary likes her. She's a good one. Pretty to boot. She could be a match for Jacob.'

'It's a bit soon to think of that... and you know he still has his heart set on going back to England and the sweetheart he left behind.'

'He does... but Ed Garth so once did you.'

Susannah closed her eyes, she could hear the distant, low pitched pounding of the surf and she let it lull her to sleep, saying a prayer for the soul of the drowned child and her mother.

****

The next day Susannah went with Ann down to the bay. Those fit enough were set the task of helping to sort the stores as they were brought ashore from the ships.

'Today after the food supplies are put into store, rations will be handed out so we will eat a proper meal tonight. You should join us.'

'Thankyou. If I'm permitted I will. I've been given lodgings with some of the other women until we find our husbands or until they find us' Ann said, smiling a little nervously at the prospect. She hoped she would win over one of the better men, someone who treated her well.

Later that afternoon when Edward had collected their food supplies, he and Susannah walked up the path that led to their dwelling. Mary was on Susannah's hip, pointing at things as they passed, including Jacob, who was working on building a verandah onto his own cottage.

'Join us for tea,' Susannah called out. Jacob looked up.

'No dried pork today. We have fresh meat and potatoes, bananas, apples, coffee and bread, and the newcomer Ann is having tea with us too.'

Susannah gave a mischievous giggle at the thought of her matchmaking, that and in delight at the prospect of eating a good meal.

'I'll wash and then come up.'

Jacob could not help but notice the pretty girl called Ann, he had seen her the day before but chastised himself for looking at her in a way that Aileen may have seen as a betrayal. She was attractive and obviously kind. Her face, beautiful even in sadness. He had reminded himself of his promise to return to Aileen but it had been over three years since he'd left England and he wondered was she still waiting for him or had she found herself another man to be her husband?

That night as they sat around the wooden table Edward had made, baby Mary slept peacefully in her crib. Susannah and Ann talked effortlessly. Ann smiled readily and Susannah thought, *yes, perhaps I have found a friend in this newcomer*.

Ann used her hands when she spoke and the expressions on her face left no-one in doubt of what she was feeling. Jacob watched, *it is as if she feels everything she thinks, not mere gestures This one speaks with her heart*. Every now and again he caught himself staring at her.

'I come from Bristol. I was an orphan as you have told me you were Susannah. They call me Ann Harper but I have no knowledge of my father. For as long as I can remember I tagged along with a family called Seine, their daughter Elizabeth was my friend.

I have some distant memory of my mother but I was told she died when I was very young. Sometimes in my sleep I can still hear her voice. She always says the same thing, *Annie, be a good lassie, we'll be together again one day...* Her voice is like a song, with a lilt that I had not heard in other voices.'

Susannah watched as Ann moved her hands about like a dance with her speech and she thought that Ann's memory of the voice of her mother was a fine one. Indeed, she could not remember anything of her own mother.

'I cannot remember mine. I wish there was something of her I knew. Sadly, if I try to remember I can only recall a feeling of being left alone.

Still I don't remember the sorrow or the time of parting. I think if I had known anything of her I would have missed her, but there is nothing of her in my mind. Did your friend's family treat you as one of theirs?'

'Not really, they were too busy looking after their own flesh and blood but luckily for me they let me sleep on the floor of whatever lodgings they could find and they shared their food, without them I would have been like the other ragged children that roamed the streets.

But I was often hungry and it was no different one morning when Elizabeth and I were on the Bristol bridge trying to sell grapes we'd found in a field. We'd often try to vend wares on the bridge, it was a good spot, the only way to cross over the River Avon without a boat. I can remember fluttering my eyelashes trying to persuade some gentleman to buy our grapes but that day no-one was interested.'

Ann seemed to be lost in her story, reliving it, her demeanour changing with each new part of her tale. Jacob thought her appealing and he could imagine her fluttering her eyelashes and turning the heads of gentlemen.

'Later two of our friends Alice Fidoe and Margaret Williams joined up with us and we ended up eating the grapes ourselves, but then Margaret said she craved some proper victuals and told us how her mother was a maid at a grand house at Denmark Street, belonging to a well-to-do lady, Nancy Clutson. Denmark Street is one of the grandest streets, with wealthy families and so much money, more than they need.

Margaret said all we had to do was cross the drawbridge, she would get inside without anyone seeing, bring out silver spoons and teapots and we could sell them to a man her brother knew, a Mr Norris on Radcliff Hill and then we could buy victuals fit for a king's supper.

So the next thing I knew we were making our way across the bridge. I admit I was hungry and wanted a feed, but I knew it was not a good idea.

We waited on the other side of the street while Margaret disappeared down the side of the house. When she came out we ran to Radcliff churchyard where Margaret pulled out the loot from inside her petticoat; nine silver teaspoons, two silver tablespoons and a silver cream jug, was what they said at the trial.

We all '*ooed*' and '*ahh'd*' and made fanciful plans about what we would do with the money. We walked up Radcliff Hill and sold a couple of the spoons to Mr Norris and Margaret gave me and Alice two spoons each and the rest to Elizabeth and her brother to sell. I remember thinking as soon as those two spoons were in my hand, I was in strife. Until then I thought myself nothing more than an onlooker.'

Jacob was taken with the way she held court. She had an air of confidence about her and the way she told her story had him entertained. His curiosity was sparked, not just about who she was and what she was revealing about her life, but by what might be revealed beneath her clothes and he found himself imagining. She was slightly built, not very tall but still the dress she was wearing pulled tightly across her breasts and bodice and the curves which lay beneath had him intrigued. *A slender girl, well-endowed and with an attractive self-assurance about her*. But as quickly as he allowed such thoughts to pervade he tried just as quickly to dismiss them, lest they lit a flame within him.

'When Alice told her Ma what had happened she was marched down to Denmark Street where she confessed to Mrs Clutson and told on us.

The constable was summoned and all of us, except Alice, were taken away. Elizabeth's mother was crying and yelling and Elizabeth grabbed at her mother but she was dragged away.'

Jacob could imagine Ann watching as Elizabeth's parents wept for her as she was taken away, just as his own parents and Aileen had, but Ann she had no-one to weep for her and he felt a tug at his heart.

'We were taken to Newgate. For months we begged through the prison bars for scraps of food. It was an evil place, but I know I'm not telling you anything you don't already know.

I used to wonder what my mother would have thought. Could she see me, was she watching over me? I'd heard talk of heaven and hell and wondered would I go to hell while my mother waited for me in heaven. I can remember silently praying to her, or God, or whatever saint or spirit might hear, that I was sorry, that I'd never wanted the spoons, that I wanted to be forgiven and somehow let out of that hell.'

Ann stood up and closed her eyes, remembering in earnest and a single tear formed and fell down her cheek.

'Yes sometimes we pray and we wonder who hears. If there is a God, then He would understand,' said Susannah. 'How old were you when you were brought before the court?'

'I don't really know my birth date but I had counted twelve summers from when I was a child and so I think I was fifteen. Seven years' transportation we were sentenced, then just outside a year later the four of us went from Newgate to Plymouth and came here on the *Lady Juliana,* they said that was July 1789.'

Jacob looked at Ann's chestnut hair and fine featured face. *Although she is small she is hearty* he thought *and holds a glint in her hazel eyes. They flicker with each expression.* He was irritated with himself, he found her quite arresting and scolded himself for not being able to stop his desirous thoughts.

'And the *Lady Juliana*, apart from the crew, was full of women. The word around the ship was we were needed as wives in the new colony of the Great South Land and that we would be made free on our arrival. We'd heard it was a distant and unforgiving place that needed women and we were ripe for the picking, human cargo they said.

The ship was wet and smelly, still not as bad as Newgate and by day we were free to go up to the top deck. Some women paired up with the crew for the whole of the journey and others sold their bodies. There was a madam who started up a brothel for the crew and for people who came on board the ship along the way, as you can imagine it was a good business for her,' Ann laughed.

'My eyes were opened, everything was at close quarters and as time went by the bellies of some women grew. There were quite a few babies born on the way. But, all these women were in their own way free, they made money for themselves, drank liquor and laughed a lot. There were no upper class ladies to bow and scrape to and many of us became like sisters.

Still there were some bad times, sometimes men crept up on me and others in the darkness demanding favours but if you resisted the older women would gather in numbers and stick up for you and kick them away.

When we finally arrived in Sydney Cove we thought we would be welcomed but they jeered. We couldn't understand it, some vicious looks came our way and many cursed at us. Later we found out they were nearly starving and wanted no more mouths to feed. Luckily our ship had enough provisions to share and the people soon softened t'ward us.

At the settlement I was kept apart with about half of the women from the ship in separate lodgings for more than a month and then we came here. I was not a grown woman when I left home but by the time we arrived in Port Jackson I was as much a woman as any of them.'

Jacob found himself inwardly agreeing, she was definitely as much a woman as any he had been in company of, *if not more of a woman than most*, he thought to himself.

'And I know it is my job to find a husband and be a wife and mother. I look forward to that as much as I want to forget the past.'

The words 'find a husband', rang in Jacob's ears. *She will be snaffled up in no time this one*, he thought.

'I have to say I was nervous to come here but when I saw the island I thrilled at the sight and was stirred at being given this chance.'

Susannah recognised in Ann her own aspirations and could see they would indeed become friends. She looked at Jacob again and almost said aloud *this is the one for you*, but thought better of it, she knew he was still haunted by memories of Aileen.

Even so, she was so young and enchanting that despite himself in the weeks that followed he kept watching her, whenever they were in proximity to the other he watched her. The way she walked, her easy smile, the way she picked and smelled every plant, the way she from time to time knelt down and lifted up the soil, crumbling it between her fingers. His gazing did not go unnoticed by Ann and she felt promise in the attention he paid her, even if it was mostly from afar.

Finally, Jacob found the courage to speak to her in private. He had wrestled with himself over this, where this would lead.

'How is the woman who lost her child?'

'She is very sad. She is still pale with grief. Perhaps it will never leave her.'

'There is always more tragedy in the death of a child,' he said lifting his hand to brush away the hair from his eyes and when he looked up he found her looking at him intently. He let his gaze drop from her to his hands. He was not usually shy but she affected him in a way that had him checking himself. He hesitated.

'I've been meaning to tell you,' and he made a small coughing sound, 'how moved I was at the kindness you showed her.'

She heard genuine compassion in his voice. It stirred a tear within her. He lifted his eyes to hers and saw her vulnerability, for all her self-assurance she was an emotional being. It jerked him from his shyness and before he knew it his hand was resting upon hers, just long enough for her to feel his warmth, just long enough for Ann to realise, if she had a choice, this was the man she would marry.

Jacob began to seek Ann out, to talk to her at day's end, to walk with her showing her the beauty of the island from vantage points he had discovered. Through the pines and gullies of lush fern trees to high points he took her, to where the pristine ocean waters could be seen below them. On one such day they spied a giant solitary manta ray beneath the sea's surface. The wind dropped and the deep water below was still and clear. Moving gracefully with water wings that spread more than twenty feet across, the ray waved its way through the crystalline turquoise, cruising gracefully. Neither of them had ever seen such a creature and when without warning it leapt from the water and flew shortly in the air both of them looked at each other astonished and open mouthed.

'What other place on earth would show us treasures such as this?' Ann said, and Jacob again took her hand.

Before that day his sleep had been filled with dreams of Aileen beckoning him home but now when he awoke, alone and wide-eyed, staring into the blackness of the night, it was the face of Ann he saw.

Chapter 6

1791

Susannah was feeling tired. As she lay with Edward upon the humble comfort of the straw and feather mattress she had made and covered with soft cotton cloth, she could hear the wheat rustling, shooshing in the summer wind outside their little house and joy permeated her mood.

She drew her hand across his chest, he was lean, his skin taut across his muscles, a stream-like vein rippled under her finger.

'I am having another baby. I think this time it will be a son, a son for Ed Garth,' she whispered. 'What do you think of that?'

Edward held her, a smile spread across his face in the darkness.

'Aye Susannah, perhaps this one will be a boy.'

Susannah saw in her dreams a boy, a son, strong and gritty, smiling yet serious. He was surrounded by water and about him were the faces of people who called him 'sir'.

****

Edward and Jacob almost always worked together, in the fields, on the fishing boats, in the building of things and in search for what were now elusive petrels. They scoured the sandy beaches.

'Susannah is having another child. She thinks a son? Do you think women know these things?'

'That is grand news Ed. And Susannah thinks it will be a boy? Aye, I think they can have an instinct for such things.'

Jacob paused then looked at his friend.

'You know Ed, it is my birthday today. I am twenty-six. I thought by now I would have a wife and children. I have longed for the day for when I could return home to Aileen but the truth is, her face is becoming lost to me and it is only in my heart that I feel her.'

'It's time you let it go Jacob. You are a world away from her now. Be part of this world, not hold on to something which is most unlikely. You are my friend and I tell you now as a friend and you should heed what I say, the yearning will pass. You have said it has already eased. You will always think after your family and Aileen back home but if you dare to let go you will see, as Susannah says, that today is more important than yesterday. I know Annie has an eye for you and you for her. She is keen. She is a pretty one and she is clever. Think about it… and tonight, tonight we will celebrate your birth date Jacob and we will have Annie join us.'

'It is true I had many women in my days at Port Jackson yet none distracted me from my yearning for Aileen. But Annie… there is something about her. I have found myself laughing more freely when she is near. Still Ed, what of my promise to Aileen. How can I just break that vow?'

126

'It is not that you will be breaking your promise, tis a promise that just cannot be kept. It cannot be helped Jacob; you must let go.'

He found himself running Edward's words over and over in his head. He knew Ann was a find but he struggled with his conscience.

That evening, the 21st January 1791 the four souls met in celebration. As she sang, Susannah felt the movement of the new life she carried. Jacob joined her in song and their voices sounded for all the world like magic in the night, the sweetest sounds Edward and Ann had ever heard.

The fields of grain wooshed in the breeze, every now and then the sound of a cow could be heard or the 'ya ho' owl hooting its sound from tree to tree and the Norfolk pines filled the air with freshness. It was warm as they sat in the open, above them the long smudge of light, the milky way, soaked the sky in all its splendour.

'Susannah, are you afraid of the birth, the pain and all?'

'No Annie, I'm not afraid. Mary came easily and I am prepared. I was a nurse to mothers on the *Dunkirk*. While I saw some mothers die and babies too, most went through the trial without too much worry, although not always without too much pain. I grew to understand the needs of a woman in her labours. The hardest thing was watching some of the babies being taken away from their mothers. You and I both had a motherless life and now after having Mary, I wonder if it would be as awful to live a childless life.'

'As I've said, I have the slightest memory of my mother and that same dream of her and her sing song voice. I can't see her face but I can hear her. Sometimes I think it is my mother's doing from heaven that has led me here and I can hear her say, 'aye Annie time is your friend and tis time that will deliver ye back to me one day'. The strangest thing I know, to hear her voice so clearly.'

'We have much in common Annie. Oh when I think of the past and think of now, what a difference! And, you know Annie what I am going to do? I am going to learn how to read and write. Will you too?'

'I will try.'

'You will I am sure of it. We will … and, we will sign our own names properly, with more than a mark. I have watched Ed, the ink from his pen runs across the page like a wave. I will do that one day. I want to write down the words I have in my head when I make up songs. I want to know what they look like.'

'You will have to teach me one of your songs Susannah so I can sing it with you.'

'I will, and if he is able to get paper and ink, I will have Ed write the words down, for I'm sure they will look as pretty on paper as they are in the way they sound.'

****

128

In the weeks and months that followed, Susannah asked Edward to write letters in the sand. Each day she learned one more letter and how it sounded. She copied them and found herself sounding out words, 'a n t, b a t, c a t, d o g, e d w a r d'. Later, she somehow convinced the master of stores to provide her and Edward with paper, ink and a quill and at night when Mary slept she wrote each letter down from a to z and practised writing her own name.

She realised how hard it was going to be to be able to spell and write the words she put to her songs. But, she would not be deterred and resolved to herself, *I will have Ed write all the words down first and then I will copy them and I will put the pages of the song in the bible with Edward's legend and one day our children will read them.*

In turn Susannah helped Ann with her reading and writing and soon with pride Ann learned how to write her name. When Susannah saw Ann had learned it straight off, she said with pretend sarcasm, 'Well Ann Harper is much easier to write than Susannah Garth. So what of you and Jacob, perhaps soon you will be writing your name as Ann Bellett?'

'Perhaps but I have only just learned how to write Harper,' she smiled.

'I have been patient. Sometimes I think he is on the edge of saying it is me that he loves, that he has let go of Aileen. He must know how I feel. I have all but said so but I am scared of holding too fast to him, for fear he may just leave when his sentence ends. I have had other men ask me to be their wife, even a marine but I have declined, wanting only Jacob.

He says things to me which makes me think he sees a future with me. He talks to me about fabrics, about the value in silk, how it is woven and how precious it can be and indeed I have imagined one day spinning my own silk, at my own spindle and weaving beautiful fabrics for a family that I hope will be with him, but my true wish is to sew and reap the harvest, at a place of my choosing. And I wonder whether he would want to be married to a farmer, whether Aileen with her spinning wheel might be the better fit for him. But then I see how he looks at me and I know there is more to how he feels about me than he says.'

'Well he is a fool if he lets you slip away to some other man! I will get Ed to have a word with him.'

The next day Ann was helping Jacob and Edward in the planting of a crop of wheat. She bent down to the earth, feeling the warm roughness of the soil through her fingers, relishing in the knowledge that in time she would watch the field come alive with the amber colour of the grain as it moved with the spring breeze.

'It is as if I have a feeling for it,' she said out loud.

Jacob heard her, 'And what is it that you have a feeling about Annie?'

'I have heard of the promises of land grants to men but I plan to convince the governor that I should also have land. I will show that I am a valuable farmer, as good as any man and when the time comes I will ask I be granted land of my own.'

Jacob looked at her with respect but raised an eyebrow at her boldness. Edward grinned at her resolution and smiled as he thought how similar she and Susannah were. *Soon I will be a father again and God willing this one will be a boy who I can teach everything I know, who can one day help me on the farm, in the building of things and, perhaps he will be the first of many boys.*

Each with their own thoughts they continued to work their way along the field, turning the clods of earth and tilling the soil, planting and watering the seed. It was work that made their backs ache but at the same time imbued them with satisfaction.

For some time, Jacob had tried to let go of his promise but whenever he thought on the possibility of never returning to Aileen a cloud of guilt hovered over him. But of late he could not deny the urge to stay was stronger than the urge to leave.

'How many people would you say are now on the island Ed?' Jacob asked.

'I'd say about a thousand and what did I tell you, just as Susannah had said, even though it was nearly disastrous with the failing of the last harvest, things did get better and now the crops are growing reasonably well again. When not long ago I despaired, now I see the livestock grows in numbers, buildings are continuing to be constructed and what is more I have been asked by the governor to start building more boats.

Jacob this is truly a good place to raise a family. Yes, it is sometimes harsh but it always seems to come good. It's not too cold or too hot and Susannah is right, we have everything we need here and so do you,' and as he looked for Jacob's attention he nodded his head towards Ann.

Ann heard the whole conversation and as she went to join in the talk she saw Edward's gesture to Jacob. She stood up, in that instant she decided she would not stay silent a moment longer, walking up to Jacob and facing him squarely.

'I arrived here in August last year,' she said. 'It is now March. I have counted seven months. For seven months Jacob Bellett I have loved you. I may not be the sweetheart you left behind but I'll wager I will make you happy. Happier than you would have ever been.'

Jacob was red-faced and silent at her outburst as Edward laughed loudly.

'Don't you mince your words Annie! Aye, tis time he got a good tongue lashing.'

'Is that all you can do, just stand there! Oh for the love of God!' Ann called out as she turned away from Jacob and stormed down the hillside, her bonnet flying off her head in the wind.

****

The silver crescent of the Easter new moon was on the horizon. It was an April evening and the coolness of the night was belied by the perspiration that beaded across Susannah's forehead.

She paced about the floor, wiping her brow, sitting down every now and then.

'Ed go fetch Annie, she will help me. Put Mary in her cot and go. Annie might as well see up close how babies are born. God willing she'll be having babies of her own one day.'

When Ann arrived, Susannah was walking around in small circles, stopping and starting at intervals, breathing with measured concentration.

'Annie the wet cloth there, every now and then it would be good if you could mop my forehead. The ache is dragging across my back, much worse than with Mary. Could you please rub it for me? It's been hours now and the pain is coming faster and stronger.'

The night drew on, Susannah wore only a thin petticoat, the air was cool but her clothing was damp with sweat from her efforts. Finally, Susannah felt the urge to bear down she crouched on the ground and Ann lay the

133

clean bedding on the floor in readiness. When the child emerged blue and slippery, the chord was about his neck. Ann watched as gently, quickly Susannah slid her fingers between the chord and the baby's throat lifting the chord over his head. He wasn't moving and Ann could not see any breathing.

Edward waited with little Mary in the kitchen. He was anxious, he had heard few sounds coming from inside the bedroom and no cries.

Doing as she had done in the past with babies on the *Dunkirk*, Susannah cleared the child's mouth, placed her mouth on his and puffed air into him, rubbing his little body in intervals. Then all at once the baby was pink and sucking in his first breaths, a crackling cry escaping his lungs.

Ann watched in quiet awe. Susannah handed her the baby as the final pains of the afterbirth took hold, within moments the discomfort disappeared and a smile formed upon Susannah's face. Ann wiped the waxy white coating from the boy as Susannah cut the cord. They shared a common thought, that all was well, Susannah had breathed life into her son and, all was well.

When Ann emerged from the bedchamber it was with a smile on her face. Beckoning Edward to come meet his new baby boy, Ann stepped aside and Edward's spirits lifted as he saw Susannah's happy face and the blinking eyes of his new son.

Susannah propped herself up on the bed against the wall, her baby at her breast.

'It wasn't easy Ed. He wasn't breathing but he is here and he is perfect.'

Edward leaned in and kissed his son and then lifted his lips toward Susannah, all the while Mary pointing and trying to grab the tiny fingers of her baby brother.

'There is something extraordinary in him, is there not?' Edward grinned broadly. 'See the way he looks at us?'

'He is like you Ed,' Susannah said. 'What shall we name him?'

'James, after my grandfather.'

'Yes, we will call him James. It's a fine name Ed.'

Edward stood holding Mary watching over Susannah who was proud and beaming nursing their new baby and as Ann watched on feeling their joy, she wished for herself that same joy with the man she loved, if only she could get him to see reason.

Ann delivered the news to Jacob, hoping it might shake him into the realisation that this is what he also wanted.

'Susannah brought her baby to life Jacob. He was limp and blue but she breathed into him and rubbed him and then suddenly he was pink. I admire her, the way she gathers her children to her, the ease with which she cares for them, the love she has for them that comes so naturally. It is a fine miracle, a family is, a fine miracle, is it not Jacob?'

Jacob smiled and nodded his head, but the crease of consternation contradicted his smile and although Ann knew his reluctance to fully embrace her came from a promise made long ago to a girl he had loved, she was despondent that he could not yet recognise her as the one person he should share his future with.

****

'Ed you must try again with Jacob. It is more than a year Annie has been here. She is the right woman for him. Tonight when they come for tea you must press him on this. We've even had a change of governor in that time but for some reason it has not been time enough for Jacob to change his mind. Annie has been patient enough. She is the one who can bring happiness to his life. She told me that almost from the first moment she met him she knew he was the man she wanted to marry but he's let himself be hamstrung, trying to remain faithful to that promise.'

'Aye, I know. The stupid thing is, it is not that he doesn't want Annie, it is just that he hasn't been able to rid himself of the compulsion to keep his vow. He thinks he is being noble.'

'Perhaps, but this 'nobility', it may end up being a foolish mistake.'

That evening after they had eaten their meal of chicken, potatoes and beans, 'a feast' as Susannah had called it, Edward and Jacob sat out on the verandah. Edward retrieved his little piccolo and began a sweet whistling tune that glided on the breeze mingling with the faint sound of the surf.

The men were alone and Edward knew this was the time Susannah would expect him to talk some sense into Jacob. He finished his melody and placed the whistle in his pocket, grabbed the sides of his beard between his fingers and smoothed his whiskers into a point below his chin, clearing his throat.

'Now that Major Ross has left and King is back as governor, we have more opportunity than ever to make the island independent. King wants us to keep working for our living but he has also spoken to me a few times about appointing constables and overseers who would receive a wage. We should both take up those jobs and continue with farming and if we are granted land we can not only subsist on what we produce; we can sell any surplus. Once we are paid a wage we can save our money and when we are given land we can plant more crops, improve our dwellings and be truly free.

And Jacob, as your friend I have to tell you this, you must make Annie your wife. If you don't, as much as she loves you, she may lose hope and look elsewhere. She's had proposals of marriage from a marine you know.

Tis a noble attribute that has impressed upon you to keep your vow but this will lead you nowhere. Annie loves you and she has been patient enough.'

Jacob blinked his eyes a few times, as if that action was somehow going to bring forth the thoughts churning over in this head out through his mouth. Finally, he spoke.

'It is a great comfort to know we can live full lives here Ed.' He paused and blinked again, 'and, I think perhaps you are right. I think I am ready to give up the thought of returning home. It is time I left England and Aileen in my past. I have thought long and hard on it and what you say is true. I will ask Annie to be my wife.'

Edward stood up from his seat, remembering the psalms, all starting with 'Praise the Lord' and said it out loud, 'Hallelujah! Praise the Lord!' thinking not only will Annie be glad but *Susannah will think I am a treasure for convincing Jacob.*

'Well no better time than now,' and without warning, Edward called out to Ann and Susannah.

As they came outside into the lamp light, Edward grinned at them and looked at Jacob,

'Well then?'

Whilst he still had the courage to be true to the words he had just uttered, he walked up to Ann and took her hand.

'So Annie,' he said kneeling on one knee before her. 'Will you do me the honour of being my wife?'

'Tis about damn time!' Susannah chuckled. 'And what is your answer Annie? Perhaps it will be no,' she laughed.

'The answer is yes and yes; it is about time! … And from tonight on I will be by your side and God willing we will have children of our own. Come here Jacob Bellett, husband of Ann Harper. Come and kiss me as you should.'

'Hip hip hooray! Thank the Lord for that,' Susannah yelled as she winked at Edward with not the least bit of shyness, in a way that meant *I will thank you in my own way later.*

****

From that day Ann shared Jacob's bed and his home and when a member of the clergy came to the island in November of 1791 Ann and Jacob were married. They celebrated with their friends, in full voice they sang folk songs from their pasts. Some joined Edward playing their Irish whistles, some had harmonicas and one brought out his fiddle, some danced and others gathered around a bonfire that threw animated shadows across the clearing. As the fire died Jacob and Ann retreated to their dwelling, the 'ya ho' owl again exclaiming his night song in celebration.

Jacob thought fleetingly of Aileen and in his heart he hoped she was no longer waiting for his return.

Chapter 7

1791-1792

Susannah loved their little house. A large apricot coloured shell adorned a shelf, draped across their bed was the bedspread she had sewn and embroidered and in the corner, stacked largest to smallest, sat baskets she had woven. These and other humble belongings were placed side by side with the furniture thoughtfully crafted by Edward and all of it filled Susannah with pride.

As she cooked the fish stew for tea, she was imagining the roast chicken they would have on Christmas day. *Perhaps I should pray more often,* she thought, *if there is a God I suppose I should offer up some thanks; after all, there would never have been fresh chicken to eat back in St Giles.* The fowl she and Edward had managed to breed were prized items, not only because they added welcome variety to their diet but because they brought good prices when sold to the government stores.

'It has been so much better Ed since Governor King has been back. And his new wife, she seems a caring woman. Even though she's just given birth to her and the governor's own child she cares for his littluns from Ann Inett like they are her very own. The governor seems happy here. But surely he must miss Ann.'

'I'm sure he does but he must have believed he had little choice but to send her away. Still he seems in good spirits. He is encouraging us all. He listens to what we say about the wages and prices on stores. But he has been having trouble with some of the newcomers and even some of his officers.'

As Susannah thought about the herbs and bread she would stuff the chicken with she heard a commotion from the coop.

'What's all that fuss? Ed there might be rats in the hen house. Quick go and check.'

Just as Edward got up from his chair Susannah looked out the window and spied a woman running away with a chicken under her arm.

'Hey you!' she called out, but the woman was gone.

'Ed, it was Elizabeth Bruce; she's lifted one of our best chooks. She's off down the hill.'

Edward was tempted to run after her but hesitated, reluctant to draw attention.

'I know what will happen to her if we report her to King. I don't wish a flogging on anyone. I'll go tomorrow and warn her myself that she was seen and not to be up to it again, and I'll tell others that they'd best watch their goods if she is nearby.'

'Aye Ed, hopefully that'll be enough to put her off doing it again. She should know better she's been here since the beginning.'

'I know the governor won't put up with thieving. I hear that he's had much strife on his hands since his return. There's some who were unhappy with Major Ross's command and the governor's been pestered with complaints about how things have been. Some of the new convicts have no skills and with the lack of tools there's been more stealing. Even though the governor has set about fixing wages and prices on goods, trying to make the island stand-alone from Botany Bay he's still got problems on his hands and he expects everyone to keep in line. She's a foolish woman, I'd have given her one of our chooks if she'd just asked. With some there seems to be little respect for ownership.'

Susannah thought back to her own desperate state, to when she was living hand to mouth and she felt sympathy for Elizabeth Bruce, but only to a point, for things on the island were not as they had been on the streets of London and what's more her husband was a lazy layabout and to date had not made any effort to better himself.

A number of days passed and even though they had not wanted King to find out, word of the theft eventually found its way to his ear. When all were told to assemble to witness the punishment of Elizabeth Bruce, Susannah could not bear to go.

'I cannot watch, even though it is a rope and not the cat, seventy-five lashes are so much to bear for a woman. I feel no comfort in this Ed. I am sorry for her. I will ask the governor to excuse me.'

143

Susannah stayed in her house but still the woman's cries echoed up the hillside, and little Mary's face turned toward the sound each time it pierced the air, her lip a quiver.

That night Susannah recalled Edward's own punishment and kissed tenderly the marks upon his back, drawing him close.

'Soon Ed your sentence will be over. We'll be truly free and this land Ed, if Governor King keeps his word … this land will be ours.'

Edward thought about the farm in Malmesbury, the rolling hills, the happiness of his early childhood, his family. *When I am free,* he thought, *I will write to them and tell them I have a wife, children and land and although they may never see me again, they can take some comfort in that knowledge.* As he drifted into sleep it was not Malmesbury that filled his dreams but the running streams, steep hills, valleys, roaring waves and the pines of Norfolk Island that pervaded.

****

Baby James was lying in the crib kicking his legs in the sunshine. His gurgling sounds and the chatter of little Mary mingled with the wooshing sound of the wheat and the distant resonance of the surf pounding as relentlessly as ever against the shore.

Susannah had brought his cot into the open air while she scrubbed the washing across the washboard in the wooden tub, wringing it and hanging it on the prop up line to the side of the house. Little Mary picked up the fallen purple flowers from under the white oak, sniffed them and then dropped them like gifts upon the feet of her baby brother.

Susannah hummed a simple tune she had heard some of the new convict women singing, but the words were what Susannah liked most and as she began to sing Mary shifted her weight from one little foot to another, jigging to the song.

'Ye London maids attend to me

While I relate my misery

Through London streets I oft have strayed

But now I am a Convict Maid

In innocence I once did live

In all the joy that peace could give

But sin my youthful heart betrayed

And now I am a Convict Maid

To wed my lover I did try

To take my master's property

So all my guilt was soon displayed

And I became a Convict Maid

Then I was soon to prison sent

To wait in fear my punishment

When at the bar I stood dismayed

Since doomed to be a Convict Maid

At length the Judge did me address

Which filled with pain my aching breast

To Botany Bay you will be conveyed

For seven years a Convict Maid'

'But twas not doom, was it Susannah?' came Ann's voice from the path next to the house, her belly heavy with the weight of her first child, a light sweat on her brow and a rose in her cheeks from the effort of walking.

Susannah turned towards the sound of her friend's voice. 'Ne'er a truer word was spoken Annie.'

Ann held in her hand a bunch of heart-shaped, dark green leaves with elongated, fleshy fruits and handed them to Susannah.

'Try these in your cooking they have a spicy pepper flavour.'

'I've noticed them in the bushes but thought they might be poison,' said Susannah as she lifted them to her noise to smell.

'Well I live to tell the tale,' Ann smiled. 'I am thinking of drying them out in numbers and grinding them up, perhaps try selling some.'

'Why not Annie, add it to your list of crops you want to plant.'

Susannah had collected dozens of palm fronds and sat with her friend in the sun, weaving them into a basket. She wore a wide brimmed bonnet because the skin on her nose had peeled so often from sunburn that freckles had begun appearing in numbers.

'I hear some of the seaman and some of the marines have chosen to stay on instead of going back to England.'

'I would never go back. Tis a bleak sky over London, so pale and weak and for months on end the days are so short and the sun barely shines. And I hear from the new convicts they are still starving in the streets. No Annie, I would never go back.'

'There's a lot of excitement about today. Everyone will be going down to see the governor's map of land grants being pinned up.'

'I know Annie! Who would have thought after only four years here that we would be allotted land of our own?'

'It's not that I am ungrateful Susannah and I am as eager as any to see what the grants are but even if Jacob receives an allotment I still want to try and convince the governor that I am worthy of my own land, once my sentence ends.'

'You're a woman after my own heart Ann Harper. If anyone can make a farmer of themselves, you can. Indeed, you should write the governor a letter yourself.'

'I know we've been learning to write but I couldn't write my own letter.'

'Surely you can. Jacob and Ed will help you. I think the governor would be taken with that. You writing your own letter an' all. I'll make sure they do that with you soon. Better sooner than later, let the governor know how you're thinking, how keen you are.'

Putting down her basket Susannah picked James up out of his crib and swaddled him in a sling against her. She took Mary's hand and they all started walking down the hill. *What an important day this is*, she thought holding her head high, *today we become landowners!*

Settlers waited for the map to be brought out and the air of anticipation drew nervous chatter from within the group. As one of the marines fastened the plan onto the notice board spirited conversation began, the calling out of names and the handing out of pegs for those to assist the surveyor to mark out the allotments. Smiles spread on the faces of men and women, smiles brought about by the keeping of a promise that many had thought unlikely to be fulfilled.

Susannah had learned enough of the alphabet to spell her own name and to recognise Edward's and saw 'Edward Garth' written inside lines with numbers on, not in just one but two places on the map.

'What does it mean Ed?' she said pointing to where she saw his name, 'here and here?'

A grin so wide drew across Edward's face that it immediately infected her.

'What is it Ed?'

'We have eighteen acres Susannah,' Edward exclaimed. 'Eighteen, and six of them are level!'

Six acres of flat land that Edward knew would be easier to clear and would more readily grow the crops.

Edward turned to Jacob, 'And you my friend, you are our neighbours.'

Jacob had been granted twelve acres just down the hill from Edward, in what was known as the First Settlers Vale.

'In Newgate we didn't even know if we would survive. I would not in my wildest dreams have thought my life would take the turns it has. You were right Ed; we have all we need.'

They gave each other a hearty pat on the back and shake of the hands, the women then embracing their men and each other.

For those who had been granted land, the Christmas of 1791 came with the celebration of freedom and fulfilment and when they toasted the New Year Susannah raised her mug,

'Ed what is that word that says things will get getter? It's like 'success'. Let's toast to that. What is it Ed?'

Edward looked to her and their children, to Jacob and Ann and out toward the valley and the ocean beyond.

'Here's to prosperity!'

'That's it Ed, yes, to our prosperity,' Susannah laughed aloud. 'You will have to teach me how to write it,' she chuckled. 'That's one word I want to remember.'

Susannah looked to her friend.

'Annie you will be able to plant fields just as you hoped and when that baby is grown and all those other babies you will have; you can teach them to be farmers.'

'I will, for I have watched the way the wheat, barley and maize grow and where it grows best. I have planted all kinds of vegetables and know which crops thrive in which soil, what to plant in sandy ground, in the black dirt or on the rockier ground and I know what plants like it wet and which like it dry. It is within me, not just to be a farmer's wife but to be a farmer myself.'

Susannah fetched a piece of paper, a quill and ink and ushered them all towards the table.

'Jacob, you have to help Annie write a letter to the governor asking that when her sentence is finished she be granted land for herself. Annie, you tell him what you want to say.'
Jacob grinned. 'These women are bossy eh Ed?' But he began to write as Ann spoke.

'Our dear Governor King,

I humbly beg your indulgence in singing my own praises but I think you would have seen the fruits of the crops I have sown, the ones where I have chosen the grain and the place to plant and I think you would have noted their success and abundance.

I hope that you will favour me with a land grant of my own when my punishment expires. Tis not that I am ungrateful as Jacob's wife for the allotment he has been granted, tis just that I have faith in my skill to become one of the best farmers on the island and this would be for the good of all, not just our family.

I beg your approval and ask this with goodwill.

Your obedient servant

Ann Harper'

'Lots of begging and obeying,' Susannah laughed. 'Let's hope that does the trick.'

Ann began copying the words Jacob had written.

'Read them to me as I write each word Jacob,' and he read and re-read the letter, letter by letter, word by word until she had written every line and then, pointing to each word Ann read the letter aloud.

'And I shall remember every word and as soon as my sentence is confirmed to be over I will say to him again the words in my letter and remind him.'

Jacob folded the note she had written out and placed it on the table.

''Tis a good plan Annie. I'm proud of you, for your gumption.'

'We're all proud of you Annie. I was the first woman to step foot on this island and you will be the first woman farmer.'

Edward looked at Jacob. 'We will help the surveyor tomorrow and peg out our allotments to mark our territories. We don't want others encroaching.'

Susannah looked up at her husband. Now that's a landowner talking if I ever heard one.'

Ann picked up the letter, at the same time running her fingers across the tabletop.

'Tell me how did you get the timber this colour Ed? I like the way it brings out the grain in the pine.'

'Now, here's a secret you can tell all, for if no-one manages to get the finish they want they can come to me and I'll make up the mix and sell it to them. I use the sap from the bloodwood tree and I mix it with my secret ingredient till it's just the right thickness and then spread it. Does a grand job I think and,' he paused, 'I am going to use it on the boats I build.'

'Yes,' said Susannah. 'He is a maker of things and a man that makes things happen is my Ed Garth.'

'I think the governor took pleasure in seeing the joy his land grants brought to us. I would say he is even proud of us, of those who have stayed and made this place better.

What now with different crops, we subsist with little help from the main colony. I have counted corn, wheat, potatoes, beans, sugar cane, bananas, guavas, lemons, apples and coffee and we have cattle, horses, donkeys, sheep, goats, chickens and pigs, all breeding well. Gone are the days of searching for turtle and hunting the petrel, eh Jacob?'

'We will always have the fish Ed and soon it will be easier for bigger boats to make land safely. I've heard said the governor has given instructions to build another landing place to the north at Cascade Bay so if the wind is too strong to anchor in the cove at Sydney Bay, they can come ashore on the other side of the island. Best of all, he is setting up a school!'

'Perhaps we will go too, eh Annie?' Susannah laughed.

'Here's a sad thing though. Did you see those poor kiddies sitting on the governor's porch? They were deserted by their mothers. Their sentences finished and they just up and went with their men on the last ship, tis a crying shame. I can't fathom it, how they could leave them behind, their own flesh and blood, when there is no-one starving here, when there are no freezing winters, it's not like England here, we aren't scraping for our next feed anymore or huddling in rags against the cold. It makes me want to cry. I would never leave Mary or James, never.' Susannah shook her head. 'Our only saving grace is the governor's having an orphan house built for the poor littluns and he says all us families are to help them.'

Ann circled her belly with her hand, looking down at its roundness.

'And as sure as I feel this baby nearly ready to be born, I am surely in love with it and would never leave it. I'm with you Susannah, I can't fathom it either.'

The next day Ann walked with purpose down the hill to the governor's house. She smoothed out her dress, tucked her loose hair under her bonnet and fixed a cheerful yet determined look upon her face before she knocked on his door.

A maid answered and Ann confidently asked that she fetch the governor. When the maid said she would hand her letter to him Ann insisted.

'I must see the governor himself. I need to see him take my letter into his own hand.'

The governor heard her speaking and came to the door, looking at her curiously.

'Good morning sir, I beg the governor's pleasure in accepting my humble request.'

She handed him the letter, not giving him time to open it or read it in front of her or make any comment.

'Thank you, sir,' she said then turned and walked away.

She looked up towards the hills and wondered if one day she would hold land in her own right amongst those peaks and valleys.

****

On the morning of the 18th January 1792 a hard southerly swept the coast, but there was no rain, the sky was a fighting blue and it pressed itself against the clouds that sailed by white and grey.

As Susannah walked down to Jacob and Ann's house she noticed hundreds of gulls facing straight into the breeze, like soldiers, standing still and lined up along the fence, all at attention to the command of the wind. Waves broke constantly along the shore and as Susannah looked down to the beach she began thinking of a story she would tell her children.

The island is a princess and the waves are her white clothed suitors, the green of the slopes her dress sweeping to the sand, the birds are winged worshipers, riding the wind that rushes up against her body and the pine trees are her ladies in waiting carrying the trail of her gown. The reef, the thousands of boulders and corals stretching out before her, they are the princess's children huddled at her skirt ends.

Lost in her own story she thought, *for this paradise is a jewel, a royal land worthy of such imaginings.* Entering her friends' home and closing the door to the wind behind her, Ann's groans jerked Susannah from her daydreams.

Jacob stood anxiously by Ann's bedside,

'Thank goodness you are here. Please is everything alright? She has been like this for some time now.'

Jacob's forehead was wrinkled in worry, his voice strained. Ann was in distress, grimacing in pain and when Susannah felt Ann's belly and realised the baby was in the wrong position, the feet presenting and not the head, she recalled mothers who had not survived such birthing.

'Everything is fine Jacob,' Susannah said reassuringly, trying not to betray her real concern.

Ann had tears streaking down her cheeks.

'What is wrong?' she asked.

'Annie, you are sitting on your baby. I want you to get onto the floor, on your hands and knees and rock back and forth...'

Ann held on to Jacob as he helped her off the bed.

'That's it...

Now breathe and bear down,' Susannah implored.

Susannah had seen how babies born this way had become stuck after their bodies had emerged and whilst she had dealt with those events on the *Dunkirk*, with women who were not close to her, she could not begin to think of the sorrow a stillborn child would bring to her friend and she dared not think that Ann would die in childbirth.

Ann began to whimper.

'I can't, I can't,' and she began to lie down again.

'Yes, you can Annie, you are doing grand, the baby is coming.'

Jacob supported her and almost at the moment she felt she could no longer go on, the baby's legs appeared, then swiftly and with great relief the head, the baby almost spinning her way from the womb. Susannah looped the chord from around the child's neck and with a robust cry the babe took her first breath.

With the wind howling outside and the new baby howling inside, Jacob laughed a nervous laugh of relief.

'All is well,' Susannah said.

Later when she left them, she looked to the heavens, a prayer on her lips.

'Thank the Lord!' she said aloud, tilting her head to the stars as the sea mist streaked fast across the darkened sky, 'thank the Lord...'

Ann held her baby girl, *what a delightful strange creature* she thought *and how I love you even though we have only just met.*

Jacob winked at his wife, a wink that said how proud he was and Ann looked up at her handsome husband, his thick blonde hair tied in a ponytail falling to his broad shoulders and she felt again the blessing of a heavenly plan far greater than a bedraggled girl on Bristol Bridge could ever have envisaged.

She did not know what had become of her old friend Elizabeth Seine but their daughter would carry her name to remind Ann always of the friendship and life she and Elizabeth had once shared.

Chapter 8

1792-1795

In 1792, the months between June and August were wetter than usual and the sound of thunder regularly resonated throughout the valleys. The streams ran full and fast, the waterfalls formed and gushed from the cliffs of Cascade Bay and when the spring came, so did the birth of dozens of litters of piglets, growing and wallowing in the mud.

The Garths' land now held some of the best crops, some sheep and chickens. Their place looked down over the valley, past where Jacob's grant was located and beyond to a row of cottages, including the governor's house, built above the flatter area that stretched to the beach and bay.

With the passing of another year came the clearing of more ground, the tilling of more soil and planting of more seed. The Garths and Belletts were always occupied, determined to seize their lives. The women's zest for life was embraced by their men and their children grew in the midst of an affirmation that life is not just to be endured but to be lived fully.

Mary and James played among the flowers. Susannah managed to strike some growth from the plants the governor was growing in his cottage garden and they had taken hold in the area beside the veranda. There was dianthus, the flowers that reminded her of her release from the *Dunkirk* that day when their fragrance had infused the air. There were also herbs, rosemary and lavender and to the side the abundant pink flowers of one of the native oaks mixed in with the yellow frangipani.

James toddled after Mary while Susannah talked to Ann who had baby Elizabeth wrapped in a bundle in front of her.

'Does Jacob ever mention his family?'

'He has done, but I think he tries to protect me. I'm sure he doesn't want me thinking that he feels he has missed out by not returning home.'

'He's a good man your Jacob. For a few it has been a seemingly easy thing for them to just leave their women or take their women and leave their children and go back to England.

Ed has talked of his family. I know part of him would still like to go back to see them, even though he says otherwise. It would be wonderful if somehow they could all just meet again just one more time. But I cannot see how that could ever be.'

'I have wondered if Jacob were able to one day save enough for his passage and if he went back to see his parents, would he see Aileen. It would be a happy day for him if he could see his parents again and that would make me happy also but if he were to see his old sweetheart I would worry that he would be carried back in time, as if they had never parted and he would not return to me.'

'Well there's no chance of that. Neither of them are going anywhere and I think you are wrong; Jacob would choose you. He may still have a place in his heart for her, but he would only ever want you now. You and Elizabeth are his family.'

'It must be hard for them. Having family and knowing they probably won't ever see them again.'

'Yes… hard, but their lives are here now, with us and whilst the memory of their homes and family, of Aileen may bring a melancholy feeling, that feeling surely must now be fleeting. Their happiness, their loyalty to us, those things say much more than any brief homesick feeling that may creep in and out.'

Jacob had thought about these things himself. The vivid dreams he had once had of the face of Aileen, had now disappeared. The powerful urges to return to England had gone. The truth was Jacob was entranced by Ann.

The longing Edward once had to one day see his parents and walk the hills of Malmesbury had evaporated into the truths that were Susannah, Mary and James and there was not one speck upon the clarity with which he saw this. He treasured them, more than any allure to somehow recapture his past.

And Norfolk Island, the dot of land in the colossal Pacific Ocean was now their home.

Time passed, ships came and went from Norfolk, some of the freed convicts left the island and some stayed. New convicts arrived and free settlers too and Governor King continued to preside. There seemed to be stability and success in the colony, some would have even said it was thriving, even Lieutenant Governor Collins from New South Wales had commented on the bumper grain crops, the proliferation of sheep, goats and swine and the availability of good limestone for building purposes on the island.

It seemed to Susannah that most of the time all was well, but sometimes things are not as they seem. In her sleep she saw visions of burning fields and dead animals but she dismissed them, as in her waking hours she could never imagine such things and she had no idea why or how the images had found their way into her dreams.

'Susannah I see the governor's new wife looks after his and Ann's littluns as well as their own new baby. She seems to be a fine woman, but so was Ann.'

'Aye, it must be hard for the lady, probably coming from some grand home in London with maids, to here taking on another woman's children in a place where things are simple and where all the children mix with each other, no matter what birthright they have. And Ed, now that we have a hospital and a school I wonder will they bring more settlers?'

'I don't know but the truth is this island can only handle a limited number and we need everyone to pull their weight. Everyone should be working hard and be inspired to become self-sufficient, but there are some in the last lot that came who seem quite hopeless. Those and some of the convicts who aren't yet free have been causing trouble. Most have not been here from the beginning like we have. Some are miserable souls and openly disobey King's orders. There's been more stealing and with more people to feed it's not easy to keep the crops up to meet the need.

A few of the marines and their wives want to stay on here and the governor is granting them land but a number of the soldiers are unhappy, they think they should be treated better than those of us who are ex-convicts, given larger grants and more supplies. But to give King his due, he tries to be fair to all.

If we just had those who want to stay and the rest just leave that would go some way to solving the problem. We who want to stay are busy trying to make things better, we're building new structures all the time and the farmland is spreading out. Things are progressing. The governor now has me overseeing work in the quarry. The new chimney's finished and we've started making mortar to bind stones so we can build a few small bridges over the streams and some walls to hold up levelled land and we've been setting stones aside for the gravestones in the new cemetery. It is the hopeless convicts, they're either too lazy or have no incentive or both.

What with them and the unhappy marines who are resentful and undisciplined it's enough to drive the governor to drink.'

Although Susannah's disposition was to mostly see the good in everything about her, from time to time she was aware of some disquiet, and noticed there was not the same universal purpose amongst the population as there had been in the beginning.

'The rangers they sent up from Botany Bay are supposed to be guarding those who are still convicts but I've seen them mixing in with the women. They don't make any effort to keep their distance from those who've been sent up as prisoners. The ones who are doing the thieving and disobeying the governor are the same ones I see the rangers living with, eating, drinking and gambling with and they show no respect for him. When I think of how you were flogged and what that lot gets away with, it makes my blood boil!'

'Aye, and what's more some of the free men have complained soldiers are luring their wives away from them. I fear there could be some real trouble about. And then as well as that the governor's been up to his neck with whinging from some officers for not treating the marines better than freed prisoners, so there is disquiet brewing between soldiers and free men.

The soldiers aren't happy that the governor only fined the coxswain Dring twenty shillings for lashing out at the marine last week. That poor man Dring had been taunted constantly by the officers about having his wife seduced away from him and after he lost his temper and gave the officer a fist full, the soldiers wanted their revenge. Some think he should have been flogged for hitting an officer.'

'Oh dear, Ed, a dark divide could be creeping in, envy and resentment may drive a wedge between us all.'

Susannah's predisposition was to be optimistic and cheerful, worry did not easily stay with her, she usually flung it aside as quickly as she could, choosing not to dwell on matters as Edward sometimes did. But these troubles did not sit well with her and without being able to put a finger upon it, a general sense of unease stirred within.

****

A stream ran straight through the middle of Jacob's allotment, it tinkled, playing its own rippling tune. The evening was balmy and the children sat with Susannah dipping their feet into the cool water. It was not long after the coxswain had taken it upon himself to deliver a beating to the soldier who had cuckolded him, when the Garths and Belletts came together for a meal. Ann was laying out the food as the sun began to shrink away behind the hills, oil lamps hung from the trees and Jacob and Edward brought the table out in the open air to take advantage of the December breeze.

There was the usual distant sound of the surf, the high pitched shrill of the gulls and the sounds of the babbling creek, but Susannah could hear another sound, the low angry sound of voices growing louder by the minute. Suddenly Susannah was on her feet.

'What's that there?' she said, pointing to a flaming torch down the hillside. 'Oh Lord it's soldiers and they're heading towards the Dring farm. Dear Lord what are they going to do?'

The soldiers were hurrying in a menacing march, angry voices grumbling about 'injustice' and 'teaching Dring a lesson.' Edward and Jacob rushed down the hillside, calling out to other settlers to join them. Susannah's unease rose and she followed after them.

'Annie please watch the children,' she yelled.

As she caught up to the men she saw them confronting the soldiers, Edward and Jacob and other settlers started to come together and were standing in front of the marines to block their path.

'Get out of our way! We're going to teach that scum Dring a thing or two, put him in his place!' the soldiers yelled pushing their way through.

As they did one of them began flaying a lit torch towards the men, Edward stepping aside just in time to avoid the fire. Then Susannah saw one of the soldiers deliberately jab the torch with full force into the face of a farmer, causing him to scream out in pain. The soldier lashed out with the torch again forcing the others to step aside and the marines burst past them toward Dring's fields.

Jacob and Edward chased after them yelling out, trying to warn Dring, the commotion caused others to emerge from their homes, including King and some of his men.

The farmer hurt by the soldier stumbled down the hillside towards the governor calling out in agony, his face burnt and bruised.

'Who is responsible for this!' King demanded and when the soldier was named, King ordered he be found and arrested.

Marines were sent up the hillside to Dring's farm, but he was gone. Edward had seen him fleeing in the bushes, his escape unnoticed by the threatening soldiers, just moments before they charged through his front door but before they could set Dring's farm alight the governor's men had converged on the scene and taken control.

Susannah with Edward and Jacob made her way back up the hillside.

'Thank heaven you were not on the end of that stick Ed. Why do you have to be the hero? You had no quarrel with those soldiers. You should have just gone straight to the governor and let him sort it.'

'There wouldn't have been enough time. A moment sooner and Dring would have been caught by them.'

'Ed's right, you saw how heated up they were. If they'd got to him he would've been a dead man. The governor has his job cut out for him now

Ed. He's got both convicts and soldiers unhappy and now he's setting marine against marine.'

'He has no choice. If he wants to maintain order he cannot punish one and not the other. If he is strong enough, and I think he is, he will do what he must to stop havoc creeping in, even if it means chastising his own men.'

The next morning Susannah heard a strange noise coming from the bushes outside their chicken coop, a low moaning sound. As she crept up to see what it was she saw a man lying still and bloodied, except for the groan that briefly left his lips, he looked for all like he was dead. She let out a shrill scream and Edward came running. Pulling the bushes to one side Edward gasped.

'Dear God, it's Dring, he's in a bad way. I'll go and get help. See if you can tend the wound.'

Susannah knelt beside him, ripping cloth from her petticoat, pressing it against his injuries, the colour red bled through the grey cotton onto her hands until they were warm and sticky, covered in Dring's blood.

By the time Edward came back with the surgeon Dring was barely breathing.

'They've all but beaten him to death,' Susannah said as they lifted him onto a stretcher.

170

Susannah was grateful that Dring did not die while her hands were pressed upon his wounds. It was enough that the smell of blood still lingered in her nostrils, she did not want it to be the blood of a dead man.

As Dring fought for his life in the hospital a soldier was arrested for the drubbing.

'The governor has sentenced Downey to 100 lashes for Dring's beating and he says if Dring survives he is to be given a gallon of rum as a present.'

Susannah raised her eyebrows.

'A present! Ed I can see that causing even more trouble, can't you?'

'Aye, I can see reprisals from the soldiers if the governor goes ahead with the flogging of the soldier Downey and as for the sharing of rum. I suppose he must think it will go some way toward making amends. Dring would be terrified of the redcoats. If he manages to live through this, it wouldn't surprise me if he begs the governor to forgive Downey. This indeed is a dilemma; I don't know how King will manage this.'

After the arrest of Downey mutterings of rebellion spread throughout the island and as days went by the tension grew.

'I hear Dring came too and just as I thought, he pleaded with King not to punish the soldiers who beat him and what's more King has conceded to that plea.'

Susannah was surprised.

'Is that so? It might let the marines think they have license to do this kind of thing to others.'

'Yes but he only conceded on the condition that when Dring is well enough the soldiers involved sit down with Dring and some of the other farmers to drink the rum together. The governor hopes this will simmer things down. But I can see it taking more than a drunken night of pretend friendship to fix this discord,' said Edward.

As he spoke Susannah noticed once again the worry line forming on his brow.

****

Although the Christmas of 1793 passed without further incident, as the New Year emerged so did the underlying friction between soldier and settlor, governor and soldier and mutterings of mutiny persisted.

At night one man could not be readily distinguished from another and some soldiers, unidentified, bitter and pugnacious, stalked about in the darkness picking fights, causing further disquiet.

Susannah hurried home from the stores. She had been speaking to some of the women and that sense of unease which she tried to put to one side stirred within her again.

'Ed, one of the women I was with today is a marine's mistress and she let slip that there is an oath been taken in secret amongst the soldiers, that should any of them again be punished for an offence against a convict they will rise up. She says, they will kill Dring and put all the convicts to death!'

Susannah saw Edward's frown deepen and a shiver of fear ran through her as she realised he would go to the governor himself with this information. As she thought about the possible consequences her hand went up to her forehead, rubbing at her temple, *God only knows what will happen to us if the marines find out it was Ed Garth who let this out*.

'I must tell King he must nip this in the bud.'

'Ed can't you leave a note with no name on it or get someone else to tell him, I'm frightened for you, for us.'

'The less people that know the better, I will tell the governor I need to speak with him under the guise of talking with him about the quarry.'

That night sleep did not come easily to either of them. Susannah, whose habit was to sleep soundly, wrestled with the night and whenever she opened her eyes, Edward was awake, staring into the darkness.

The next day Edward met with King in secret.

'It will be a very delicate affair to quell this. I cannot lightly disarm on mere suspicion a group of soldiers, who are supposed to owe their allegiance to me.'

Edward could see the concern in the governor's demeanor, but as decisive as ever King hastily formed a band of civilian militia. He chose forty-four rangers, comprising free settlers, all former seamen and marines, not emancipists and they set about rounding up suspected mutineers.

Edward watched from his verandah as a number of the marines were marched down the slopes to the governor's house, grumblings of discontent and mutterings of 'the hide of the governor' to arrest his own.

'Susannah, I am so disappointed that King thinks that ex-convicts the likes of myself cannot be trusted with a musket. And this rounding up, I know he has no choice really but this is going to cause even more tension between the soldiers and freed convicts and there may be a backlash. We have no arms to protect ourselves and no proper prison for those soldiers to be held in. I've no doubt those marines will continue to try and sway the others. I don't know that guarding them with the rangers is going to be enough. We'll all be living in fear. We need them off this island quickly.'

Susannah felt the reality of Edward's worry. She watched him rub the crease between his eyes, down to the bridge of nose, back and forth and across his eyebrows, one then the other.

When she and Edward went to the stores a few days after the soldiers were brought in, they heard talk the soldiers were encouraging a full blown rebellion.

It had been nine months since a vessel had arrived at the island. Susannah looked out to where the sky met the sea, wishing for a ship to appear. Just as she was about to turn away she saw the billowing sail of a schooner being blown towards them and with great relief, as she had done once before, she let out a loud call into the valley.

'It's a ship!!' *a ship that will take those mutineers away from here and leave us in peace.*

****

Some of the settlers came down to the beach to watch the soldiers board the vessel to be taken back to Port Jackson where Governor King had ordered they face a court martial for conspiring to plan a mutiny. The governor displayed his authority, standing in full uniform in front of them all, insisting they salute as they walked past him. As the boat sailed out of sight there was an immediate sense of relief, not just from King, but from those who remained.

But the reassurance and comfort felt by the settlers at the removal of the rebellious marines was in deep contrast to the rage with which the news was received by Lieutenant Governor Grose when the soldiers reached Sydney Cove.

No provocation that a soldier can give, Grose wrote King, *is ever to be admitted as an excuse for convicts striking a soldier. They are to understand*

175

that they are not on any pretense whatever to stop or seize a soldier, even though he may be detected in an unlawful act.

'I heard when the marines arrived in Botany Bay that King's superior Grose sent orders back to him that civilian guards were never to arrest a soldier for an offense against a convict or even an ex-convict, an atrocious order!'

'Oh no Ed, that would mean they would run riot here, over all of us.'

'But thankfully King did not accept it. Nay he went above Grose's head and wrote direct to London telling the authorities why he did what he did and London directed Grose that his order must be withdrawn and what's more he's been made to apologise to Governor King.'

'Well, thank the Lord for that! What a dreadful thing that would have been if that had been left to stand.'

'Speaking of the Lord, the other matter I have word on my dear is that a Reverend is going to be permanently settled here next year and there will be a church built for those who want to go.'

'Well Ed Garth, perhaps it will be time.'

'Time for what my love?'

'Well, time to make a legal wife of me!'

Smiling, Susannah shook out her hair from under her bonnet, flinging her cap across the room. Grabbing Edward's arm she led him on to the porch, where she sat upon his lap, cupped his face in her hands and kissed him. A salty breeze ruffled their clothes, the voices of their children, the sounds of the ocean and the night creatures could be heard around them.

'Yes indeed, I think it is time you made me Mrs Edward Garth.'

****

James, Mary and Elizabeth played together in the February warmth, Edward and Jacob nearby. Susannah was with Ann in the Bellett's cottage, encouraging her as she laboured through the birth of her second child.

When the baby girl was born, this time with relative ease, Ann looked at her friend with genuine gratitude.

'This one I name after you. She is Susannah. What would I have done without you? Next to Jacob, you are the dearest friend to me in the world.'

'Oh heaven, my namesake eh… I've a lot to live up to now,' Susannah winked. 'Best be a good example to her then, hadn't I?' and she called out through the window to the others. 'Come see your new daughter Jacob and … Ed Garth! when is that Reverend coming?' she laughed.

****

By the time Reverend Marsden arrived in 1795 Susannah had given birth to another son, calling him Edward after this father. Mary was five and a half,

James four and new baby Eddie just months old when they all came together with their friends and the Belletts for the wedding ceremony.

In her typical boldness, after the Reverend had decreed them man and wife, Susannah made a little speech interrupting the final part of his ceremony.

'Good fortune has delivered us to this place, this tiny speck of an island. The new Easter moon is above us and tomorrow the sun will shine on a new day. This is my whole world. I don't care one iota what lies beyond this place. Here is where I belong and now ... now I am a legal wife!'

It was a proclamation to all present and when the Reverend had finished writing out the marriage certificate Susannah stood up tall, dipped the pen into the ink and waved it above her head for attention. She then leant over the certificate and proudly signed her own name.

Chapter 9

1795-1796

In his Easter services Reverend Marsden promised everlasting life, 'The Lord's resurrection means we will not die but we will live with him forever in paradise.' Susannah thought, *paradise? If paradise is half as beautiful as here I'll be happy.*

She tried to be God fearing but the truth was fear did not come easy to her, still the part of the Bible that talked about loving thy neighbour, she found that easier to abide by, after all, her neighbours were her best friends and she did indeed love them. Some prayers also didn't come easily, not the laboured, submissive ones, but the prayers of thanks and prayers to keep her family safe, they came readily. Not in a kneeling down, head-bowed fashion but a looking to the skies open-eyed way. Still she taught her children to close their eyes and hold their hands together and imagine God was listening to them each night as they said His prayer.

With the April new moon and the Reverend's promise of resurrection came new life, Jacob and Ann's third daughter, Mary.

Susannah brought her children to meet the new baby, they crowded around wanting to stroke and touch her. When she began to cry Susannah watched amused as James tried to lift her up.

'Sit down James, I'll hand her to you.'

179

Ann lifted her up and placed the baby in his arms. He put his face against hers, whispering soothing words, *Shhshing* and rocking her and to everyone's surprise she ceased her grumbling and snuggled against him.

Ann looked at him. 'She likes you.'

James grinned a proud boyish grin, 'Yes, she's clever, is Meh,' he chuckled.

The name stuck for from that day on, everyone called her Meh. As she grew, blonde hair and hazel eyes emerged and, from the genes of her unknown maternal grandmother, so did the clear olive skin of her French heritage.

Whenever she saw James Garth she flapped her hands and grinned cheerfully.

'I don't know what it is with you but you have the knack for brightening her.' Ann would say when James cooed at Mary, and for all to see, even though he was only a child himself, it was as if he possessed a magic that worked upon the baby. Whenever she was near him she seemed to want for nothing more.

A year after Mary's birth, Susannah walked with her own children down the slope where the fields of the two families' properties ran end to end, along the well-worn path to the Belletts.

Ann looked up from weeding the vegetable garden and the older children ran to greet each other. In the weeks before that day Ann had given birth to yet another child. They named her Ann but called her Nelly. Four daughters in four years, growing up alongside the Garth children, in a place so far removed from the streets of London and Bristol that had it not been a reality Susannah and Ann would never have conceived it.

Ann seemed to have a slight look of disquiet upon her face, her eyes downcast. 'Susannah my sentence has ended.'

'Now don't be dejected,' Susannah said, remembering Ann's request to the governor for her own grant of land. 'He's probably just forgotten; you know with all the trouble he's had.'

'Perhaps he thought me too bold?'

'Not a bit, he sees your gift. You're a natural Annie. Tis all of us would benefit from your talent.'

'I hope you're right but I am a woman and land ownership is a man's domain.'

'I'm sure you will have your wish Annie. I have a feeling for these things. I'll come with you to see him.'

Ann was quiet for a moment. 'And Susannah, why would I want to do that?'

Susannah looked at her quizzically.

'Why would I want to do that, when the governor has granted me my own land of thirty-nine acres!'

She ran to hug Susannah, a grin wide and bright illuminating her face.

'Ahhhh Annie!' She squealed and grabbed her friend, their embrace turning into a jumping dance with both of them laughing and spinning in such a way that had all the children stop playing their games and looking at their mothers' crazy, whirling, noisy jig.

'Jacob says that's fifty-one acres we will hold, side by side. And the crops, oh, they will be plentiful! Hard work ahead but Susannah what a dream come true. The governor sent for me last evening and I have been bursting to tell you.'

'It is the finest news Annie. What a prize that is. I am so happy for you.'

Ann showed Susannah the map and in a lively fashion began pointing at spots on the allotment, telling her friend where she would grow what.

'I am so very happy for you, especially since Ed said the governor has so many grants to fulfil he may not give any new grants. Ed says that we cannot hope for another. But one of the marines who was given an allotment not far from ours is returning to England and Ed has requested a bargain from the governor. If the government will pay the marine out for his land, Ed has said he will pay back the government in produce. If the deal is taken up Ed says it will mean, we'll have sixty acres.'

'Imagine that Susannah, the Garths and the Belletts like the landed gentry, our children inheriting like blue bloods.'

They both laughed aloud, the children going back to their games, oblivious to the benefits their mothers' imaginings would bring to them should they become a reality.

The women rested for a while and watched the children. Edward had given James a ball. He had cleaned out the bladder of a pig to make it, blowing air into the sack and tying it off. James and neighbouring children played with it, Susannah marvelling at them. They were creatures of the sunlight, they wore skin as gold as honey and grew taller and stronger than the fetid air and lack of food in London would have allowed. They were blessed as any children could be. They frolicked in the open air, on a spot on the planet that tilted at just the right angle to the sun, delivering to them a temperate climate, free of the bitter cold from which their parents had come. There was so much joy in watching their happiness, in those moments there was nothing that could bring greater delight.

****

The earth spun upon its axis, days came and went, a year of farming, of making things, of times of plenty and of some times which were lean, a year of songs resonating up the hill from the Belletts in Music Valley.

Sometimes, like on this day Susannah caught the sound of their voices on the breeze, and she joined in their songs like an echo across a canyon.

When Edward began working as the overseer she started taking the children to where he built the boats. Edward's hands moved with the timber in a way that others might envy, for to see his hands working the wood was to see that the timber and his hands belonged together, he brought it to life. He cut and moulded small crafts, often with James by his side watching and helping. In places he carved designs into his work, feathers and swirling patterns like the waves.

Susannah was proud of him and often she found herself in a silent prayer looking at the night sky, thanking the heavens that he chose her. She never took for granted her good fortune. She sometimes held her hand up to the firmament in gratitude, imagining she could sift the stars through her fingers, *it's like touching the face of God* she thought, *perhaps the stars are His eyes upon us.*

She walked with the children to the shore of Sydney Bay where Edward was finishing his day's work. There was enough light from the milky way to catch the whitewash on the shore break and as the waves crashed and hissed she sang to the children who danced on the sand. The moon was rising full and silver, the ocean shone like mercury, heaving and glistening in a mass of movement.

'Look there,' she said pointing for the children to see. In the distance, beyond the bay, a whale was breaching 'Again there.'

Time and again it breached, leaping into the air, defying the sea then crashing back to the surface. The children's faces lit up with excitement. It was a moment to savour, a moment sweeter than most, the kind that elated her, the kind of moment she would always remember.

That evening Edward was drawing a sketch of a vessel.

'The governor says I have a natural flare for building and design and I'm now well placed as overseer of sawyers to oversee the task of building more boats for the colony. He is allocating labourers to work our land so that I can be freed up for the task.'

'Ed Garth, the maker of things and the man who makes things happen. I'll not ever forget the fine figure you cut whilst felling the timber at Botany Bay. I knew then you were special.'

She watched him, the way his hand moved across the paper and affection welled within her. She still felt the kind of ecstasy that came with being in love with a man who made her want him in every way. Their children had been born out of love, their love sustained them. Edward had not attempted to reign her in, he had let her remain herself, never trying to tame her or make her something she was not and she loved him all the more for it.

Edward had surrendered to her optimism and her words, there was as he said, a truth in her which infected his being. She had once told him, 'all the deep valleys of my heart hold my dreams and with you Ed Garth they can be delivered.' This was a reciprocal truth which he held on to. He thought her heart complex, yet simple all at once. Sometimes her words were charged with love, sometimes with passion but never with resignation.

The day had been warm and as the sun sank, the air cooled and the hum of the cicadas died away. Once again the far off slapping and hissing sound of the ocean could be heard.

Edward stopped his drawing, an earnest look upon his countenance.

'Governor King has ordered the construction of a new vessel. A large sailboat which is to be called *Norfolk,* just as he has named his son. They are bringing in sailcloth for her from Port Jackson and we will use both the pines and wood salvaged from the *Sirius* to build her and I've a few ideas for the new boat.'

'What a challenge that will be Ed.'

'And the *Reliance* anchored in the bay, she is in a dismal state of decay. They are going to try and use her to retrieve the guns from the *Sirius* but that might just pull her apart in the process. One of the jobs the governor has set me is to help oversee repairs on the *Reliance* to make sure she is seaworthy.'

'That is good news for you Ed, for us, he will pay you for those efforts.'

'But it is not all good news. You know how the governor has been poorly. Well, if we can get the *Reliance* into shape, he will be leaving on her and going back to England with his family.'

'You didn't tell me that before Ed.'

'Well I didn't want to worry you. Who knows what his replacement will be like?'

'That is sad news indeed but I'm not the one to worry. You are the one that worries. Let's hope whoever comes to replace him will learn to love the island as much as the governor has.

But yes what a sad day it will be when he goes. Oh Ed, and what about the bargain you sought with King about the marine's land?'

'A reasonable man is our governor. And this is the good news my dear, the bargain was accepted. We will soon have another twenty acres. A legacy for our children, should they choose to stay.'

'This is their home. They won't ever want to leave.'

'The island can only hold so many my love, there will come a time when the people will outgrow her.'

'Well that may be Ed Garth, but it will be a time long after I am gone from this world.'

Susannah had trimmed Edward's beard and cut back his hair. She thought his profile handsome in the lamplight. He went back to his drawing, his broad shoulders moving slightly with the movement of his hand. She reached across his back and drew her hand from one shoulder to the other, then slid her hands up under his shirt, feeling the scars beneath her fingertips. Whenever she did this it reminded her of that dreadful day, but it was her way of letting him know she would always share the pain of his ordeal with him.

Other than the day Edward had rescued Jacob and taken off his shirt, she could not remember him removing his shirt and exposing his body in places where others could see. It was the brand of a flogged convict, a permanent legacy for others to judge him by and he didn't want to give those who didn't know him any such opportunity.

The man who had ordered the flogging was leaving the island. He was a man Edward respected and admired and this was not the only irony, for Edward believed his own heritage hailed from royalty, whilst Governor King had been the son of a mariner. In another place and time Edward was sure Governor King would have counted him an equal amongst his friends.

****

When the day of the governor's departure arrived, they came in droves, walking in lines down the hillside, hundreds of the inhabitants, including those like Susannah and Edward who had been there from the first. They

188

congregated on the shoreline to bid their governor farewell. The horizon blurred between ocean and sky, silvery grey, the sea was smooth and beckoning and sadness appeared on the faces of the women and the men as they stood together as one.

Susannah thought about the last eight years. Despite the flogging, despite the forever altered flesh on Edward's back, she had grown to like the governor for he had let them make this place their home, he had watched over them as they grew older, as many children were born, as farms had multiplied and as their town had been built.

People had come and gone and those who had wanted to stay, remained. She knew the governor was going home, some may have thought him lucky, but to Susannah it was those who stayed behind, it was they who were the lucky ones.

Phillip Gidley King was rowed out to the *Reliance*. As he climbed from the longboat to the deck, Susannah called out loudly.

'Governor, sir! You'll not be forgotten!'

And a resounding three cheers spontaneously rang out from the beach.

King removed his three cornered hat and lifted it towards the crowd as the breeze filled the sails of the *Reliance* and pulled the ship out from the cove, bound for England.

That night Edward sat at the table, the lamplight again shining over the letter he was writing. The children slept and Susannah embroidered, the thick blue thread making the shape of scallops along the edge of a cotton tablecloth.

In the top right hand corner of the notepaper Edward wrote *October 1796.*

'Read me your letter Ed.'

My dearest Mother and Father,

I have no way of knowing how you are, or even if you are alive, but I hope my letter will indeed find you alive and well.

I am living at a place called Norfolk Island. This tiny piece of land is like a diamond in the vastness of the South Pacific Ocean. Now I am free and hold land in my own right. I was granted an allotment here for farming and have now acquired more land. I hold over sixty acres on this island of salvation and with crops and livestock now growing in abundance I am indeed a lucky man. And dear parents above all things that bring me happiness are my wife, Susannah and our three children, two boys and a girl. Mother we have named our daughter after you and she is now seven and as pretty as a princess. The boys are James, who is six and Eddie, just one and they grow strong in the healthy air.

I have joined the Progress Society here and our community continues to do well. I grow grain, pigs, sheep and chickens and I build, all manner of

190

things, including boats. So you see I am a success. Not what we may have imagined but a success nonetheless.

For so long I yearned to return to you but my destiny has brought me to this place and I am content. I may never have the opportunity to return to visit you again but I want you to know I am well and safe, that I have found the answer to why I was unjustly convicted. The answer being my beloved Susannah and what she and this island have brought to me.

My hopes of a fresh life have been fulfilled. Susannah and I are surrounded by the beauty of our island, with good health and respect from others and we are content to live out our lives on this small piece of earth. I am a trusted and productive member of this community. I have been made an Overseer of the sawyers and am rewarded for my efforts by being supplied with clothes and food and with labourers to help cultivate our land and I am paid a wage for other tasks I undertake.

I hope I will receive word from you and if it is not in God's plan for us ever to meet again I hope you can take comfort from what I have written here. Although I will always miss you terribly, I am grateful for the place I am now in and content with my lot in life and I'm sure you will be glad for me.

From distant shores

Forever your loving son

Edward

Chapter 10

1797-1798

Edward walked the hill home at day's end, Jacob by his side. The year was no longer new and the November breeze blew cool and gentle down the valley from the east.

'The *Norfolk* is taking shape my friend. We will show those back in England we can build boats as good as any built at Portsmouth. Since Townson has been acting governor he's made it clear he wants the vessel finished. I'd say she'll be ready to launch by the middle of next year. We were lucky they didn't bring a new man to the island to be governor. Townson's been here since the year after we arrived so he knows first-hand how hard we can work and the progress we've made here.'

'Yes it is true Ed, but I don't see he has the enthusiasm King had. I am hoping King becomes well enough to return. I know the island is dear to his heart and I think he would be keen for us to maintain what we have and continue to improve things.'

'It would be good to have King back here, he has been the best leader for us.'

'Tomorrow we celebrate our wedding anniversary. It will be six years since Annie and I married. Come and join us for tea. We will have a little rum, you can bring your whistle and we'll sing some of our tunes and dance a while with our girls.'

'That I will gladly do.'

Earlier that day, Susannah ventured with the children to the other side of the island to Cascade Bay. She had only ever seen the bay from the water, in those days when she had first arrived on the *Supply*, but now a track had been carved between there and Settlers Vale. She knew it would be a long walk so she set out early. Her favourite cow was tame so she tied a rope loosely around her neck and loaded the children upon its back, little Eddie in front, then Mary and James behind. She led them up through the hills. *It is one of those magnificent days*, she thought, *when the island really is like a princess seated on her throne, looking down on the waves, as if they are worshipping at her feet.*

Susannah still found herself lost in the island's beauty. Not only was the coastline spectacular but the gullies were full of palms, tree ferns, lush green plants and trickling streams.

As the sun rose higher in the sky they finally arrived, emerging through the pines high above the bay. Susannah looked around her, on either side of the bay ragged rock faces rose up from the sea below her. An eagle soared above the cliffs, gliding on the thermals. This was the place where she had seen the rainbows in the mist of the waterfalls that had cascaded over the cliffs in those days when they had first arrived. Today the streams flowed gently, not overflowing and flooding but moving steadily, trickling through the gullies and over the ridges, down the face of the bluffs and into the sea.

When the wind stilled a little they could hear the streams babbling and gurgling and Susannah thought it was like the voice of glee, as if the water knew it was free, as if in running to the ocean the stream knew it would become part of something greater, something mightier. The thought personified her own feelings, feelings of nostalgia. She remembered the excitement and anticipation she had felt when she first saw the island and the feeling of hope at the prospect of becoming free and part of something important.

They rested on the slopes above the bay, in the shade of the pines and looked across the shimmering water. Susannah pulled out from her apron pockets rolls of bread she had made and they sat and ate as she recounted to them how in those rainy days the streams gushed into waterfalls and how the colours of the rainbow were painted across them.

James turned towards her. 'Mumma, how is it that you and Pa came to be living here?'

'Yes Mumma, I heard you and Pappa talking about the convicts and how you were not like them. What does that mean?' Mary asked.

Susannah drew a breath of courage before telling them her story, not the details of her crime but of how she came to be where she was, of how suffering, disease and shortage of food and shelter had led people like her

195

to do whatever they needed to do to survive. It did not mean it was right to do what she had done.

'It just meant I had no choice but to steal,' she said. 'Here it is different, we want for nothing here. We have all we need now. And your Pappa, he did nothing wrong he never did what they say he had done. He will tell you about it, but it was a mistake that he was sent to prison. Still I am glad, for if it had not been we would not be together and you children would never have been born. It is what they call fate.'

'Fate?' asked James.

'Yes it was not chance or luck, it was meant to happen. Like the sun rising and setting, it could not be stopped, it was a certainty, your Pappa and I coming together, falling in love, it was destined.'

They listened intently, even Eddie with his eyes wide and thumb in his mouth.

'And now it's time for home, up you get, it's downhill this time,' she smiled.

'The world beyond this island is different. It may be hard here from time to time but the wider world is harder.'

'But Mumma, there must be other places like this but bigger than here, where you can't walk from one side of the island to the other. One day I want to see those places.'

'And how would you get there James?' asked Mary. 'That's a silly idea,' she added.

'I will build a boat and sail there.'

Susannah could see his earnest yearning look. It was the desire for adventure she saw in him. She had known what it was like to feel such a thing but she neither encouraged nor discouraged his want, *lest fate be tempted*, she thought.

They stopped and drank from one of the many streams on their way home, the cow grazing a little on some grass that had sewn itself in a sunny spot in a clearing.

They arrived home just as Edward emerged from the pathway. Eddie ran to his father to be lifted, arms outstretched and Edward picked him up and hoisted him above his head, Eddie laughing as he was lowered to the ground, Edward tickling him as he did.

'And where have you been my lovelies?'

'We've been on an adventure. To Cascade Bay where the story I told today was the one about my life.'

Edward with eyebrows raised, flashed a glance of curiosity her way.

'I'll tell you about it later Ed Garth. There's tea to be made.'

****

197

Early the next morning the rooster crowed his wake-up call as Mary and Eddie watched their mother milk their two cows. Gently she eased the milk from the teats, five squirts into the wooden bucket and one into young Eddie's mouth, a game for him and a way to make sure he got 'more goodness into him', as Susannah would say. Warm and trickling from the side of his mouth he licked at the milk, then he wiped his face with the back of his hand.

When the cows' udders were empty Susannah poured the milk into a clay pot, sat the pot in a tub filled with cold water she had collected from the stream and let it sit. While they waited for the cream to settle on top Mary helped her mother make loaves of bread while Eddie sat up on the table watching.

After Susannah had made the dough she and Mary kneaded their portions, occasionally Susannah threw the dough into the air for show before dropping it and pounding it on the bench. Eddie helped spread the flour all over the table top and Susannah punched down the dough, then she set them it into two neat oblongs which she covered with cotton cloth. Eddie always thought it magical when they took the cloth off some time later and the dough had grown to twice its original size.

Susannah took pleasure in these simple things, to be able to make food, to create something from what they grew on their own land.

'Where I came from little was fresh. You kiddies are lucky to be able to taste the milk from a cow, to eat fresh bread and as for jam, I only ever had that once and I'd hardly ever seen a fresh strawberry before coming here.'

She used a ladle to skim all the cream from the top of the bowl of milk, dropping it into the cream jar, then she poured the rest of the liquid into the clay churn and began moving the dasher stick up and down constantly.

'Come on Mary your turn,' Susannah said after a while with a chuckle. 'Get those arms working.'

Mary copied her mother, up and down, up and down with the dasher until perspiration began to form on her top lip and she sighed deeply.

'Argh, Mumma your turn.'

They continued until the yellow fat separated from the buttermilk, the whole while Susannah singing a churning song she'd learned from some of the other women which beat time with the rhythm of their effort.

When the job was finished, they looked into the churn where chunks of butter mixed in with the buttermilk floated on top. Gathering the chunks and the buttermilk with a ladle, Susannah put them into a large bowl and began her mixing, moving the spoon back and forth, back and forth quickly until all the liquid disappeared into thick smoothness.

'And now … we have butter!' she said, as she did every time she finished the process.

That afternoon the breeze wafted through the apple trees either side of the pathway as they all strolled down to the Belletts. Over her arm Susannah hung one of her weaved baskets filled with warm baked bread wrapped in cloth and fresh butter in its little wooden box, the delicious smell of the bread whetting their appetites with every step.

Little Meh waited on the porch of the Bellett's home, her golden curls loose around her shoulders and her cherub smile upon her lips, ready to greet them.

As Ann came out of the front door, followed by her other daughters, Susannah called out.

'You shall have the best women farmers Annie, you and your four girls, you'll have your fields not only filled with crops but with petticoats!'

Jacob and Ann had laid out a table in the open air, a few oil lamps again hung from the trees. Above them, the Milky Way in her usual splendour smudged the sky and the brighter, closer stars shone their astrological symbolism over the southern hemisphere.

It was November, the time of celebration of the Bellett marriage and spring in its final month. Susannah looked to the heavens. Just visible to the south was the emerging Southern Cross, the group of stars which she was now familiar with and higher in the sky another constellation which, if she had known the name of what she was looking at, she would have called Orion's belt and there also was the bright star 'Sirius'. Again, had she known, Susannah would have thought it no co-incidence that the brightest star in the sky shone like a beacon over the shipwreck of its namesake which lay beneath the glistening water of Sydney Bay, once the proud flagship that had carried their commander, the determined and gallant Arthur Phillip to the Great South Land in that First Fleet nearly ten years before.

As she stood with her hands crossed, her back to the others and her face looking skywards, Edward placed a caring arm across her shoulders.

'And what thoughts have you so occupied that you stare into the heavens as you do?'

'It is just wonder Ed, wonder that fills me up. I wonder at everything, how this all came to be, how we came to be here. Just a while ago when I heard one of the children cry out my name I wondered at what had happened to the small girl who disappeared that night I was taken into the cells. I wonder will she end up like me. Our children Ed, I wonder at them, their futures.'

Then she lightened her mood, kissed the hand that rested on her shoulder and turned as Eddie came bounding towards them.

After feasting on pork, potatoes, beans, bread and butter and a little rum they started their singing and the children joined in the chorus. Later Susannah sang a cheeky tune, which made the men laugh, grateful that the children did not understand the few lewd words which she sang with gusto, a wink and grin. Then she rose to her feet.

'Now Ed Garth it's time for you to play that whistle of yours.'

The children followed Susannah's lead, held hands and skipped around, circling and dancing, the little ones squealing with happiness. The contagious delight of just being in that moment spread amongst them and Susannah and Jacob's voices could be heard above all others, the sounds of their joyful song carrying throughout the valley.

Meh toddled around behind James. He sometimes relented to her want for him to pick her up and he struggled with her on his hip. When they sat in a circle to their games, it was James who Meh pushed herself in beside.

When Ann made up beds for them all, the small ones fell asleep beside each other, Eddie Garth's own long curls mingling on the pillow with the curls of all the little girls, all except for Meh who rested her head on the pillow next to James who was sleeping, oblivious to Meh's hand wrapped about the braces that crossed his chest.

Ann and Susannah looked at the sleeping children.

'Some images remain in our minds forever Annie, this will be one of them. Look at them, each of them perfect, Eddie all snug with your girls. I was saying to Ed before; I wonder about the life ahead for them. Now all is well but we know how fate can be. Sometimes we choose our path, sometimes the path chooses us. What mixture will it be for them?'

****

'These past months have been good ones Ed, the best. Yes, it has been hard work but it has been worth it. Our toast to prosperity has come true has it not?'

'Indeed it has my dear. Since the workers were given to us by the governor it has meant I have been able to put most of my time into overseeing the sawyers and the building of the *Norfolk*. James watches and he is keen to learn. He comes after school and looks on, asking all manner of questions about how a larger ship is made. He says he wants to be a boat-builder but not just a boat-builder, he wants to captain his own ship. Big dreams our boy has. But yes, my dear these months have been good.'

Placing both his hands upon each of Susannah's shoulders, he turned her gently to face him.

'You my love you are the greatest prize of my good fortune,' and he kissed her lips softly, catching her breath.

She did as she often had done, reached beneath his shirt, tracing her fingers across the scars on his back, whispering into his ear.

'No Ed Garth, tis you, you are the prize.'

****

James watched as the *Norfolk* materialized. During the months after Governor King had left, the building had continued under Townson's command. James took mental note of how she was being put together, the hull, the bowsprit, the gunwale, the intricate rope ladders, the small bridge but most of all he watched the way the timber had been cut and fashioned, the bending of the wooden planks around the centre rib and the way his father used the natural curves in the timber to make them fit. He watched as the chines and inwales were cut from the same pieces of timber to ensure that each of the halves bent in the same way, to make sure both sides of the hull were symmetrical.

For Edward it was as much a labour of love as a practical construction, turning the timber of a few dozen trees into a thirty-five-foot sloop-rigged boat with her deck and hull polished all shining from the application of his special bloodwood oil.

When the time came James helped his father apply the oil to the hull, the rails and deck, revealing the grains of the different wood. He loved the way the oil brought out the wood's character. The pine was lighter in colour, with yellow and red hues, straight, uniform grain and a fine texture but the teak timber that had been salvaged from the *Sirius* held a dark golden colour with an occasional wavy pattern and uneven texture. The pine revealed a creamy lustre whilst the teak a darker richer sheen and James, although only seven, saw art in the contrast, a lovely variance that even as a child he recognised as pleasing to the eye.

When he thought about his life ahead, what the grown up James would become, he saw himself among unfamiliar forests of trees and on boats, not as a farmer and he wondered how this imagining could ever be.

When the *Norfolk* was complete and the time came to launch her, Edward was worried. There was no way to test her seaworthiness before putting her to sea. With no port she would be launched straight into the bay and have to set sail immediately so as not to be hurled back to the shore. Still, whether she proved to be leaky or not Edward took pride in the ship he and his fellow workers had built.

'She is the first vessel of her kind ever to be made on this island and she has great escapades ahead of her,' he said to James. 'And with that mainsail and the two jibs, she will cut through the water with great speed.'

'Aye Pa, I wish it was us that could sail her. I wish she wasn't leaving the island.'

'Perhaps one day, son. Perhaps one day you will sail upon a boat such as this one.'

The community gathered at Sydney Bay, there was to be a public celebration, Lieutenant Governor Townson had directed it.

Susannah thought, *this will show them in Port Jackson and back in England. Not only can we grow crops but we can build ships.* Eddie tugged at her skirt and she lifted him to her hip, pointing to the sloop and the pomp and ceremony that was assembled about them. She looked at James, little Meh was as usual by his side, but he was absorbed in watching the event, his face a mixture of concentration and joy, a thinking line on his forehead and a smile upon his lips.

Susannah stood next to Ann and her other girls.

'The governor has declared that the boat must be christened, just as tradition would have it. So we'd best get closer so we can hear the Reverend.'

'Aye Annie wouldn't want to miss what the Reverend has to say,' Susannah winked. 'Perhaps it will be a toast to the *Norfolk's* 'prosperity',' she grinned. 'No talk of fire and damnation today I hope.'

As the crowd settled, the ocean seemed to still a little and the Reverend's voice lifted above the sound of the waves crashing on the sand.

'A reading of Psalm 107

They that go down to the sea in ships
That do business in great waters
These see the works of the Lord, and His wonders in the deep…

May God bless this ship and all who sail on her.'

206

James felt the hair prickle on the back of his neck, there was something about the occasion that filled him with awe.

The governor stood at the *Norfolk's* bow, the stern of the ship facing the sea. He held in his hand a large metal cup filled with wine, took a sip of the wine and threw the rest over her bow.

As James watched on, the men heaved the *Norfolk,* 'one! … two! … three lads,' the governor called out and with the men's effort she shifted and began to slide, then gravity took hold pulling her down the makeshift slipway, creaking and splashing into the bay. Those on board hurriedly hauled up the sails and with relief the wind filled them moving the sloop out of the shallows and into the narrow channel towards the open sea. The crowd let cry three cheers, and with the last 'hip hooray' hats and bonnets were thrown into the air.

What adventures will you have? James thought as he watched the billowing mainsail. He recalled his father's account of the journey from London on the *Scarborough* upon the high seas and the way he had spoken of sailing into the mighty harbour that is Port Jackson. *One day,* he thought with all the adventure that was bursting from within him, *I will build a boat like the Norfolk and sail it to places no one has ever been and just like Mumma did here, I will be the first white person to walk on another land.*

Chapter 11

1799-1801

Susannah discarded her heavy petticoat and her loose summer dress filled with the breeze, flying up and catching a splinter on the bark of the white oak. She had finished her day's work and was strolling with the children through the bushes pointing out the cicadas clinging to the tree trunks. They watched as one struggled free of its crusty shell, emerging green and shining, rainbows on its wings.

Gingerly James took the fragile shell in his fingers, initially having to pull at it to free its lifelike grip from the bark and then, surprised at its weightlessness dropped it, grasping at it as it fell. Meh looked at him.

'It's not alive?'

Her lash heavy eyelids stared at James and the corners of her mouth dropped. Susannah stroked Meh's golden hair which fell in curls about her shoulders. *She is a child who holds the glances of all who see her*, she thought. *My own Mary is as pretty as a princess, but Meh, she has the face of an angel.*

'Don't worry Meh, the cicada has just taken off its old coat and left it behind,' he said. 'It's still alive look?' pointing to where it had flown.

'Mumma, tell Meh it's alright.'

'Of course it is, don't you be worrying, that cicada is as free and alive as he'll ever be,' said Susannah. 'There's no reason to be sad. Anyway, it's getting late, time to go home. There'll be more cicadas tomorrow.'

Susannah looked at the children as they turned to walk down the hill. *James, he is like his father, becoming tall and skinny and he has Ed's straight nose and lean look. I wonder what my father looked like? Was he in love with my mother? Was I born out of love like my own children?* It was not often she pondered such things but when she did it was with a mind full of unanswered questions and imaginings of sad images and sorry tales filled her answers.

Meh took James' hand. *It's always his hand she takes,* Susannah thought. *He's definitely her favourite, even above her own. Of all of them he is the one she is drawn to. And he humours her in a way he does not humour his own brother and sister.* Susannah thought the child bewitching, that her fascination with James seemed to come from some unearthly place. Whenever the child looked at him she always showed more than just a flickering of gladness at being near him.

Susannah could smell and taste the salt in the atmosphere, that afternoon the air was thick with it, it was so much a part of her world now that she could scarcely remember the fusty air of London or the putrid air of Newgate and the *Dunkirk. I pray to God that our children will never know those hells...* she said to herself and then her thoughts digressed. *I wonder if*

I should keep the full story of my past a secret from the children or whether I should one day tell them the whole wretched truth. It is one thing to confess to being a starving thief, she thought, *forced to steal to survive but it would be another thing to try and explain why I chose to sell my body, especially with the Reverend preaching against 'fornication'! Oh dear the hideous visions of hell with all the gnashing of teeth and fiery furnaces... I have lived my hell on earth and surely God will give me credit for that. And, besides I don't believe in it, fire pits and beasts! But Heaven?... aye perhaps. If my spirit remains in this place, that would be enough heaven for me.*

She looked across to Nepean Island, plush with dark green, covered with pines and for an instant she thought she should also be the first white woman to step upon its sand. *A daft thought perhaps.* Then as fleetingly as the notion came, it disappeared, gone along with the thoughts of her old life.

Ann had just finished giving instructions to her workers on where to plant the latest crop when Susannah and the children appeared.

'I've been planting some different crops this time. After the last successful yield, I've told them to till and plant peas in the newly cleared fields. I've even had them plant the native pepper in a cluster so I can crush and dry more to sell as seasoning.'

211

'Well Annie it sounds like your efforts are paying off. You're not only a good mother but a good farmer, just as we knew you would be.'

'There is enjoyment in making things grow. And a kind of peace that comes with surrounding myself with living things that cannot speak but which flourish when nurtured and reward you with full and splendid harvests.'

Just then the peace was broken by a child crying.

'Indeed there is Annie, pity about the screaming children,' Susannah laughed.

Ann at first laughed along but then a thoughtful looked appeared on her face, a serious thinness came to her lips.

'You know those convicts who have been assigned to us whose sentences have not expired? They are grateful for the work and that we treat them well but they tell me of convicts allocated on other farms who are resentful of working on land belonging to folk they think are no better than themselves. The newer convicts don't have their own land, they don't have houses of their own and haven't been here long enough to know how things work. Not everyone is as content as we are Susannah.'

Susannah recalled Edward's fear at the time the mutinous soldiers were being held on the island.

'At least the convicts don't have muskets.'

'No, but they have axes and tomahawks and scythes.'

'Oh Annie stop! We have to trust that they will want to be like us, that we are an example to them. Perhaps we should start up a group and include the new women convicts to re-assure them of the success that can be had here.'

'But Susannah that is not the only problem,' and Ann paused, deepening her frown. 'Jacob has said there is other trouble brewing.'

'What is it now? Jacob and Ed, they are fine pair, always worrying.'

'No, it is not just them. You know it's been four years since Governor King left us and it really hasn't been the same since. Captain Townson and now Captain Rowley haven't showed anywhere near the interest in the place that Governor King did. It seems they were only here to mark time. Some things have been left to run down, even the governor's old house and his beautiful garden.'

'We built the *Norfolk*, that was a fine achievement, Captain Townson was keen to see that task finished and besides I have heard they are sending us a new governor.'

'I hope he takes to the place. It's been sad Susannah to see the way the government buildings haven't been cared for. After all the effort it took to build them. I know Jacob and Ed are trying to get a working party together to fix things up but that is not all and this is the really worrying part, Captain Rowley says there's no point repairing the buildings.'

'What do you mean there's no point?'

Ann's forehead furrowed and a tear began to gather in the corner of her eye.

'For the Lord's sake, what is it Annie?'

'Captain Rowley, he says the island's too remote and that it's too hard for the authorities to keep things going.'

'What do you mean?'

'There are rumours they are closing the island down.'

Susannah could hardly believe what she was hearing. At first she was quiet, then a look, which was unusual for her, a steely look, a crease between her eyes, a tightening of her lips, a look of both anger and dread came over her, and when she spoke it was as if the air was being squeezed from her lungs.

'What! That cannot be! That's just them believing we need them to look after us. Surely not! Someone needs to get that through their heads. We don't need them. We just need someone the likes of King to persuade them to leave us be. We have order, we have laws and constables and a gaol now. We have food and water. We can look after ourselves.'

'I think so too but even though we work hard and look after our farms the town itself is being left to rack and ruin and they say the governing of the island is too costly.'

'That's not a good enough reason. That is easily fixed. We can govern ourselves. And what's more, they need this settlement. We are a port of call for traders and whalers. We make money from the whalers who come here for fresh water and food and we sell our produce to the government stores which help the settlement at Port Jackson. Surely this is just a hitch. When the new governor comes he will see. I'll have Ed and the lads in the Progress Society make special point of talking to him about it.'

Although Susannah tried to convince herself this was nothing but a hiccup and that the attitude of the authorities could surely be altered, the whole conversation left her unsettled and with an unfamiliar worried countenance.

In the months that followed the dream of burnt fields returned to Susannah's sleep, unwelcome and foreboding.

****

Winter came and Joseph Foveaux, an officer with a friendly reputation and a knack for organisation, arrived at the island, bringing with him the good wishes of Phillip Gidley King who had returned from England and taken up the role as governor for New South Wales.

'And what does our new Governor Foveaux say about our island Ed?'

215

'He was disappointed to see how things had not been kept up but he is pleased that the settlers are faring well. He's straight away on to choosing workers to repair and do up the government buildings and the roads. Tis a weight off my mind my dear.'

'That's such good news. It seems then that the rumours of closing down the island, were just that and nothing more.'

With that thought, a look of delight lit up her face and with no frown furrow to be seen on Edward's brow Susannah relaxed back into the chair, her pregnant belly raised before her. The child within, impatient to be released into the world, sent waves of movement across her stomach and she ran her hand across the front of her dress, circling its roundness.

'Perhaps another boy, this one's playing rough games with himself, and I'm ready for him to join his brothers on the outside.'

'Yes, tis a lively one, I can see the baby moving from here.

But with Foveaux has come some bad news. It's about the *Norfolk* sloop.'

When James heard this he lifted his head from the writing he was practising.

'What is it Pa?'

'The story goes that when Governor Hunter first saw the vessel sail into Port Jackson he thought her an excellent boat and directed that she be

216

commanded by Captain Matthew Flinders. He is said to be a renowned navigator. He sent Flinders off in the *Norfolk* to survey unmapped areas and it was discovered Van Diemen's Land was an island apart from the mainland, completely separated by a strait of water.

After these exploration journeys she was used to voyage north of Port Jackson to carry provisions and grain to new settlements on the Hawkesbury and Hunter Rivers. It was on one such journey that she was seized by fifteen desperate runaway convicts. The word is they meant to sail her thousands of miles north to islands called the Moluccas. But when they were stopped by authorities in at a river north of Broken Bay, they drove her ashore.'

Susannah saw Edward's expression of disappointment.

'Oh Ed, that is a sorry thing indeed. All the effort that went into her'

'Pa, did they fix her?' James asked.

'The governor put out an immediate order and despatched with all speed an armed boat to the Hunter River but when they found her she was bilged. Tis a crying shame. They could not salvage her and she fell to pieces in the surf off the point where the river meets the sea, a point they have now named Pirates Point.'

'And what of these pirates Ed?'

'Governor King's men gave chase after some of the desperate men secured a trader's vessel. They were pursued and captured, taken back to Port Jackson and were condemned to death. They were in bad shape when they caught up with them. Two of them were executed straight away but seven of them are being sent here.'

'Here! Dear heaven, they'll not be welcomed here.'

'Will they hang them Pa?'

'If they were going to hang them they wouldn't be sending them up here. Not that it's any consolation for the *Norfolk*, I hear Governor King has now issued a general order that vessels are not to venture to those remote places unless accompanied by at least another boat and should there be any attempts to seize ships, those who are in charge of the boat are to cut away the masts and rigging before the pirates' board and not only that, they have been directed if they can, they are to run the vessel ashore and bilge it. So all ships must have an axe for the purpose. What a waste that would be; in the name of trying to stop convicts escaping!

He has also sent out a warning to all, that should any others attempt such a scheme that only inevitable destruction awaits them.'

James' memory of the sloop was of her slipping into the bay and sailing out of sight, with all the promise of adventure aboard her. He reckoned from the sound of it that she had indeed had much adventure in her short life, still he was dismayed at her fate.

****

Within a week of hearing about the sad end of the *Norfolk*, Susannah gave birth to another son, John, *a good strong name* she thought. He was big and healthy and loud, a strong cry to match his strong name. Soon Susannah was up and about, back into her daily tasks, with John wrapped in a sling that rested over her shoulders against her back. There he snuggled, often rocked to sleep by the rhythm of her walk, leaving her hands free to do whatever the day presented to be done.

At night John slept in his crib beside Eddie's cot. Eddie talked to himself, at the same time his chatter soothed his little brother. As she tucked John into his crib, Eddie peered over the side, thumb in mouth.

'You're getting too big to be sucking that thumb. You're five Eddie, and your little brother here, you don't want him to be thinking you're a baby still.' Eddie immediately pulled his thumb out and stuck it behind his back.

Susannah lifted Eddie up and kissed him on the cheek.

'I'm not too big for a kiss Mumma?'

Susannah set him down and ruffled his hair.

'You'll never be too big for that my boy. Now it's time for you to sleep too. So say your prayers and close your eyes and try to be quiet.'

Susannah closed the door to their room and slid into bed beside Edward, he reached for the bottom of her nightgown and lifted it up over her head, then dropped it on the floor. Not much more than a month had passed since John's birth but the fervent love that she and Edward still felt for each other manifested itself in a way that even surprised Susannah. Her urges to be held and made love to were more intense than ever.

The next month when she found she was again pregnant she wondered whether it had been nature's trick that had not only made her desire Edward so passionately but at the same time had made her more fertile than before, for even with baby John at her breast she still managed to conceive.

****

Within the year, on a day when the rain fell in torrents, the sounds Susannah made during her labour could be heard mingling with the pounding rain. The bedroom door was closed but every now and then Edward could be heard calling out to the children from inside the room.

'Everything is alright. Don't be worried.'

'Are you sure Mumma's not hurting?' Eddie asked from time to time.

'Eddie,' Mary told him, 'Mumma says it's an effort to push out a baby,' and with that, Eddie would grimace and sneak in a sucking of his thumb.

As the rain eased the baby was born. The sound of pelting rain was replaced by the pattering of showers and the comforting voice of Susannah as she nursed their new son.

'Well Ed Garth, four boys now to carry on your name and what shall we call this one?'

'We shall call him, William. Another good strong name.'

'I wonder whether my body will now give up bearing babies? I don't mind, it's just that it happened again so soon. Annie is the same, what with her Johnnie only six months, she is now expecting another.'

'Well, we have food to put in their bellies and a place to live, and it will make more hands for work in the future. So as long as your body can deliver, then so be it,' and he grinned his familiar grin.

Susannah looked at him, *other than his once pale skin, now darker from the sun, and a few creases about his eyes, he is still as lean and handsome as the moment I first spied him.*

She had no regrets about the frequency with which the children had come but the truth was, the more children there were the more it kept her anchored and she railed against not being able to escape the confines of the house.

When Edward saw her frustration he decided to build a pushchair from the lightest timber he could find, with wide wooden hollowed out wheels and a

221

carriage big enough for the two little ones to be moved about in at the one time. When he surprised her with the contraption Susannah was thrilled, a smile so broad revealed her pleasure, a feeling of gratitude so deep it warmed her heart.

'Oh Ed Garth, you are indeed a maker of things and a man who makes things happen and what you will allow me to make happen with this wonderful gadget is for me to be able to visit Annie and walk down the path through the vale and to the seaside with the littluns. Thank you, you know you have made me very happy.'

On a day almost too beautiful, Susannah stopped in at Ann's farm on her way to the bay.

'Tis too grand a day to be inside Annie. The warmth is just right, the breeze not too strong.'

'That it is Susannah but I don't have a pushchair like you and my Johnnie is too heavy to carry all the way down the hillside and back, especially with this tummy of mine.'

'You and I Annie, we are as fertile as the ground beneath us,' Susannah chuckled. 'I'll have Ed show Jacob how to make you a pushchair and soon you will be able to join me.'

Later, as the afternoon shadows began to fall across the south eastern side of the island, Susannah wheeled the children down to Mary's school. From

222

there she walked with them along the road that lay parallel to the bay, to where James' and young Eddie's school had been built, between two enormous pines whose towering shadows cooled the yard below.

When they arrived at where Edward was working, James stayed helping his father, learning the skills, watching the harmonious way Edward's hands worked with and transformed the wood. James thought about the sad end to the *Norfolk* and he continued to commit all he could to memory about how the boats were being built. *One day,* he thought, *I will build a boat in her honour.*

The other children swam in the bay and played in the sand. Susannah took off her shoes and hitched up her dress and as she stood in the shallows the small waves lapped about her ankles and knees and she resisted the urge to remove all her clothes and submerse herself in the refreshing swirl of the waters that heaved and retreated along the shore.

As she watched the children play Susannah felt a happiness deep in her heart, that same kind she had felt the first day the *Supply* had put down anchor in Sydney Bay. It was elation that rose up from a well within her, a well that held all the love for her family and the love for this place. She saw them as one, the family and the island, all intrinsically connected and the joy of these images washed over her senses leaving her lightheaded with gladness and a feeling that all would be well.

Chapter 12

1802-1803

'I remember being on the streets of London, a place far away and very different from here, where there were lots of buildings, very many people, no forests and no oceans to be seen. I am an orphan like you and I remember seeking out other urchins, so we could band together to steal food and clothes. We had no-one to look after us. I always wanted to believe my mother had died and that there was no choice about me being left alone, but the truth is I remember that feeling of being deserted. I can't remember the place or time when it happened, I only remember the feeling that I had been left.'

Some of the girls began to cry and quickly Susannah thought she must change the subject, so she started again with the instructions of how to make and bake the bread, the task which she had been allocated to teach the girls. She had been distracted with recounting her own tale and the curiosity of some of them who asked questions sent her off on a tangent. She saw no point in avoiding the answers and she felt perhaps they would identify with her and see there was hope. The truth was the girls were sad and they would cry, because their parents had abandoned them, or perhaps their mothers were alone and could not cope. Whatever the reason, someone they had once loved or could have loved had left them.

'So what did you do ma'am?'

'Well there was no Governor King to build me and the other urchins a place to live, where we could get a feed and be clothed. We had to fend for ourselves, sleeping wherever we could in the filthy and freezing alleys, in falling down houses with rats all about and sickness everywhere. But God had a plan for me and that's how I ended up here.'

Susannah thought perhaps if she described her destiny as God's plan the girls may take comfort in that, for she wanted for all of them to see she was now happy with her life.

'Sometimes we think things will never get better and we can't see our way, but it is like the girl who set out to find the pot of gold at the end of the rainbow but got lost along the way. She walked through dark forests, was chased by ogres, became frightened and hungry but just when she wished she had never started her journey she woke up and found herself surrounded by colour and at her feet was the key which opened the door to her new life and she realised all the time she had been standing at the rainbow's end.'

Well I never, she thought, *I sound like a preacher* and she chuckled proudly to herself as the girls smiled at her story.

They listened to Susannah as John sat in the pushchair next to William who was sleeping. Occasionally John tried to wake his brother up but Susannah would scold him and Eddie, would repeat after her 'yes, stop it

Johnnie, that's naughty' and the girls would giggle before settling down again, watching and listening.

After the lesson on bread baking was finished and Susannah had told some more of her tales, the girls waved goodbye to her and the boys. She pushed them across the yard to the roadway, the ride was always a bumpy one and hard work when the wheels got stuck but whenever she became irritated by the effort she chastised herself, *think yourself lucky Susannah, at least you have a pushchair* and her thoughts turned back to the orphan girls, *I still can't fathom how their mothers could leave them… but who am I to judge… fear and desperation can force our hand, Lord knows it forced mine.*

'Come on Eddie, help Mumma push the chair up the hill. Let's see how strong you are.'

She wondered about the girls in the orphanage and how perhaps some of them one day may make good wives for her own boys, but then she thought of the Bellett girls and knew there were no better matches than the daughters of her friend.

****

The winter, more like autumn, came and went, and spring came bringing with her ten new chickens to Susannah's chicken coop. Johnnie and William toddled amongst them, the hens pecking at the boys' feet, making them squeal and trip.

227

The air was filled with fragrances which burst forth from the new blooms of the season, the salty air wafted on the breeze with the songs that resounded up the hill from Music Valley. Edward leaned back in the rocking chair he had made and it creaked its rocking sound in time with his words.

'The year has brought with it mixed fortune. Governor Foveaux has proved to be a capable commander for us, making sure the public works were undertaken and he's tried to build the island back up. I'm sure Governor King would be happy that he is trying to make things work here. But the way he deals with some of the convicts who are not yet free is harsh and unyielding, and I know he has gone outside the law in his punishment of them, which in turn has led the marines to think they can treat the convicts with contempt and cruelty. And, some say he has even sold some of the convict women off.'

'What! I wonder what Governor King would think if he knew these things. Surely Foveaux would not sell any of the older orphan girls. Dear heaven! Well perhaps he will leave soon, he is not a well looking man you know. He has an unhealthy pallor about him and he is always wheezing and coughing.'

'There have indeed been some queer stories about him, you know he has inveigled himself into the affections of the wife of one of his non-commissioned officers and has taken her as his own. The only good thing about that is she at least seems to have had some influence over him. I think it is her doing that he has not used the lash so freely recently. Some say in the past he was guilty of torture and at least until she came on the scene he showed an ardent appetite for human suffering.'

Susannah had made regular trips to the girls' orphan home, teaching them to sew or cook and sometimes she convinced Ann to go with her to talk to them about farming. The thought of the girls being treated like slaves enraged her.

'If he tries that with the orphan girls there will be uproar, I will band the women settlers together and we will take a stand,' she said raising her voice.

'Calm down my dear. The girls are not convicts, they are orphans. I don't think he would do such a thing.'

'Well Ed Garth I hope you're right, for if you aren't it's a stand we will have to take. I just wish Governor King were back here. What does Jacob say?'

'He has been taking on jobs as a constable and he has heard more rumblings of closing down the island. He's also not been happy about some of the orders he has had to follow. I've said to him he should just go back to working the farm with Annie but he says the extra earnings are needed, especially with yet another baby to be born soon.'

229

'Closing the island down… that rumour again. Why does it seem that some are just so set on that idea? I hope it is put to rest once and for all. It's unsettling for everyone. As for Jacob I can understand him taking on whatever he can to earn more, after all Annie is expecting their sixth soon. He's got so many mouths to feed. Quite a brood and it wouldn't surprise me if there's another before the next year is out. Still even though he needs the funds I hope he doesn't get caught up in having to carry out some of the governor's terrible orders.'

James was on the verandah listening to the conversation. It all sounded quite grim and suddenly he had the urge to sail their little boat out towards the horizon. It was summer and he knew the twilight would be long. Whenever he had sailed out to sea with his father it had been for a purpose. They always pulled down the sail and let the boat drift and they would fish, laying lines out of the stern of the boat, but never losing sight of the island. And when they sailed they took turns on the tiller and the sail but he was sure he could handle both on his own.

The urge he felt this day was not to fish, but for the pure pleasure of sailing and he was sure he could sail the little boat alone. *Perhaps I can just push her out into the bay and sail her in the cove between the islands.* But in some ways this was more precarious than heading straight out to sea because he knew if he were to only sail in the bay he would have to be very careful to avoid the shallow reef.

He had heard the stories of the sunken *Sirius* that had come to grief on the rocks*, but she was a huge boat* he thought, *our little boat is easy to tack and turn and her hull can float on next to no water. If I could just get someone to help me push her off the sand and into the bay, I'd be right and when I come back I can sail her straight up onto the shore, the keel will slide into the sand, then I can tip her on her side.* It was an ambitious plan, to land the boat in this way and he knew there was a risk of damaging the keel, but the urge was strong and the more he thought about it the stronger it became. In the back of his mind he knew his father would not be happy about this adventure but he thought perhaps he could get away with it and his father would never find out.

It did not occur to him that a strong wind may gust and tip him and the boat over at sea, nor that he might hit some submerged rocky island in an area he was unfamiliar with, or that a storm might force him over the horizon. All that he thought of was the freedom to sail and the feeling that would bring with it.

He hurried down the hillside and enlisted the help of another bigger lad to push the boat off the sand and into the shallows. The boy tried to insist on going with him, but James knew the lad could not sail and would be more of a hindrance than a help. Once afloat James began to hoist the sail, letting it flap in the breeze, then as he tightened the mast he grabbed the tiller with his other hand, the wind caught the taught sail and suddenly he was propelled away from the shore.

There was no thinking at all, he sailed straight across the reef and out to sea, just as he had wanted to, towards the horizon. His sinewy body was relatively tall and strong but he still strained to keep the sail in, the boat began to lean and James manoeuvred himself up onto her side, balancing the boat against the pull of gravity. Faster and faster she sped through the water, the further out from land the stronger the wind became. The wind roared past his ears, the ocean spray saturated him and the boat dipped and bounced beneath him. Occasionally he would ease the sail, slowing her down a little, but the rush of blood he felt with the speed the boat made led him to sail it almost horizontal to the ocean surface, his muscles tense and his heart racing. He had been taught the skill by his father but now he was sailing on instinct. It was he, the boat and nature, water and wind that fired his being and if Susannah had been able to see him, she would have recognised those feelings of exhilaration.

From outside Edward and Susannah's cottage came a call.

'Garth! Garth I saw your sailboat being sailed out of the bay. If it was a convict trying to escape he won't get far on her.'

Edward rushed down to the beach and saw indeed his boat was gone. He looked out to the ocean but the vessel was nowhere to be seen.

He stood in disbelief, surely a convict would not be fool enough to think he could abscond on that little boat, still strange things happen and for the moment Edward thought it a pity his boat had been stolen and that he would have to build another in its place. Just then a voice bellowed at him from the pathway above.

'Mr Garth sir, James took her.'

Edward could scarcely believe his ears. James had never sailed the boat alone, not even in the bay.

'How long ago lad?'

'Twas about half hour ago.'

Edward's immediate thought was to commandeer one of the other vessels and take off out to sea after him but he had no idea which direction he had gone, instead, he began to climb to the nearest high point to see if there was any sign of the boat, calling out to the lad as he did.

'Fetch Jacob Bellett lad, tell him what has happened and tell him I need him to bring as many people as he can to help look out.'

'But sir, Mr Garth, James said he would be able to sail her out to the horizon and that he would just sail her back in.'

'Lad just do as I ask, there is not a trace of him. If I am to go and find him, I need to see if he is within reach.'

The boy turned and ran to find Jacob, muttering to himself *but he said he would be fine*.

Edward was afraid and his rush to the high point above the beach had left him gulping for air. Scouring the horizon, he looked for the sail, the veins in his temples throbbing, his breath laboured and loud in his ears.

When James had realised the island was out of sight he did not panic. Although there was no beacon to guide him back, he knew the direction the wind had taken him, he knew the position of the sun and he tacked her back around to face what he thought was the exact same direction from where he had come. Every nerve in his body was alive. Whilst he looked keenly for the island, he relished the excitement of being in the middle of nowhere with nothing but water and wind about him. But soon his limbs began to ache and the thought that he could be lost crept in. When he finally saw again the island in the distance the relief gave him the courage to sail her even faster still, daringly close to tipping.

By the time Jacob had joined Edward on the hilltop, word had spread that men may be needed to take out a boat to find the eldest Garth boy who had sailed his father's little yacht out to the open sea and a crowd began to gather. Susannah left the little ones with Ann and dashed to the bay, all the way praying that her boy would be found, tears of trepidation blurring her sight and alarm gripping her heart.

She held tight to Edward's arm, standing with the congregation, silently gazing out to the ocean. Susannah implored Edward with her eyes, seeing her fear he said.

'I cannot wait any longer, the sun will be setting soon. I need two other men to help me sail the bigger yacht. Come Jacob, down to the beach we'll need to row out now, there's only about an hour of sunlight left.'

Just as Edward turned to walk down the hill came the cry.

'There, there!' one of the onlookers called, pointing to the east. Edward looked in the direction and amongst the whitecaps could be seen a lone sail. Closer and closer the sailboat came until there was no doubt.

'Yes it is he!'

But the relief was tempered for by the time the boat was seen to be approaching entry into the bay it was heeling at an acute angle and looked dangerously close to capsizing.

Susannah held Edward's hand tightly. 'He is going full out!'

'Once he gets into the lee of the southern island the wind will drop somewhat and he won't be able to sail so fast.'

'Ed you mean he is deliberately going so fast and leaning like that?'

'Yes, that is what I mean.' Despite their fear Edward and Susannah could not help feel a hint of pride in the daring James had shown in his somewhat reckless action.

James sailed into the bay, wet and exhausted, muscles screaming with the ache of his efforts and he tacked the boat toward the shore, loosening the sail a little to slow her down, gently manoeuvring her into the shallows. Edward waded knee deep in water with Jacob to save the boat from having to be run onto the sand.

James pulled the flapping sail in and looked briefly up at his father and his mother on the shore and the dozens of people and knew it was not a time to talk about the wonder of it all.

His father helped him off the boat and although his look was stern, his embrace was loving. 'I'll be giving you a hiding later, but for now I just thank God you are alive.'

Susannah held James by the shoulders and shook him, sobbing at him to 'never do such a thing again.'

But James knew then he would one day do just that and that it was the best thing he had ever done.

Although Edward had promised James a hiding he could not bring himself to beat his son.

'You're not to sail the boat until I permit it again,' he said 'if you do the boat will be sold and not another will ever be sailed by you.' James knew that despite his father's love of boats his word was true and that was enough.

Still he bided his time, waiting for the day when he would say to his father. 'Pa it is time for me to sail out to sea again, alone.'

****

'Twas a grand Christmas celebration yesterday Ed Garth, my voice's a little hoarse and my legs weary from all that jigging but it was a grand day indeed.'

Susannah noticed Edward's demeanour change, he had become serious, *that wretched crease between his eyes,* she thought, and all her happy thoughts for the coming New Year of 1803 receded to the back of her mind.

'What is it Ed?'

'My dear I worry for us all.'

'Ed you have worried before for nought, what is it now?'

'The word is… that indeed Major Foveaux has brought with him the duty to tell us the government does intend to close down our island. I fear this possibility is going to hang above us like a wretched sword.'

'Oh Ed, I thought by now they would see we are doing fine. And why would he direct us to go about repairing things if he had orders to put into action such a plan.'

'I don't know but Jacob tells me the governor has already asked for the names of those who are prepared to leave willingly. They have started up

237

another colony, on Van Diemen's Land and he is asking for those who would be prepared to resettle there to come forward.'

'Perhaps they will be satisfied to just limit the numbers here. Perhaps they will change their minds once they see that governing the island is less difficult with fewer people on it. And Ed, I can't see them getting many volunteers, there's only a few who don't have their own land here. Why would anyone with farms and land want to leave? I think this madness will pass. Once Governor Foveaux gets word back to the authorities that we are doing well here surely they will let us be.'

'I hope you are right my dear.'

****

On New Year's Day Edward allowed James to join him fishing, sailing the small sailboat out from the island, to a spot where a deep hole lay in the ocean floor, the territory of large fish.

They sailed her with some reasonable speed but with the two of them she was heavier.

'Pa you know I can sail. You have seen I can sail on my own.'

'Son, you are not yet twelve and you know if you were to capsize at sea you would be lost.'

238

'What if I promised to only sail out to Nepean Island and back, would you let me?'

'Let's get past your next birthday and then I might be able to convince your mother.'

Although Edward meant what he said, he secretly wished the child had no such ambition and hoped he would lose the urge, for he could not see James being satisfied with sailing in the confines of the bay.

They returned at the end of the day, sunburnt and tired. James spoke with animation as soon as he walked in the door.

'Ma you should have seen the size of the tuna we caught today. It was as large as Eddie. Pa says it was the live bait we used that brought it in and there were thousands of fish around. At once the water was black with them, masses and masses of them. And then I felt the pull on the line, it felt like a whale, it was so strong it nearly reefed me off the boat. It took pa and me near on an hour to pull it in. We cut it into steaks! It was so big. It's now in pieces in the smokehouse and it will feed us all for weeks.'

Susannah smiled, a smile that belied her consternation. She knew the fish were plentiful in the deep reefs that surrounded the island, that the waters were temperate and the air fresh, she loved the island but to think there may be the possibility of having to leave, that thought stirred a sick feeling inside her.

When James was out of sight she sat down on the steps of the porch and gazed toward the two southern islands. It was not her usual inclination, to pine and worry and she became more disconcerted when she realised her own forehead was now furrowed in an Ed Garth-like frown. Their future had seemed solid, indestructible but this possibility had left her sharply aware that her future may be beyond her control and she wondered what hand fate may have ready to deal them. She had believed that destiny had brought her and Edward together, that everything that had happened had been a part of some greater plan. Optimism had carried her thus far but it was an optimism that had grown from her new beginning on Norfolk. The thought of being shipped off the island choked at her positivism and a grim uneasiness began to dwell within her.

'Ed, this is our home, our children's birthright, I cannot face the thought of leaving here. I can't believe it Ed. Tell me it's not true.'

'I am holding on to hope Susannah, I and others like me and Jacob are making it clear to the governor that we do not accept it as a fait accompli. Although Foveaux asked for volunteers to leave, less than fifty people have offered to go. He knows the rest of us will not go willingly. Those of us who have been here from the beginning will not be giving up our land. How could they expect us to just walk away from here? We're hoping our resolve will make the authorities change their minds.

The governor has made me the acting gaoler and Jacob is to assist me. He has appointed a number of us freed convicts into jobs like this. Perhaps it is a sign that even though he may have been told to prepare us for shutting the island down, he is resisting or changing his own mind about whether that should happen and perhaps he can convince them back in Britain. The word is that Governor King is strongly against it and thinks we should be allowed to stay. If he and Governor Foveaux have any influence, then there is a chance we won't be made to leave.'

'Well Ed I for one won't be leaving without a fight. This is our home and I'll not be going anywhere!'

Chapter 13

1804

'Pa I am nearly thirteen...'

Edward knew what the statement meant. James had waited longer than Edward had expected to bring it up. James's expression was earnest, his eyes looking directly at his father.

'If your mother allows it then you can sail alone, but only if you go no further than the southern waters adjacent to Nepean Island and only when the weather is fair and you must ask my permission every time so I know where you are.'

Edward knew James was a good sailor but the waters could be treacherous and sometimes the weather unpredictable and no matter how fine a sailor he was he and Susannah both held the fear if the boat capsized he could be drowned. Still he also knew it was something he had to allow James to do again, to sail alone and give him this pleasure. It would be a hard to convince Susannah but he banked on her own love of freedom to help her see the way clear to allowing the boy to enjoy this passion dwelling within him.

They both came into the kitchen wearing purposeful expressions and as Susannah shifted about preparing their meal, she felt their eyes fixed upon her back. When she turned and saw undeniably that they were waiting for her attention, she brought her hands to her waist and resting on one leg she tapped her other foot.

'Yes…'

'James has something he wants to ask.'

Susannah knew before the asking what it would be. She had rehearsed the answer so many times, but the answer in her practice was not the answer she knew she had to give, still she let him ask.

'Ma, I am older now, I am more sensible. I will be careful. I want to take the boat out again… on my own. Pa says it is up to you.'

'And what am I to do with my heart should anything happen to you? It would be useless to anyone, your father, the others… How could I ever look out to that ocean I love and know you had been swallowed up out there? Tell me!'

'But Ma.'

'No, there are no buts. You must not. You must not ever go out in the ocean without telling us first.'

And on realising what she was saying James wrapped his arms about his mother. He had grown taller still, taller than his mother and she let her head drop into the crook between his head and shoulder, part of her proud of her young man and excited for his own adventures and part of her wishing for her little boy back.

Later, in the quiet of another Norfolk night Susannah dared for a moment to think what it would be like for a child of hers to die before her. She had seen the grief such tragedies brought and to contemplate the possibility sent an ache to her heart. As she shook the thought from her mind, she tried to sniffle up a renegade tear that was forcing its way down her cheek,

'So tell me Ed Garth, what other not so good news do you have for me?'

'Well my dear, right now I cannot say I have any bad news. It's now been two years of passive defiance by the settlers in the face of the rumblings about the island being closed down. We have taken our pleas to the authorities that we be allowed to remain and indeed it seems that through our determination and efforts to maintain our self-sufficiency the government has perhaps lost interest in going ahead with moving everyone off and, although some have left and returned to Port Jackson, the majority of us stay and carry on as we always have.'

'Well Ed Garth, I have some news for you. Just when I thought perhaps there would be no more babies…' and she placed his hand upon her belly.

He held her.

'I love you my dear, my lovely.'

And Susannah thought, *when love comes from some unearthly place, when it comes from a place where forces unseen bring two people together, it has an unstoppable force, stronger than anything that can be seen or touched, stronger than our mortal flesh*, the kind of love that transcends matter and time, *this is our love*.

That night, as they lay in bed, a tangle of arms and legs and with the sounds of Edward's sleeping breaths against her ear, she fell asleep and dreamed of still water and brown hills, of peculiar animals, of black men and fires.

When she awoke she looked out from her porch, the distant roar of the ocean was what she heard, high flying birds, the blue vastness of the ocean and the green valley was what she saw. *Was it Botany Bay she had dreamed of*, she thought, *or was it this Van Diemen's Land that had been spoken of?* To her the dream fit what she had heard about the place and the thought of it raised the hairs on her arms.

Despite her dream, the first week of the New Year brought no talk of evacuations and by the time Edward went to work eight days into 1804 Susannah had forgotten the images of still water and the goose flesh she had felt at the thought of it. Edward was engaged in duties he had taken on as a constable, Susannah attended to the cows then the chickens, had some words with their workers and set about making a new loaf of bread, the little ones obediently sat at the table watching.

Edward was standing at the wicket gate looking across the gaol yard watching as John Morris, one of the inmates was pacing up and down in an agitated way. Jacob noticed Morris' unsettled demeanour and walked over to Edward.

'What's he up to?'

Edward knew John Morris could be a violent man.

'He has a reputation for getting worked up and being easily angered. He has brutally beaten up his wife Sarah Bird many times. Susannah says Sarah has regularly been on the receiving end of one of his swift back-handers or a knee in the back and he's a trouble maker. The governor says he must be confined due to his desperate character and conduct.'

Morris saw Edward and Jacob looking at him and he strode up to Edward aggressively, standing toe to toe with him.

'I want to go into the cells and get my trunk off the loft where I left it.'

Edward was suspicious at what he may have in his trunk.

'No, you don't need anything out here and I don't think I can trust you. Just settle down.'

'Damn you Garth, I want my tools, just let me get my trunk and stop being a lickspittle.'

When Morris began to yell abuse at him Edward kept his composure and turned to Jacob.

'Can you get Morris's trunk and bring it down.'

Jacob looked at Edward, concerned at Morris's still angry demeanour. 'Maybe he can accompany me while I retrieve it,' thinking this may placate Morris.

Edward reluctantly nodded his agreement. The two men went into the cells, appearing some short time later with Morris's trunk. Morris was still riled, he muttered angrily under his breath, his face twisted and the whites of his knuckles showed on his clenched fists. Jacob set the trunk down in the passageway and Morris began extracting items, all the while hauling abuse at Edward. When Jacob took the trunk back into the cells Morris looked up at Edward.

'Who do ye think ye are Garth, restricting m' liberty. You're nothing but a convict ya'self. Bugger your soul to hell you bloody bastard!'

Around the yard others began to show signs of agitation and Edward was worried Morris could incite some kind of riot. He looked Morris squarely in the eye.

'Quieten down or I will put you in the cells.'

With that Morris ran towards Edward full speed, his hand raised above his head, his face red with fury. Edward held up his left arm to screen the

248

coming blow. He believed it to have been a punch, but when he reached for his elbow where he had taken the full force, Edward saw blood and knew he had been stabbed. Initially there was no pain and as Morris raised his arm again to deliver another blow Edward with both hands took hold of Morris's arms. They fell to the ground, churning up the dust around them. The strength in Edward's left arm weakened and as he called out to the watchman his arm gave way completely allowing Morris to plunge the knife deep into Edward's stomach.

There was again no initial pain and with a rush of adrenalin steeling him, Edward managed to push Morris off him, he rose to his feet and began to run. As the pain set in he staggered down the passageway and struck his shoulder against the jamb of the door, which slowed down his attempts to flee. Morris caught him, he was grunting, staring wildly and sounding like an animal he thrust the knife into Edward's loins. Still Edward did not stop, he kept going towards where the pistols were kept, blood pouring from his wounds until he became so weak he could stand no more. As he slumped to the ground Jacob reached Edward with one of the constables causing Morris to take flight, knife still in hand. Jacob picked up a hammer and threw it at Morris with all his force, glancing Morris's back but not stopping him.

As one of the gaolers pressed against the blood gushing from Edward's wounds, Jacob ran out of the gaol pursuing Morris.

'Stop him!'

Edward could feel the wetness of his blood, tacky and viscous about him, warm and sticky. A wave of agonising pain, rising, tearing into his grown and stomach engulfed him as his sight began to fade and, as a blurring greyness crept in, his head became light and he could hear nothing but the sound of his own hard beating heart.

Morris ran like a possessed demon, Jacob could not catch him but as he pursued him he saw him reach Sarah Bird's house and thrust his leg against the door, forcing his way inside.

Sarah had heard the commotion and saw Morris running towards the home. She had placed a table across the inside of the doorway to prevent the door from being opened but Morris burst in pushing the table clean aside. Screams shattered the air, bringing people out to see what the melee was all about. Sarah Bird retreated to a corner of the room, Morris lunged at her attempting to cut her throat. She held her hand up to her neck, he again slashed at her cutting through her wrist. Just moments later as Jacob reached the house Morris retreated out a rear window. Sarah fell against the doorway in a gore of blood. Constable Symonds took flight after Morris, firing his musket once as Morris headed to the swamp and Jacob rushed to Sarah's assistance trying to stem the blood-flow from her neck.

Constable Symonds was catching up to Morris and exhausted Morris fell. Jacob saw Symonds level his musket at Morris and then he heard loud pleas.

'Mercy, Mercy, I had lost my mind! Have mercy!'

Symonds did not fire upon him again but pointing the musket at Morris between his shoulder blades, he marched him back to the prison cells.

Susannah had heard the distant screaming and musket fire and rushed to the gaol. She saw people gathered around a figure on the ground.

'Oh dear Lord. What has happened?'

When she realised it was Edward she felt a crushing pain in her chest, and began to tremble and her legs became weak as she forced her way through the crowd.

Edward heard her voice and tried to open his eyes, but his eyelids were heavy and he only managed it briefly.

'I'll be alright.' The strength in Edward's words betraying the fact that all he could see before him was blackness.

He drifted out of consciousness. Susannah stayed near as the surgeon began to pack his wounds.

'Prepare for the worst,' was all the doctor could say, but Susannah would not think of such a thing.

'He will live. Don't give up on him.'

She watched on as the dressings became blood soaked, as the colour of the dressings deepened and the colour in Edward's face washed away.

When Jacob arrived with James, Edward was pale and still, the smell of blood in the air. Susannah sat ashen faced by his side.

'Tell the children your father has been wounded but don't frighten them, tell them he will be right. You tell Mary to keep the children away until I say to come. You and Mary must look after the children for now. I am staying here with your father. He has lost a lot of blood but he will not die.' *I won't let him* she thought.

That day and the next and the next, Edward slipped in and out of consciousness and Susannah continued to pray her silent prayer to God, to Jesus, to Mother Mary, to the stars, the heavens, to the spirits, she prayed, the same words in her head over and over again, *I will give anything for him to live. Please, let him live! I will give up everything, if you just let him live.*

He lingered on the brink of death, thin breaths, his chest barely rising and falling, Susannah watching intently, sitting next to his bed resting her head against his pillow to nap. She rarely left his side, moistening his lips, dripping water into his mouth which he swallowed in a half sleep and from time to time she whispered to him,

'You cannot die. You will not die. This baby needs to know his father. Your children need you. I need you Ed Garth. We have not come this far for you to die so soon. You listen to me. You will not die.'

Gradually, as the days passed, Susannah could see the slightest hint of colour returning to his cheeks and then one morning, as the roosters heralded in the sunrise, he opened his eyes.

'Thirsty' he mumbled, his tongue sticking to the roof of his mouth. Susannah held a mug of water up to his lips to sip at.

When he saw her, he smiled a small smile and Susannah's fears began to subside. She grinned back at him.

'Ed Garth, you're going back to your boat building, enough of this guarding criminals. I'll not allow it; you hear me?'

As she breathed a sigh of relief she thanked God, for it seemed her prayer had been answered.

That morning she sent for the children. When James and Mary arrived with the younger ones, John and William had to be held back from jumping up on to their father and needed to be satisfied with a kiss and ruffled hair. They could not understand why he was lying down barely moving. James looked closely at his father, he could not see how he would ever recover, when he watched the dressings being changed all he could see was angry red flesh and jagged black stitching across the wounds.

Through a long February and March, Edward's wounds sometimes swelled and oozed puss and blood and he shivered with a fever from infections that came and went but Susannah bathed the lesions with salted water and left the dressings off just long enough to allow the wounds to dry and he began to recover. After the waxing and waning of another Easter moon, Edward's injuries healed and finally he was able to walk… back up the hill to their home.

It was April before he felt well enough to be able to work again. He was surprised he had recovered so well, although now his elbow was tight and he was not able to straighten it fully, there was no longer much pain. At the end of his first day back in his old role as overseer of sawyers, as he took off his work clothes Susannah looked at his scars. The stripes across his back now competed with the new scars left by the knife wounds. Some were raised and bumpy, some deep in the valleys of his skin.

Susannah half-filled a cast iron tub with cold water then poured boiling water in to warm it. When Edward climbed in, his knees drawn up, she began sponging him, across his forehead, his neck and back, down his arms and then under the water to the places where the new lesions resided, on his stomach and loins. Edward rested his head forward, tired at the end of his first day back at work.

'And what of Sarah Bird?' he asked.

'Twas savage what he did to her too Ed. Cut her from one collarbone to the other, like you, a wonder she survived. And you know how Governor Foveaux was away from the island when Morris attacked you, well since he's got back it's been reported to him what Captain Wilson did to Morris after they caught him. Wilson hit him so hard across the face with a stick that he broke his jaw, then he had him flogged and had salt water thrown over his wounds and hot leg irons were fixed to his legs which burnt through almost to the bone. I did not see it but those who did said it was a cruel punishment. And now, now that you and Sarah are well enough you must give evidence at his trial.'

'Aye, tis next week. If he is found guilty of attempted murder, he may be hanged.'

Edward did not want him dead but he wanted him punished and locked up where he could not go on the rampage again.

Susannah sponged his back, soft purposeful movements across his shoulder blades, Edward leaning his head into his chest.

'How are your injuries Ed, you seem weary?'

'Aye, I am stiff and sore… but it will pass.'

****

As the trial approached Edward was plagued with nightmares, the same over and over. It was the crazed face of Morris that came at him, the

255

frenzied look and the motion of Morris' arm as he stabbed Edward time and again. But when the trial began Morris did not have the look of the madman Edward remembered, he sat quietly in the dock, his face expressionless, a broken man, his jaw askew, the burn marks and mangled flesh about his ankles plain for everyone to see. Edward thought he saw Morris mouthing to him that he was 'sorry', but he wasn't sure and when at the end of the hearing Morris was found guilty and sentenced to death neither Morris nor Edward showed any sign of emotion.

That night and in the nights that followed Edward's sleep was finally free of the manic nightmares of Morris' attack and Susannah was thankful that he no longer awoke agitated and damp with perspiration.

Susannah leant back on the verandah chair, hands resting on her growing belly, Edward standing against the rail of the little porch at their home.

'Governor Foveaux has allowed Morris to appeal to Lord Hobart against the hanging. He says what Captain Wilson did was an 'atrocity'. Ed I can't bring myself to say he should be hanged but I'll not ever forgive what Morris did. He nearly took you from us. I'd have been tempted to hang him myself if that had happened.'

'I find it hard to think clearly about Morris. He did seem to be crazy with rage, perhaps he really had lost his mind. So long as they keep him locked up and away from me I don't care what they do with him.'

Edward was glad to get back to his work but his body was battered, not only from the attack but from the years of hard work and the physical trials he had endured and he tired more readily. But James was encouraged, after seeing his father nearly dead he was surprised he could even walk again.

Some weeks later James noticed there was something that was affecting his father, his spirit rather than his flesh. Edward sat at the kitchen table, grim look upon his face.

'I have something I must tell you. Mary, James this news is for you too. Morris' appeal was successful. He will not be hanged, he may be out amongst us again, perhaps before too long…but, that is not all… On his return Governor Foveaux brought with him final orders. After all our pleading and even with the support of Governor King, the word is they are pressing ahead with the closure of the island.'

Susannah's shoulders sank, she exhaled long and slow, closing her eyes She retreated into herself momentarily and thought about the deal she had made with God, *Dear Lord, is this the price I have to pay for you saving Edward's life…*

Chapter 14

1804-1807

It was coming on spring and Susannah's new baby was eager to make its way into the world, it kicked about inside her, sending the skin on her stomach rippling, especially when it heard the voices of its brothers and sisters.

Susannah wondered what the consequences of carrying out these supposed final orders would mean for her unborn child, for all of them. She tried to distract herself, fussing about the house, washing and folding clothes, changing the sleeping arrangements of the children and giving instructions to everyone, trying to put things in place for the arrival of the new baby.

She visited Ann and did not talk to her about the sword hanging above their heads and as if in denial that such threat existed, they both went about their business, doing what they had always done.

The first week of spring saw lambs being born to the ewes of Edward's flock. Ann's maize was ripe for the harvest and as the pink hue of another September sunrise rested offshore, Susannah gave birth to her second baby girl.

She had been so used to boy after boy being born, she had chosen another boy's name but when a baby girl hurriedly entered the world with a cry as hearty as any she had heard, Susannah saw the girl was a child who possessed gusto and the babe reminded her of herself.

'Susannah is what we will baptise you. But Sassy is what you are and Sassy is what we will call you.'

****

During that same spring, at the end of one of their long day's work Edward and Jacob rested and yarned in the shade of the palms nestled in Music Valley.

'What do you think of Lieutenant John Piper as Governor Foveaux's replacement Ed?'

'He seems ambitious but still an affable Scotsman and although he is said to have had disagreements with Governor King in the past, he is also said to have one thing in common with him. He sees merit in keeping the island open. He looks upon those like us as first class settlers. He sees those of us who are freed convicts who have made good with their lives as valuable settlers and he recognises how important our roles are.

When I have spoken to him he has talked with admiration for what we have all done here. He knows it has been no small feat for us to have made a home for ourselves in this remote place. After all we are all on our own in the middle of a large wild ocean and we have more than just survived. He

260

sees us as a thriving settlement and he is going to somehow try and convince the authorities that the orders to close are a mistake.'

'That is so heartening Ed, but Governor King has been trying to do that for years. Why would Piper make any difference?'

'It is true Governor King has tried and he has at least succeeded in delaying carrying out any such orders. We should not give up: we should keep lobbying the authorities ourselves. Meantime Jacob, we carry on with our lives, working our farms, growing our stock and earning our livings in the hope that they will give up on seeing the orders through.'

****

For near on a year the Garths and Belletts continued to do as they had always done, in their work and in their leisure, in the hope that somehow the orders would be abandoned.

They moved seamlessly between households, helping each other, looking out for each other, the children learning from their parents that satisfaction could be gained from the simple pleasure of working and living side by side with people who were of the same mind.

James listened to his parents' conversations, the talk of not giving in, of staying on. He understood their love of their home and he tried to understand their want to stay but when he looked out to the horizon it was

261

not a limit to where he could venture that he saw, it was a blurred line that beckoned him to come closer, to go beyond.

Since that day when James had sailed at full speed out of sight of the island he had again ventured out to sea on his own, but only as his parents had demanded to Nepean Island and no further but the urge to keep sailing was strong, it was the same urge that had him thinking about what lay beyond that horizontal line.

It is a joyful thing, Susannah thought as she watched her children with the Belletts. *We are more like family than friends. They want for little and they love their lives. Oh to have had such a childhood.* They had developed a love of the sea, they swam in the ocean, danced in the valley, played and laughed together in friendship and with affection. *We are all part of the fabric that binds us. We and the Belletts, the island, we are all woven together.*

Young James felt it too, the way the families were intertwined, but there was something else within him, something stronger than the thread that bound them to this place, it was a want that lived inside him and it drew him beyond his field of vision. *One day,* he thought, *one day I will see for myself what is past that thin blue line.*

****

Mary Bellett loved James Garth and whilst she was only ten and James fourteen, she felt she knew this more than any other thing.

262

'When will you marry me James?' Mary asked tirelessly and faithfully, always her head dipped to one side, eyes looking for affirmation.

'You're like a sister to me Meh, besides you're only a littlun,' was his usual response, but Mary would not be dissuaded.

All her life she had followed him about, at school, after school, while he worked, while he played and whenever he was nearby to her she placed herself right behind him, asking him questions, 'What is this James?', 'What is that?', 'How did you catch that fish?', 'How do you build boats?', and when she was not asking questions she was echoing his remarks to others, 'James says' this, 'James says' that, 'James will know the answer', 'James', 'James', 'James'.

Susannah could not help but see the way the child shadowed him whenever she could. She had seen Mary sitting on the shore, watching James sail out to sea, watching him come back, watching as he and Edward selected the best timber for the boats they built, watching while he sang with their families.

Susannah saw that Mary not only watched but waited and she knew that the girl meant it when she said she wanted James to marry her, even though the words came from the mouth of a child, they came with an unmistakable truth that the child believed. It was a truth Susannah could understand. But whilst James loved them all he had a restless soul and Susannah knew he was a young man who would not be corralled. When she found him gazing out at the ocean she knew his gazing was driven by the desire to venture much further than the eye could see.

James was not a stranger to the utterings of the island folk, he listened to all their chattering and yarns and he knew of the rumour or so called orders that the island was to be closed. With this in mind he took note as another 250 people were induced to leave with promises of land grants in Van Diemen's Land, another island he knew to be far bigger than Norfolk and even in his youth he wondered what opportunities might lie in this other larger place, with more open spaces, more land to be had and more waterways to sail.

He overheard his parents talking but he knew better than to interrupt, so he waited.

'Ed, I have tried to block the thought from my head but if there is a real chance that this is going to happen then I suppose I should not keep denying it to myself.'

'Whilst not defying orders there is no doubt Lieutenant Piper is delaying things in the hope Governor King is still able to argue successfully against it.'

The Garths all sat around the table, a noisy mix of talking, the scraping of plates and babies' babble.

'Whilst there is still some chance that they won't go ahead with the order we will keep making it as difficult for them as we can. Jacob and I are drafting another plea but I fear the stubbornness of those powers that be in England will prevail. They refuse to open their eyes and ears to see and hear what Governor King and Piper have been telling them.'

James could not hold back any longer.

'Pa, those who have just left were promised land, building supplies, clothing and provisions to be given them when they arrived in Van Diemen's Land or Port Jackson, wherever they choose. I know Norfolk is our home but if we don't yield and go freely and if we are made to go anyway, we may not get the best pickings for land.'

Although somewhat taken aback by James's interjection, Edward saw merit in what he said.

'James even with all those promises I can't see how we would get proper recompense for what we have here,' Susannah said with passion in her voice. 'Besides this is our home, every nook and cranny in this house has been built by your pa and you, and you both know this island like you know your own skin. We belong here. Think of all we would lose.'

'Ma, we may have no choice,' James said and as he did Susannah caught what she thought was a look of more than just acceptance upon his face, it was a look of anticipation.

She continued to ponder the thought of it, the possibility, an awful prospect to her and she wished she could gather the problems up like fallen leaves, throw them into the air and have the swirling mix settle and resolve itself in an orderly way, without fear and hurt. She had been liberated from her past by this island, the magnificence of the place mingled with the freedom and security she felt in being there, *these highbrows,* she thought, *what do they know, they would shatter our lives from the distance of their ivory towers with the wave of their manicured hands.*

****

Susannah knew she had an ally in Ann. Ann had nothing but contempt for the idea. She had also just given birth to her third son, her seventh child and this only sought to make her resolve stronger,

'What of his birthright Susannah, what of all our children's? This is their home they did nothing wrong. Why should they be made to leave? The thought of my fields lying barren is too terrible.'

'Indeed it is a terrible thought Annie,' Susannah said staring out of the window, down toward the two southern islands, the images of her dreams of burnt pastures intruding upon her thoughts. Then, without warning the words came out.

'We have to have the courage Annie to face what may lay ahead.'

She could not really believe she had said those words, they were almost like a concession, a kind of acceptance and she was as surprised as Ann to hear herself say them.

She had always tried to smooth the frown of the serious Ed Garth, always tried to avoid allowing the likes of such a frown to crease her own brow but it was true, this dilemma had caused her to wear worry on her face.

Of late she found herself looking out to the sea. She remembered Edward doing the same all those years ago, in their early days. But his had been a longing for another home left behind, hers was a longing to stay in this place they had made their home. Her consternation came about from a yearning to remain, not like Edward's had been, not a yearning to leave.

Her holding on to that want to stay had been like a need, an intense preoccupation which had not allowed her to entertain the thought of moving. This need came from a place deep inside her, it had been a heart and soul commitment to the island. Then out of that same place came a thought as clear as the crystal water that ran in the Norfolk streams. There was a sudden silence, the sea hushed, the wind stilled, the children were quiet and at that moment the answer came to Susannah, out of a jumble of unrelenting thoughts or, perhaps it was not so much an answer but more a remedy.

She remembered that cold day when she had emerged from the *Dunkirk*, squinting at the sun in that collective group of wretched women, and all at once she knew, if they were made to leave the island, it was not the price of the deal she had done with God to save Edward's life, it was Edward's life that was God's gift which would help them start again.

She had Edward and her children. She loved them more than life itself and in the sharpness of that truth she remembered what the Reverend had once said. 'Love never fails.' She said, breaking the silence.

'What was that Susannah?'

'I have to go and talk to Ed,' she said, suddenly standing up and striding away, wide-eyed. With a determined look fixed in a line across her forehead and with purpose she resolutely made her way up the aromatic pathway between the fruit trees, leaving Ann somewhat open-mouthed.

Susannah could see Edward working with the sheep and when she was close enough she called to him loudly.

'Petition the Governor to raise the price of our produce, drive a bargain for land the same size and quality as what we have here in Van Diemen's Land. Write that we want all the building materials we need to make a home such as this. Set it in writing that we want to take as much stock as we can. Tell them we want our debts forgiven. Write down that we want funds to buy whatever we need in this new place that they would send us to, enough funds to put us into the position we are in now. I tell you Ed Garth, if they want us to leave this island without a fight that is the bargain they must reach. Be humble, beg and obey but tell them that is what we want.'

Edward knew not to say anything. Susannah almost breathless looked at him and he simply nodded his approval.

****

When a sense of inevitability is allowed to creep into the equation events sometimes take on a life of their own and it was as if the island knew she was to be abandoned, for no sooner had some more of the settlers begun to leave, than part of the crops began to fail.

Nature appeared to be in alliance with the British authorities to force the abandonment. More harvests came to nought, livestock started to escape from their holds, fleeing to the cliffs and ravines, goats and pigs and fowl broke loose and became wild, hardly able to be recaptured and people in the community began to suffer more hardship.

A number became desperate and resorted to robbing which led to stricter discipline by the officers, which led to tension and the atmosphere on the island was altering before Susannah's eyes.

'Ed our community is falling apart.'

Ed nodded. 'Some of the settlers in defiance of the authorities are joining with some of the prisoners,' he said. 'There has again been a sense of mutiny in the air. This is what has come about from the authorities' lack of support, from them trying to force us to leave. Men have lost their enthusiasm, their drive to continue and they do desperate things and have resorted to thieving.'

Little by little order began to crumble. In retaliation for stealing and rebellion the marines began to hang and shoot people and put them in irons for their transgressions.

Edward and Jacob set about gathering support for a further petition to have prices for their produce increased and they and other settlers requested they be allowed to take their convict workers with them when they left or be allocated workers once they arrived at their allocated lots in Van Diemen's Land.

The evacuation was gathering momentum and in its wake more disarray was creeping in. In the ensuing year lists were made. Lists of every man woman and child, on and off the stores. Lists of articles belonging to the settlers and to the crown. Terms of bartering were drawn up. Accounts were updated and stocktakes undertaken. Memorandum of claims of settlers were presented to Captain Piper and after the failure of some of the wheat and maize crops every settler remaining on the island signed a petition which was presented to the Captain.

The humble Memorial of the Settlers and Landholders of Norfolk Island –
Shewith,

That your humble memorialists, deeply impressed with a sense of gratitude for the many marks of attention to their interests which have individually and collectively experienced under your administration, request your acceptance of their most sincere acknowledgements.

They, with respectful deference and developed respect, beg leave to address you ...

This petition, was one of many requesting considerations of those matters raised by Susannah and the other settlers and they all hoped it would give rise to a deal that would go some way to satisfying them if they agreed to move away willingly.

But still there were some who said they would never leave and although Susannah had once been in their number, she saw that leaving her beloved island behind armed with what they needed for the future, was far better than being on bad terms with the authorities without a thing to begin again with.

For twelve more months Governor King kept pleading with the British authorities to keep the island open. For twelve more months the settlers continued to petition and request, and the powers that be debated and considered the settlers' appeals and plight. Resignation seeped into Susannah's being and she tried to unearth the positivism within her to counter the sadness she felt.

She considered all manner of things. Her dreams. The persistent images of burned out fields and how those dreams were now mixed with visions of hills, of still water and of endless twisted trees.

'And what of the orphan girls? What will become of them? God forbid that they may end up on the streets or given over as nothing more than slaves in the guise of maids.'

'Surely Phillip Gidley-King will make sure they are looked after.'

'I hope so Ed. Those girls are doing well. They would make fine wives and some of them good farmers. They can read and write. They are valuable.'

'Of course they are. Governor King will make sure they will have somewhere to go. I'm sure of it.'

'And the farms Ed, it is so sad to see no replanting, the farmhouses deserted and left to ruin. All that work Ed… it truly breaks a heart to see.'

Edward tried not to contemplate it, he tried to face every day in the way Susannah had shown him, living it as best he could, knowing that tomorrow held no certainty.

It was a Sunday and although people of late had been reluctant to venture out, apprehensive that renegade settlers or prisoners might steal their food or animals, the officers and constables for the moment at least seemed to have things in hand.

Susannah gathered the children together to walk down to the bay, Sassy in the pushchair, being pushed by James, the other children nearby. They walked the track towards the Bellett's farm and Susannah called out for them to come to the beach with them.

Edward held Susannah's hand, in her forty-fifth year she was expecting another child. She did not feel at all old but it had been seventeen years since she'd given birth to her Mary and now Mary herself was ready to marry and have her own children.

The Belletts joined them, the two families were like a clan and as one they moved down the hillside. Susannah pushed thoughts of being away from the island to the back of her mind. She looked across to Ann, she was feeling sentimental. People on the island had recently set against each other, had set against the authorities but the Garths and Belletts were strong together.

'We may not have the same parents but we are sisters. You and I Annie, indeed we are.'

'And you are my brother Jacob and whilst we do not come from the same place there is much about us that is the same, we have a like history. Ours is a tie that has grown from our common experience, our trials and triumphs, our shared dreams and realities.'

'That's right Ed Garth, I like that! Remind me to have you write that down,' Susannah smiled. 'I will write down next to it love never fails.'

Young Mary hurried along to catch up with James, she went to place her hand upon his, but James wriggled it away, pretending he had to scratch his forehead.

'Look there,' called Eddie. 'Porpoise!'

A pod of dolphins had appeared in the bay, jumping and flipping above the waves, chasing one another. James pointed to them.

'Look Sassy, see how they love to play.'

'How do you know they are playing,' asked Mary.

'I've seen them up close, when I've sailed out there. They ride the little bow wave and leap out of the water in front of me. There is no need for it, they do it for fun.'

'You are so sure of everything James,' and she smiled again trying to place her hand upon his.

He looked at her, 'Meh I cannot hold your hand like that.'

'What do you mean? Why not?'

'Because that is what sweethearts do.'

'Aren't I your sweetheart?'

'You are eleven and I am fifteen.'

'And one day soon I will be fourteen and you will be eighteen,' she said, nodding her head in defiance, 'hmpfing' at him, blonde curls loose on her shoulders, eyes looking up at him from under her dipped eyelids.

He imagined one day she would indeed grow into a splendid young woman. But she was a child and he not yet a man and James thought there would be much life to live in between. He thought he could not promise or predict anything, let alone the direction their lives may take.

The families settled on the grass above the beach. It was a hot day and others in the community had also come down to savour the cooler air near the water. A feeling was about that perhaps there would be little time left to enjoy the island. In the gruelling reality of their day to day lives there was limited leisure time but now, in the knowledge their days on the island were running out, friends who had been there for many years came together.

Susannah looked around her, amongst them were those like she and Edward, like Jacob and Ann, who had worked hard for their livelihood, who had built farms and homes from nothing and whose sweat had run from their bodies and blended with the soil as they had carved out a place for themselves, *indeed* Susannah thought, *even Ed's blood is mixed with this land...part of us will forever remain here.*

It was easy to take the island's beauty for granted, she was dressed in her grandeur everyday but today the air was almost still, the sky a soft blue and the ocean smooth and inviting, Norfolk invited them to put aside their toiling and join her for pleasure.

Some of the children ran to the sand to build castles, or splash in the shallows, the older ones joined their friends. Mary followed after James until he dived into the bay, swimming across toward the lone pine that now marked the eastern most tip of the cove.

Susannah began to sing a soulful song, her honeyed voice filled the space around her with feeling and Jacob and others began to follow in chorus. Before long Edward brought out his whistle, another person fetched a fiddle and the mood was lightened, there was dancing, laughter charged the air and for one day they managed to forget their collective troubles.

Chapter 15

1807

When Susannah and Edward's seventh child Richard was born, she wondered if she would live long enough to see this son grow to be a man. She had known many who had died of diseases at earlier ages than her forty-four years.

She wondered where she would be when she died, not in a morbid or gloomy way but in a real and practical way. She wondered where her children would be, how far they would wander from her and she found herself thinking more about James, her first born son, the child whose eyes reflected places he had never seen.

'There are now fourteen children between us and the Belletts. Fourteen Norfolk natives. It could have been the making of an empire. Imagine that Ed, landed gentry our children could have become, yet perhaps they may still, in some other place…but I cannot help thinking this whole business is unnecessary, if the government had just had some faith and listened to Governor King and let us govern ourselves we would make it work.

'It is a sorry thing. They are distant and out of touch, they have no idea really and with all the uncertainty that has come about from the vagaries of those orders over these last few years there is confusion and disorder.'

'Ed I know and I have tried to accept that our lives will be lived out somewhere else but I just can't yet imagine it.'

'Things here are not as they once were. Those like us who were the first settlers, have in the main lived as free people, most of the time in harmony, but we are now among the minority.'

It is true, Susannah thought, whilst the island remained steadfast in its beauty, she had to admit the community had evolved into something far less than perfect.

'I know, yet I cannot help but think if they had just let us be years ago, things would still be well.'

Susannah saw James making his way up the hillside, every now and then he picked a flower holding it in a bunch as he came back to the house. He seemed to be almost glad at the thought of leaving and, as was Susannah's predisposition, she allowed herself to be buoyed by the positivity she saw in him. Yes, she was sad to be leaving but she saw in him the same optimism she saw in herself and she knew he had faith, in the face of the unknown he could see a bright future.

'James's eyes are full of promise. He is like I was before we came here. I did not know what the bottom of the world would deliver but I saw it as my new beginning and James, he moves forward in the same way, with openness. I can see him on another shore, looking around him and toasting as we did in the beginning to success. Do you remember Ed? I remember you saying, to 'prosperity.'

Edward and Susannah smiled at each other.

'No Ed Garth I have not forgotten that word.'

****

The fruit tree blossoms growing on the edge of Ann and Jacob's land again formed a fragrant corridor and as Ann and Susannah walked along it with their young children, Ann's heartache at the prospect of having to leave behind all she had lovingly planted was making it hard for her to speak. She pulled off the small apple blossoms, handful after handful and scattered them behind her. It was a melancholic gesture, as if she was scattering her past to the wind.

'I too can hardly believe we will be leaving. But Annie we will start again. We've chosen to go to Van Diemen's Land instead of Port Jackson, after all it is an island and that is what we are used to.'

'But we have been here for nearly twenty years. All our children have been born here. It is part of us.'

'I know. I have thought on it so long and hard. I, more than anyone have loved this place. When I first saw her tall green pines, the colour of her shores and her heaven of new stars, it took my breath away. I thought there could be no more beautiful place on earth. I will miss her from the depths of my soul but I will not let the leaving make me bitter.

The government is pitiful and insensible on the point and with all the uncertainty disorder has arisen, our settlement is not what it used to be. If we can strike a good bargain with the authorities for leaving willingly it will be better for us all. Annie, you are like me. We will make the most of things. And besides, we aren't being shipped off yet, we have time to prepare ourselves as best we can.'

Ann's crops were ready for reaping, the wind whipped grains of wheat into the air, sunlight glinted through the pines and shone upon the sea, *one last harvest*, she thought to herself.

Edward and Susannah also had one final harvest to reap. The Garths and Belletts always treated their convict workers well and tried to reassure them they would do all they could to be able to secure their move with them to their new allotments when the time came. Ann had the respect of her few workers, she and Jacob paid them a little for their labours when they could and she dearly wanted to take them with her, particularly as Jacob spent most of his working hours in his duties as a constable.

'You know they have the same desire, to one day own their own land and with good commendations from us, their chances of being granted allotments one day is more likely. Isn't it strange Susannah that our character references may carry some weight? Did you know when they described us on the lists, they did indeed write us down as 'First Class Settlers', not ex-convicts, not emancipists…there is pride to be taken in that.'

Ann looked on as the workers laboured their way through the fields, sickles in hand, thrashing methodically. As she moved across the hillside watching them cutting and then bundling the wheat, she seemed oblivious to everything else because in her mind this event was momentous, sadly momentous, the reaping of her last crop of grain.

Edward was fully engaged in overseeing the loading and shipping of timber. He could barely believe there would be no more trees felled, no more structures built and the boats, those which were not large enough to endure the long voyage south or not small enough to be hoisted on board the tall ships, he had been told they would be destroyed. The sweat of his brow that had formed over the years from the efforts of his labours was now replaced by the tears he shed in the knowledge that some of the fruits of his work would soon be demolished. Even the boat James sailed so passionately to the horizon would be amongst those ruined. It seemed so absurd that they would destroy that which had taken so long to build.

Jacob had taken on full duties and among his tasks was trying to keep the renegade prisoners and disgruntled and disorderly settlers in line. This task did not come naturally to him but he did not consider himself a farmer, or a builder the likes of Edward, and whilst his occupation was a far cry from the aspirations of his youth to become a master silk merchant, he was not unhappy with the job. His work demanded respect and as a law officer he knew he would be amongst the last to leave the island but he was as determined as Edward to ensure his request for land and provisions in Van Diemen's Land was confirmed sooner rather than later.

He thought back to when they had first come to the island, when there had been no need for a gaol, to when Governor King had given them a large degree of freedom to do what needed to be done, without treating them as criminals. Even during the initial times of hardship, when the crops had failed and food was scarce he remembered the common sense of purpose that had brought them all together.

When he had left Sydney Cove the settlement there had been near to starvation, they had not been able to grow crops of any great quantity, the natives had become problematic for Arthur Phillip and things had indeed been dire. He wondered how much things had improved over the years. When he had left the town was nothing more than a makeshift village and the buildings there were overall little more than humpies. He also wondered what Van Diemen's Land would be like, whether it was the same, whether the settlement was more established than Port Jackson had been. Even though Norfolk Island had endured harsh times, in Jacob's eyes these problems had been much less serious than the troubles and poor conditions he had left behind.

Susannah wondered what Governor King would make of it, all of his good service in establishing the island coming undone. The considerable advancement the settlement had made seemed to have been for nothing. At one point there had been just over a thousand people living on the island and she found it a difficult thing to believe it may soon have not one living soul upon it.

'When we came here Ed, we all had to rely upon each other. What a beginning we had. Just those fifteen of us. It's hard to believe that was how many of us there were and those few marines and just the surgeon and Governor King. What an order that must have been for him, to start something from nothing.'

When the last harvests were complete the promises of land grants in Hobart Town were forthcoming from the authorities.

'The allotments are supposedly proportionate in size to our land here and they've also promised enough funds, provisions and tools for us to be able to erect a residence of equal value to the houses that we will be leaving behind. As well food and clothing for two years at the public expense and the labour of convicts. It seems Susannah our requests have been heard.

The stamp of approval has been firmly sealed upon the agreement and so the inescapable truth is here, that we must go. The plans are in place and we have been allocated space on the *Porpoise*. She leaves on Boxing Day.'

'That's just two months from now,' Susannah's voice caught in her throat.

'We'll arrive at Hobart Town into the New Year. The officers have taken note and put values on all our assets so that when we get there we will be properly compensated.'

Susannah wanted to believe that true heed had been taken of their demands and the promises would be kept. She looked around her house. It was all she could ever want for, all they really needed and the feeling tugged at her heart again, but she straightened her back and lifted her chin.

'1808 will be a good year Ed Garth. We must have faith that it will. It is a heart wrenching thing but it is what we must do.'

'My dear even if we had decided to dig our heels in we could not have stayed, it would have been for nought. King is no longer the governor of New South Wales and the new governor there, Bligh has threatened that anyone who tries to avoid resettlement will be shot.'

'Dear Lord Ed, what a sorry state. To think people would be shot for that. Free people who have done their time. What an unspeakable thing and what a loathsome man that Bligh must be. I'm glad we have chosen Van Diemen's Land and not New South Wales!'

'We must be selective in what we take, there is limited space upon the transports and Susannah I have to tell you, I have asked to be able to take livestock with me in place of material things. The sheep will be more valuable to us than any chair or cot.'

She looked at the carved backs on the chairs, the cot and pushchair Edward had made, the bedhead and chest of drawers.

'Surely we can take the pushchair and one of your other chairs Ed. The pushchair can be used to store and carry things.'

'We will have to see.'

'Pa what of the boats you have made, what of our little sailboat?' asked James.

'I will try and sell them to the public store. What will become of them after that I do not know.'

'We will make others Pa. When we are on our new land, we will make others.'

'James I don't know where our land will be. But I do think it will be near a decent waterway. I am told Hobart Town is a port town up river and that it lies in a cove at the south of the island. They say it has a deep sheltered harbour which means easy access and it has a fresh water supply.'

'It sounds like it has promise but it is a new colony isn't it? All the progress we have made here Ed. In those twenty years, our school, our church, the jetties, the buildings and we are going somewhere which has only just begun.'

'I'm not entirely sure how long the colony has been there but it is a least a few years and as I said there is a proper port, a safe harbour.'

James began imagining what the new land would be like and the adventurer in his heart had his mind building a boat and sailing him from that safe harbour to places where no port yet existed.

****

The breeze wafted gently, it was a warm Sunday afternoon in November and James and Mary rested in the shade of pines. She was approaching womanhood and James found himself looking at her differently. When she released her hair from her bonnet it fell shining like honey down her back, he saw a lovely young woman and it caused him some disquiet, for she was no longer the little girl who had tagged behind him, the girl for whom he had felt childhood affection.

The earth was tipping and the sun was going down and the clouds that gathered off the western shore were blazing red and orange over the water, setting the sea on fire with colour.

'*We are leaving in just a few weeks*,' James said in a quiet voice, his eyes fixed on the ocean.

Mary began to cry, not loud sobs but quiet tears of resignation. Her heart was weighed down by sadness. Not only was it sadness for the imminent separation from their island but more so for the separation from James. In her twelve years she had spent part of every day with him and her mind was now full of doubts about whether they would see each other again.

James tried to change the subject.

'Do you remember when you were very little, probably about five and I told you about how once upon a time natives had lived on the island and how some of their ghosts remained? I had remembered hearing the story after the governor had brought the Maori from New Zealand to make the flax and they had discovered some oddly shaped stones down near the bay which the natives recognised as ancient tools. Do you remember we went there and when I heard the howling of the wind through the trees I told you it was their spirits and you screamed so loudly it started the governor's dogs barking and even though you were scared you said you would run home without me?'

James began to laugh but Mary frowned.

'It was a mean thing to do.'

'It was, but it was funny. You should laugh about it now. Besides, everything was alright. There was nothing to be scared about.'

More tears fell. James felt a pang of guilt that his plan to divert the conversation had only made things worse and so he hugged her gently.

'All will be well Meh. Think of what is out there. It is exciting.'

James thought about his lessons, what he had been taught about the world that lay beyond the shores of Norfolk and he thought of the place they were going to, a place that had barely been explored by the Europeans, an island only recently known to be separated from the mainland and all the wonders it held. He was inwardly thrilled but tried not to show this to Mary as he truly did not want to upset her any further.

'But we are staying on. Papa has been given the job of waiting behind to make sure everything is moved off or destroyed. I can't believe they are ruining everything James, it's so very horrible to think it. They've given orders that before we leave we must burn down our own homes. I can't bear to think of it, and Mama, she is filled with grief about this.'

'I know, it's a strange thing that the British should be so worried about the French moving on to the island once we have all gone, yet they a breaking their necks to abandon it. It makes little sense to me.' James again paused, looking out to sea,

'But Meh … perhaps it is for the best that we are going.'

'I don't know James. I hope we will be given land close to you. They say Van Diemen's Land is a much bigger place than here. Our families have always lived side by side; we have always been together… it may not be like that… it may not be easy to find each other.'

'We will meet again I'm sure of it.'

288

Mary lowered her eyes, 'You may find a girl James.'

'Meh, I've told you. You are too young to be thinking of marriage and you are already my family. There are going to be many young men who will be chasing after you. Even with that pouting, crinkled up nose and unhappy look on your face you are still the prettiest girl on this island and you will be the prettiest girl in Van Diemen's Land. Why an officer or some important person will snaffle you up in no time.'

Mary gave James a look of defiance and her tears stopped. She was annoyed and he knew at once he should not have said it, but it was too late.

'I know what I want James Garth and you know it is you!' she said and she stood and stomped away.

Chapter 16

1807-1808

Susannah now knew her dreams of burnt fields were premonitions of the island's ruination. But she also knew the island had enough strength in her to renew herself over time, she knew that the charred remains of whatever may be claimed by fire would one day be reclaimed by the green of the plants that would grow again and tangle themselves amongst the ruins and cover the once scorched earth.

She believed it would be only a matter of time before another band of settlers would be brought back to the island to try and tame her again but whilst she could see the island would one day again be inhabited, sadly she thought she would not be among those who would build their homes there. Susannah could not conceive that a paradise such as she had found the island to be would remain empty and forsaken.

Christmas Day 1807 was not the same kind of celebration as it had been in years gone by, the cloud of the unknown tomorrow hovered over and in all their hearts there dwelt an ache for what they had and what they would leave behind.

It was the last time they would sit on their little porch and look across to the sea. The packing had been done, the pushchair loaded with their most needed belongings and Susannah had made Edward give all but one of his

291

crafted chairs to one of the marines in the hope they would not be destroyed.

Edward had sold what he could, his few little boats, most of his stock and stores. He had trained a dog and it kept watch over several sheep he had holdup in a makeshift yard. These sheep were his treasure. With them and the provisions he had been promised he would make his farm again on unfamiliar ground. He had built a few large crates down on the bay for the sheep to be transported in and he would steadfastly care for and guard them on the journey. In the morning they would leave.

The whole family crammed onto the verandah and despite their consternation about the future and the sadness about having to go, there was acceptance, even from Susannah.

'I had almost tortured myself to the point of despair at the thought of leaving. I have had to dig deep within me to find the right mind about this…Ed this is the only real home I have ever known.'

Edward remembered how Susannah had embraced her new beginning on Norfolk Island with vigour and enthusiasm and he also knew that whilst she had accepted this new fate and tried to be optimistic, any positive emotions were truly tempered by sadness.

'We were flung into circumstance not of our own making but you and I, together we seized what command we could of our lives. As you have said my dear we started from nothing. We have made what we now have out of

292

love and necessity, a faith in our future. We have our family, we have those things we have bargained for and we will start again.'

Susannah looked at her husband, the love she had within her for him murmured, stirring her, making her want to hold him tenderly and lightly stroke his hair. She reached out for him, letting her hands drift under his shirt, feeling his body beneath her fingertips. He was not the young man he had once been, his body was lined with the scars of hardship, scars which he bore for both of them, yet still with all he had been through and with the trial of what would be ahead of them, he pledged his confidence in their future, just as she hoped he would.

Tomorrow they would set sail from one small island in the Pacific to another larger one, south of the mainland, surrounded by the Indian and Pacific oceans and separated from the continent by a deep wide strait of water where the winds of the *Roaring Forties* rushed through.

That night Susannah told the younger children again the story of the princess island and said they should keep those images in the minds forever so that they would only need to close their eyes to remember and also that they may one day tell their own children about the home they once had.

When the rest of the house was quiet, when they all lay in their beds, some sleeping, some restless with nervousness, Susannah and Edward both lay wide-eyed in the darkness. Outside the island's familiar sounds impressed upon them, the 'ya ho' owl's call, the whistling wind through the

293

pines, the distant crashing surf but now missing was the hissing of the fields, the comforting whooshing of the wheat crop... that sound was gone.

The half-moon had waned and only a sliver remained, not enough light to make the ocean shimmer brightly. Susannah could not resist, she got up and went out onto the steps and looked at the stars. She hoped she would still be able to see them all from her new home, at another place somewhere else at the bottom of the world.

She had heard from someone, she could not remember who, that Norfolk Island was a place 'of angels and eagles', a place so hard to land upon that you would have to fly there. Whilst she and the others had somehow been delivered there on transport other than by pinion, she thought one day her spirit would fly back there, perhaps on the wings of an angel.

****

Governor Bligh had given the settlers a choice between Port Dalrymple at the north of the island or Hobart Town on the Derwent River to the south. Most of them like the Garths and Belletts chose Hobart Town.

Governor Collins presided over Van Diemen's Land and he had been sent some extra supplies to provide for the 386 new men, women and children arriving in the coming months.

David Collins had been in the marines from the age of fourteen. He had been with Arthur Phillip on the *Sirius* when it had been the flagship of the

First Fleet. He had a legal, analytical mind, he liked order and kept meticulous records. Many a night he had spent by candlelight stabbing his quill into ink and scratching out his accounts, his proposals, and in those days before the new arrivals, he wondered, dare he now write his aspirations for this new colony, this place he himself had suggested should be settled, the place of which he had now been made Lieutenant-Governor. Five years before it had been founded as a penal colony and now he was trying to make it an outpost for England, a place not just for convicts but emancipists and free settlers.

  He was informed most of the settlers had been living in a comfortable manner, in well-established homes on Norfolk Island, possessing every necessity of life and some luxuries which Van Diemen's Land did not offer. He had been told that every one of those resettling had stock of their own which they had given up to the stores on Norfolk Island on the pledge that it would be returned in kind on arrival at the Derwent and, as a result of what he had been told, he was worried, deeply worried because he did not in fact have to give them what they had been promised...

****

The *Porpoise* waited at anchor off Sydney Bay. The Garths, Susannah and Edward, Mary, James, Eddie, John, William, Sassy and baby Richard were about to walk away from their home for the last time. With them they took the money that had been acquired through selling what boats they could sell to the public purse, their most important personal possessions, amongst them some of Susannah's embroidered cloth, her woven baskets all fitted into one another, the pink conch shell that had rested for twenty years on her kitchen shelf, a section of the carved bedhead that Edward had made and which Susannah intended on mounting on the wall of their new home. Packed in amongst the belongings was Edward's bible, his best axe and a few tins of his bloodwood oil, all loaded onto the pushchair and a cart jam-packed with the fifteen live sheep that Edward had been allowed to take with him.

The moment was finally real and as Susannah shut the door of their home behind them, the thought struck her sharply, there was no point closing the door. Although she knew this it did not seem right to walk away leaving the door flapping hopelessly in the breeze. She took the final steps off the porch onto the pathway, turning her head once more to imprint the image firmly in her mind's eye, their two level home, shingled and boarded with timber floors and stonework so meticulously laid by Edward, its little verandah empty, the door closed to the nothingness inside. The plants in the garden that had grown up from the cuttings from Governor King's garden seemed to bend their heads in sadness.

Her eyes swept over the acres of cleared land, the fences and outhouses, the chicken coop where the fowl still pecked at the ground. They had sold their other animals to the government stores but she hoped the chickens could live out their lives on the island. She knew they would not stray far from the house and at least she thought there would be some life left behind. It seemed to her the sounds that came from the remaining emptiness, the creaking of the buildings and whistling of the wind through now hollow spaces, were like the cries of a loved one being left behind.

They had been ordered to demolish everything but they could not bear to. They simply walked away, leaving it for some other person who could stomach the task to do the deed, to destroy what they had so lovingly built.

They trudged the path to Music Valley where the Belletts joined them. There was silence at first, a sombre parade to the bay and Susannah thought, *if I had a funeral for a loved one this is how I would imagine it to be, no words ...* It would have been trifling to speak, she thought, *to try and find words for the occasion would be pointless* but Susannah began to sing, a sentimental tune which she had heard some of the new convicts sing and her voice echoed though the hills, a last goodbye to her beloved island.

Should auld acquaintance be forgot
And never brought to mind
Should auld acquaintance be forgot
And auld lang syne
For auld lang syne, my jo
For auld lang syne,
We'll take a cup of kindness yet
For auld lang syne

Jacob joined and in and then the family, singing along in chorus. People came out of their homes, stopped what they were doing, first listening and watching and then, together with the others who were making their way to the ship to leave, they all lent their voices to the song.

Jacob and Ann, their children beside them, stood on the shore. One by one the families embraced each other. Ann handed Susannah a small hessian dillybag. When she opened it there was a mixture of soil and seed. Ann looked at her solemnly.

'For your new garden, a little piece of our island to take with you.'

Jacob and Edward shook hands then each wrapped a brotherly arm about the other.

'You will have no-one to bid you farewell when you leave my friend, but hopefully we will be at the other end to welcome you.'

Mary held on to James, lingering as the rest of his family boarded the longboat.

'We will meet again in Hobart Town James,' Mary said smiling weakly.

'Yes we will Meh,' he said returning a smile that belied both sadness and excitement.

She leaned in to the side of his face, whispering softly.

'And, don't be falling in love with any of those other pretty girls while we are apart.'

James did not answer, for to him the future was yet to be revealed, a mystery to be unravelled, a story yet to be told and he would make no promise he could not keep. But still it was a bittersweet goodbye for in that moment James too recognised there was a love there beyond family, beyond friendship.

Jacob looked on as his daughter wept her open tears and he remembered the despairing farewell he had said so long ago to his childhood sweetheart. He fleetingly wondered…what had happened to his Aileen?

The sea, as it often did, threw off a pinken hue, silken and sweeping to the horizon enticing the *Porpoise*. It was Boxing Day morning and as they waved goodbye to their friends from the deck, the vessel's sails filled with the wind and Susannah's eyes filled with tears.

Around the shoreline, across the reef and at the base of the cliffs the white foam of the familiar crashing surf, boomed and hissed. The air smelled like Norfolk always did, a mix of pine and sea, but it did not abide, as the ship sailed from the island the fragrance was swept away as quickly as the next gust of wind. And, as surely as Edward and Susannah had left the shores of England more than twenty years before never to return, so now they left the shores of Norfolk Island.

Susannah thought back on the day she had waded to the sand, that first day and as the island disappeared from view she turned to face the wind and lifted her face to the sun.

Her children gathered around her. 'Look there,' she said pointing south. 'There, further than you can imagine, that is where we are going.'

Chapter 17

1808

James was wonderstruck by the way the *Porpoise* cut her way through the swell. For such a large ship she made good speed. He looked around him admiring the beauty of her fashioned timber and the lines in her shape. Whilst his parents had endured the long voyage from England to the Great South Land and from Port Jackson to Norfolk Island on tall ships, James had never sailed on such a vessel.

 He found himself examining her, she was a quarter-decked sloop, 100 odd feet in length, with a beam of over thirty feet. He had seen ships like this anchored off shore in the bay but never stood on the deck of one. He counted at least nine sails and he watched intently as they were hauled up and down. These were things he wanted to commit to memory, for in the future he would build a boat such as this.

 One day he lent upon the deck rail marvelling at the vastness of the sea, with nothing in sight but the deep teal blue of the ocean and the pale cornflower blue of the sky. He had seen a globe of the earth, the one in the school room on Norfolk Island that Governor King had brought back with him from England, so he knew the ocean wrapped itself in a sphere around the lands and he knew if he sailed in any direction he would eventually make land somewhere, whether that be in the far reaches of the wild icy place they called Antarctica or the islands that dotted across the equator and as he thought on it, he admired those who had sailed the seas in search of lands unknown to them.

This place Van Diemen's Land, he wondered, *what will the forests be like? What trees grow there from which I can build my ships? Will there be huge waterways to sail upon?* He wondered what a wilderness would be like and let himself believe in limitless possibilities.

The *Porpoise* carried with her forty-three families, 187 persons and a menagerie of animals, crowded as could be. Once in the open sea the passengers were given rations and a roster was put in place for guarding the stores and livestock. With so many passengers on board some of the animals had to be held in one of the longboats. It was not an easy job to keep the cattle, goats, pigs, sheep and fowl in order, let alone the dozens of children. It made for a noisy, smelly and lively zoo.

'It's just like Noah's Ark,' Susannah said to the children. *Filled with life and hope*, she thought.

For over two weeks they rode the swells, coursed along with the winds and sometimes lulled in the troughs. The vessel sliced through the water and James found himself admiring those who had built the large boat.

The weather was favourable, thankfully encountering no storms for if that had occurred the congestion on board would have meant deplorable conditions. Despite the crowded circumstance James was one of those who could truly say he relished the journey. Others however could not say the same. Some of the settlers had not been careful enough with their water ration or were not able to inveigle favours from the crew for more water, and their stock died.

'Ed I see Crowder lost five of his sows and six sheep. What a waste, as the animals perish, they are having to just throw them overboard. Thank goodness you are sensible and measured. Your common sense is keeping our sheep alive.'

'Aye my dear, and Mitchell has lost seven sheep and three goats and some of the others the same. It has been quite a carnage. But I mean to make sure our sheep arrive alive. I have taught the sheep how to drink from a bottle and they have mastered it, so none is wasted. They will be so important for a start on our new land. They are more valuable to us than gold right now.'

'I wonder how harsh the countryside will be?'

'We will find out soon enough my love. But we will manage whatever is delivered.'

'Now, that's what I want to hear, so be wiping that crease away from between your eyes Ed Garth.'

'It will be a struggle to move our stock and the provisions that are to be given to us at Hobart Town to our allotment. Still we have been promised men to work for us and we have Robbie our convict worker with us. I will purchase a horse and cart for the job but I think that will be the least of the problems, for untamed land again awaits us.'

'We will manage Ed. We can do it again. You have said so yourself. Even though we are older, we know more than we did back then. And you Ed Garth, remember, you are a maker of things and a man who makes things happen,' Susannah said with the optimism Edward knew would sustain them both.

They had heard of the treachery which could be whipped up by storms in the waterway they called Bass Strait and how sometimes the seas were so wild ships had been dashed upon hidden rocks and sunk, but the passage of the *Porpoise* was relatively calm and seventeen days into the New Year they sailed up the Derwent River.

It was extremely hot, very little breeze and an unexpected heat haze hung above the little town in the distance. On the northern shore, further afield Susannah could see a thin spiral of blue smoke rising amidst the trees. Despite the surprise of such weather and the enormity of the task that lay ahead, as they came along the river Susannah did allow herself to think the scene was quite pretty, not like her Norfolk, but still quite pretty. But, as they came closer to the port the orange glow of the bushfires beyond sent a menacing chill through her and she wondered just how much of the island was alight.

The *Porpoise* anchored in the harbour, straight ahead behind the dock was a towering mountain, its peak hidden in the smog. As they waited for the word to come ashore seamen rowed to the vessel providing them with greatly needed fresh water. They stayed on board overnight, the menagerie of men, women, children and animals waiting for the sunrise that would usher in the start of their new lives.

When they came ashore the next day, they could see the settlement was far more primitive than the one they had left behind. Susannah looked about her, there was not much to see in the way of structures. A dock had been built, a government store building, a number of small thatched cottages and a grand expanse of olive green trees that stretched out to the foot of the mountain which lay behind the village and rose up behind, with smoke and a red glow about it.

There was the hustle and noise of the new arrivals with their belongings and what was left of their livestock all being offloaded on to the dock. Locals and officers moved about in the melee of newcomers and their possessions and there seemed to be little order.

Some of the Norfolk islanders who had arrived at Hobart Town earlier were there to greet others but Edward immediately looked for the officials who would provide them with directions to their new land. He of course carried the crease of worry between his eyes.

James's demeanour was one of nervous anticipation, open-eyed, fidgety. He saw the place as a door to a new world, as new as any place could be and he imagined the prospect.

Susannah was a little distracted by the chaos, but despite this she held on to her hope, like James she believed this was the genesis of their new life.

****

At Norfolk Island Mary waited impatiently for their turn to leave and she hoped the sadness of leaving her home would be washed away by a reunion with James.

Jacob and Ann wondered what awaited them. They had not heard from the Garths but there had been the sad news that their advocate Phillip Gidley King had died in England and Jacob hoped that word of his death had also reached Edward.

'When we arrive at our new place, we will name our home after the governor for he was the only one who truly had faith in us. He had faith in me Jacob, I will always be truly grateful for that.'

Ann's eyes gazed over their land. 'The day I found out about my grant of land was the proudest in my life. It was the governor's belief in us and our hard work that let us prosper on Norfolk and this has in turn given us standing and promise for the future.'

'Mother do you think James will know we are coming? Do you think he will be there to greet us?'

'I don't know my dear but even if he does know we are coming it may not be as easy as him simply walking down to the bay as it is here.'

Mary wondered if James had found a girl, from what she imagined was a large selection of eligible young women at this other colony, a girl who would see straight away see the qualities James had and latch herself to him and Mary hoped she would not be too late. It had been eight months since James had left, over two hundred days and she had written to him and sent them on other transports, care of Hobart Town in the hope that somehow her letters would make it to him, but she had heard nothing back.

She had turned thirteen. Since she last saw him she had grown some inches in height, her body was evolving, a waist now thinner than her hips, her breasts becoming larger and the cycle of womanhood, which had taken her by surprise and sometimes made her teary and frustrated. She understood that now she could bear children and all she could think of was that one day, if she were to bear babies, that James would be their father.

She ventured on her own to the ground in the shadows of the pines where she and James had sometimes rested. From there she looked out at the dark blue line at the end of the ocean, as far as the eye could see, where the *Porpoise* had vanished from her sight. She too had learned of foreign lands and whilst some part of her was curious about those places, she knew she did not have the urges that James possessed to go further, to travel beyond the home she had always known, but now, with the reality of boarding a ship and sailing to an unfamiliar land where she had heard natives roamed and wildfires raged, she looked to the imminent change with trepidation. In her heart she believed the only thing that could make it all better would be James.

When the day finally came to leave the island, she walked with her parents to the bay, the frowning faces of her brothers and sisters wet with sorrow. She looked at her mother, she was the saddest of all. Ann who could not remember her own mother's face, only the distant lilt of her lost mother's voice; Ann who'd had no mother to wipe her tears, now dried the tears of her own children as they left the home they had built.

Just as Susannah had, Ann closed the door to their house behind them and as she walked through what remained of their forty-five cleared acres the remnants of her crops and gardens that she had passionately tended, the flowers seemed to sag, as if reflecting the grief she felt. The fruit trees remained, the aromatic pathway perhaps would withstand time, *and perhaps also* Ann wondered, *perhaps the trees will continue to bear fruit and the birds will feast on them. My legacy* she thought.

Their two level house which had been built with pride by Jacob, boarded and shingled with care, their sturdy stone fire place, the floored barn and the two log outhouses, tucked away in the hills of Music Valley, remained standing. Again, even though Jacob like all the settlers had been given direction to pull the dwellings down, he could not suffer the pain of doing such a thing and he secretly hoped that because his dwellings were tucked away in the valley they may be overlooked in the final demolition.

Just as the Garths had done the Belletts waited on the southern shore of the island. Jacob and Ann, pregnant with their eighth child, stood with their children, Elizabeth, Susan, Mary, Ann, John, Jacob junior, and William.

Jacob hoped his standing as a constable would mean a good start for them in Van Diemen's Land. He hoped too, the land granted to them would carry the richness of soil of the farm they were leaving behind so that Ann and the workers would be able to clear and till the soil, plant and nurture the crops just as they had done in Music Valley. For a moment he thought *what if we were taking a transport back to England. I wonder if my mother and father are still alive. I wonder would I have been able to go back to building the business I once thought I would. And what of Aileen...* But it was only that, a momentary thought, tinged with a fond emotion instead of the yearning he once held.

Ann kept thinking that the unborn child within her would be different from the others, born in another place. This child would call another place their home. She considered them all natives of Norfolk Island, herself included. Even though she had been born in a country that others still called 'home', it was Norfolk that had been her true home.

It was the third day of Spring 1808 and as they climbed aboard the longboats to row out to the *City of Edinburgh,* Ann remembered the day she had arrived eighteen years before, the day when the high swell had taken a sad toll and the child who had been swept from her mother's arms, a child whose spirit would always remain nearby to the shores of Norfolk Island and she thought to herself, *I was delivered to my destiny that day, to Jacob.*

Ann looked up at their valley, the valley that was once filled with music. The hilly fields which had once been bursting with the golden colour of grain were silent and empty, as empty as the cloudless sky that spread before them as they boarded the ship. Mary was the only one, the only one who had a light in her heart. A light that she kept alive for James.

Once on board they waited to depart, it seemed a cruel thing to delay pulling up anchor and sailing away, for the longer they waited the harder it was to look back at the shore and stay composed, to not succumb to the temptation to row back to where they had just come from but some of the settlers, who were supposed to board the ship had taken off and were hiding in the bush.

With orders to hunt down any person who did not arrive for debarkation, marines set off in pursuit to seize them and bring them on board by force. As well as delaying the departure the sight of people being dragged onto the longboats, being held as captives, and then restrained on the ship, with nothing more than the clothing they were wearing, was an awful sight and made them all the more dismayed.

'They should have made a deal,' Ann said. 'Susannah was right those who didn't have been forced to leave anyway, with nothing and no guarantees of anything when they arrive at the other end.'

'Perhaps they thought if they were able to secrete themselves away on the island until the last officials departed, they would be able to somehow rejuvenate the ground and occupy abandoned residences, for they had made no bargain with the authorities. And you are right, no they will have nothing when they arrive at Hobart Town.' Jacob wondered if his duties as a constable on arrival at their destination would include guarding convicts who up until that day had been free to walk Norfolk as they had pleased.

The ship sailed away but there were still some who remained on the island, some who had not yet been allocated a passage, or who had been delayed because they did not want to leave, some who still believed they would be allowed to remain but Jacob knew better. There were those constables and officers who had been ordered to stay on to the last, to make sure that when the final boat left nothing would remain. It may not be within the next few months but Jacob knew the island would eventually be left empty, that no-one would be permitted to stay.

The settlers of Norfolk Island had endured much in their time there. They had faced starvation, been saved by the 'birds of providence' as Susannah had called them, built farms and livelihoods for themselves and now they were faced with the burden of rebuilding their lives, stepping onto unfamiliar ground and starting again.

Some of the passengers on the ship were in a poor state and others like the Belletts had reasonable provisions and held on to promises they hoped would be fulfilled in the trade-off between leaving their homes and relocating. For over a month they battled the seas and bad weather and the *City of Edinburgh* was driven further out into the Pacific. Many were wretched with sea sickness and just when they were told their destination was not far away the ship made its way into Bass Strait, that sometimes savage stretch of water that during storms whips up steep waves which grow steeper as tidal currents rush against the wind.

It was a storm such as this the ship sailed through, dipping and swaying, lurching and falling down the sides of waves and some on board wondered if they would even survive. A mixture of treacherous seas, wild wind and partly submerged rocks and reefs made the conditions perilous and frightening. Ann stayed with the children below deck, Jacob above assisting in keeping order and Mary wondered whether she would be drowned, and that if she did, whether James would cry for her. When the ship finally sailed into the mouth of the Derwent River there was great relief on board. The ship levelled in the calm water and the seasickness of the passengers began to ease.

The Derwent was wide and still and they had been told parts of the river were so deep as to rival Port Jackson. In the distance Mary could see on the banks of a sheltered harbour a small township and she turned to her mother.

'So that is Hobart Town,' Ann said and she looked keenly around at the gently sloping hills and valleys that stretched to the water's edge on both sides of the river, hoping that within that soil lay the riches that would make her future.

Compared to Norfolk Island, Van Diemen's Land was enormous and Mary gazed across the wide expanse of water towards the forests and seemingly endless hillsides wondering, where in this vast place is James Garth?

****

After Norfolk Island was laid to waste. Nothing of value was left, for the British feared if any dwelling remained the French may claim and inhabit the island; buildings and jetties were burned, stones pulled down, stray animals killed and except for those whose bones would lie beneath the soil for eternity, the island was left deserted.

They did not know that in the years to come the island's native shrubs would grow and overtake the cleared fields, vines would enmesh and entwine themselves in the remnants of what had been left behind and as if in defiance wheat and barley seeds would sow themselves and grow amongst it all.

They did not know that more than a decade later their paradise would become hell on earth. Even in Susannah's dreams there was no premonition, no foreboding omen of what was one day to become of their home. But for now, it was no more than a year since they had left and sometimes at night Susannah thought she could hear the island tempting her. In her dreams the 'ya ho' owl called, the Norfolk pines whistled with the wind, the waters of Sydney Bay sang a luring siren's song and the eagles that soared above the cliffs cried out her name. But with daylight came a softer sound, of waters lapping at the edges of another sandy bay, the sight of strange creatures and black people amidst the dense bushland and the scent of the native peppermint tree.

As she pondered their future in this foreign place, a place so different from that which they had left, Susannah looked back on her life with fondness and forward to tomorrow with her usual hopefulness and resolve,

Norfolk Island released us from our shackles...Van Diemen's Land will bring us true liberty.

Postscript:

Governor King had done his best, Susannah knew that. He had brought with him to the island his small band of felon pioneers and they had succeeded, but what Susannah did not know was that when Governor Hunter had come to rule in New South Wales he had looked unfavourably upon Norfolk as a settlement. He saw its lack of natural harbour and its remoteness from Sydney as major pitfalls and reported so to the British authorities. He had been Court-martialled as a result of the wrecking of the *Sirius* and although later re-instated, he blamed the conditions on Norfolk Island for the shipwreck.

By 1803 Hunter had set his sights set on Van Diemen's Land as a more suitable place for a colony. Van Diemen's Land had been glowingly reported upon by Matthew Flinders who had explored the waters around the island. Ironically Edward and his fellow settlers having themselves built the very vessel Flinders had used in his exploration, the *Norfolk*.

Note: The Orders given to Phillip Gidley King in 1788:

After having taken the necessary measures for securing yourself and people, and for the preservation of the stores and provisions, you are immediately to proceed to the cultivation of the flax plant, which you will find growing spontaneously on the island; as likewise to the cultivation of cotton, corn, and other plants, with the seeds of which you are furnished, and which you are to regard as public stock, and of the increase of which you are to send me an account, that I may know what quantity may be drawn from the island for public use, or what supplies it may be necessary to send hereafter. It is left to your discretion to use such part of the corn that is raised as may be deemed necessary; but this you are to do with the greatest economy; and as the corn, flax, cotton, and other grains are the property of the Crown, and as such are to be accounted for, you are to keep an exact account of the increase, and you will in future receive directions for the disposal thereof.

You will be furnished with a four-oared boat, and you are not on any consideration to build or to permit the building of any vessel or boat whatever that is decked, whose length of keel exceeds twenty feet; and if by any accident any vessel or boat that exceeds twenty feet keel should be driven on the island, you are immediately to cause such boat or vessel to be scuttled, or otherwise rendered unserviceable, letting her remain in that situation until you receive further directions from me.

The convicts being the servants of the Crown, till the time for which they are sentenced is expired, their labour is to be for the public; and you are to take particular notice of their good or bad behaviour, that they may hereafter be employed or rewarded according to their different merits.

You are to cause the prayers of the Church of England to be read with all due solemnity every Sunday, and you are to enforce a due observance of religion and good order, transmitting to me, as often as opportunity offers, a full account of your particular situation and transactions.

You are not to permit any intercourse with any ships or vessels that may stop at the island, whether English or of any other nation, unless such ships or vessels should be in distress, in which case you are to afford them such assistance as may be in your power.

Author's Note

While the *Garth Trilogy* is based on real events and people, it is nonetheless, a work of fiction. I was drawn to writing the story of Edward Garth, Susannah Gough, Jacob Bellett and Ann Harper as a way of finding answers to the many questions that arose from my discovery of being a great, great, great, great granddaughter of these four souls. In doing so, I have travelled thousands of miles with my maternal aunt, retracing the steps of my ancestors and researching their history. In the process of finding the answers, the *Garth Trilogy* was written.

www.ingramcontent.com/pod-product-compliance
Lightning Source LLC
Chambersburg PA
CBHW071242170626
46809CB00001B/50